C. L. PATTISON

C. L. Pattison spent twenty years as an entertainment journalist, before embarking on a career in the police force. She lives on the south coast of England.

ALSO BY C. L. PATTISON

The Housemate

C. L. PATTISON

The Guest Book

VINTAGE

1 3 5 7 9 10 8 6 4 2

Vintage is part of the Penguin Random House group of companies
whose addresses can be found at global.penguinrandomhouse.com

Penguin
Random House
UK

Copyright © C. L. Pattison 2021

C. L. Pattison has asserted her right to be identified as the author
of this Work in accordance with the Copyright, Designs and
Patents Act 1988

First published by Vintage in 2021

penguin.co.uk/vintage

A CIP catalogue record for this book is available from
the British Library

ISBN 9781529113617

Typeset in 10.1/14.8 pt Scala Pro
by Integra Software Services Pvt. Ltd, Pondicherry

Printed and bound in Great Britain by Clays Ltd, Elcograf S.p.A.

The authorised representative in the EEA is Penguin Random House
Ireland, Morrison Chambers, 32 Nassau Street, Dublin D02 YH68.

Penguin Random House is committed to a sustainable future for our
business, our readers and our planet. This book is made from
Forest Stewardship Council® certified paper.

THE GUEST BOOK

My legs are aching and my heart is pounding so hard I think it's about to burst. But I can't stop running; you're right behind me. Another thirty seconds and you'll be able to reach out and grab my arm. The thought sends a dark tide of panic racing through my body. I can feel it clawing at my throat, making it difficult to breathe.

'Please come back,' I hear you shout. 'I don't want to hurt you, I just want a chance to explain.'

I know you're lying. You've been lying to me this whole time. My head is spinning like a merry-go-round and I can feel a sort of thunder in my chest, a shuddering sensation, like something breaking open.

At the edge of the bluff I keep going, straight down the rocky steps that lead to the beach. The steps are wet after the rain and I have to force myself to slow down, or else I'll twist my ankle. The wind's picking up too, it's blowing my hair all over my face.

'Stop running,' you cry. 'It's no good; you can't get away from me.'

I can and I will.

Only when I've reached the bottom step do I risk a look over my shoulder. I can't see you, but I know you won't have given up the chase; you're too single-minded. I used to like that about you.

I stop for a moment and bend over, resting my hands on my knees, trying to catch my breath. At first, I don't know what to do – I just know that I need to get away, to get away from *you*.

And then I see the lifeboat station in the distance. You won't risk a confrontation there; I'll be safe.

I climb up onto the sea wall, intending to drop down onto the beach below. That's when I realise I've fucked up: the tide's in. The sea is fierce and the waves are smashing against the wall, but I've made a plan and I'm sticking to it.

I start running; one foot in front of the other, that's all I have to do. I'm so focused on the lifeboat slipway up ahead that I don't see it until it's too late: the rogue wave that rises twelve feet into the air and comes crashing down on top of the sea wall.

As the wave swallows me, my body feels heavy, weighed down like ballast as if the sea has found its way inside me, filling me up. In that moment, I realise I've just made the biggest mistake of my life.

My second biggest mistake was trusting you.

I

GRACE

I can tell from the look on Charles's face that he's starting to enjoy it: the feeling that something bad is about to happen. Ever since he was a little boy, Charles has loved storms. He told me once that when he was eight, he seized the opportunity to watch the weather gods unleash their fury, sneaking out of the house in the middle of the night as his unsuspecting parents slept. For the best part of an hour, he crouched under the eaves of his sister's Wendy house, watching open-mouthed as lightning bolts carved zigzags across the sky. I love his fearlessness and hunger for new experiences; it's one of the reasons I was attracted to him in the first place.

Judging by what I can see through the rain-lashed window, there's a storm brewing right *now* over our heads; no wonder Charles is looking so pleased. The sky is big and black and even though it's only four o'clock, the landscape is already beginning to lose its definition. Meanwhile, the wind that began as a stiff breeze when we boarded the train at Salisbury has developed into a full-blown gale.

Naturally, Charles and I checked the weather forecast before we set off, but we weren't about to let a little old 'severe weather warning' spoil our plans, not when we had booked and paid for our first-class rail tickets and boutique hotel with its rainfall shower and two AA Rosette restaurant. In any case, who cancels their honeymoon?

'I hope we're not going to spend the entire fortnight stuck in the hotel room,' I say, sighing heavily.

Charles reaches over and takes my hand. 'Actually, I think that would be rather romantic … the two of us, holed up together, some place warm and cosy.'

'But you hate being stuck in one place for too long; you'll be bored.'

He draws my hand to his lips and kisses my knuckles. 'Grace, my love, I could be stuck in a lift with you for a hundred years and never be bored.'

My heart swells absurdly at the words. I love Charles so much. Not smugly or sloppily, but with a great thumping visceral certainty. We met two years ago at a sponsored bungee jump, organised to raise funds for a local leukaemia charity. Charles was behind me in the queue as we waited to plunge from a crane platform 160 feet above the ground. When he saw how nervous I was, he offered to take me through some deep breathing exercises to calm me down. It proved to be a highly effective distraction, not least because of his impressive physique and his eyes that were like trap doors, dark and deep. Once we were both safely back on terra firma, he proposed celebrating our achievement with a drink in the pub around the corner. I thought about it for all of two seconds and then I said yes.

The more we talked, the more I liked him and, as day turned into night, something shifted in the air and I felt our bodies draw towards one another, magnetic and irresistible. Later, as we swapped numbers outside the pub, I leaned into his chest and my ear found his heartbeat. I knew there and then that this was the start of something special.

Although our relationship became serious fairly early on, I never entertained any thoughts of marriage, or even a joint mortgage. Back then, the very word 'husband' smacked to me of tedium, of entrapment, of constant petty bickering about whose

4

turn it was to empty the dishwasher and, if I was lucky, crap sex (if I was *un*lucky, there would be no sex at all). I was convinced my life was perfect just the way it was: a well-paid job as a senior HR exec for a global tech company, a beautiful apartment over-looking the park, and a large and loyal circle of friends, many of whom I'd known since school. I had absolutely no intention of giving up my independence any time soon. But last summer, Charles and I went to Turkey and everything I thought I knew about myself turned out to be wrong.

It was only our second foreign holiday together, a three-centre break that was weeks in the planning. Up until then, I saw myself as young, strong, fit ... in other words, *invincible*. It never occurred to me that I might need to rely on anyone for anything. But sometimes, even the most charmed existence can change in the blink of an eye. That's exactly what happened to me when I had my accident. I understood for the first time that I *did* need someone; I needed Charles. Because if it wasn't for him, I would be dead.

Recuperating from my physical injuries was a slow and often painful process, but much more difficult to deal with was the psychological fallout. Before the accident, I was confident, ambi-tious, eager to step outside my comfort zone. Afterwards, I changed completely: I became cautious, jumpy, overly sensitive. Night-times were the worst. Alone in the darkness, coiled tight with fear, I squeezed my memories into the murkiest corners of my mind as I tried to forget just how close I came to death. Every part of my body seemed to jangle and my head throbbed with the effort of blocking out all the thoughts I couldn't allow myself to think. While the fear has receded, it's still there, an ugly, misshapen thing lurking in the shadows, waiting for the next opportunity to sink its teeth into my neck.

Even now, five months later, I don't like reliving what hap-pened that day in Turkey ... feeling vulnerable, feeling mortal, knowing I was utterly alone. Waiting for help that might never arrive. So mostly, I push it to the back of my mind. Charles and I haven't even talked about it. Maybe one day we will, but not yet.

I should point out that the fallout from the accident wasn't all negative. Before we went to Turkey, Charles and I had been living on opposite sides of the city. But after I was discharged from hospital I found that the pleasure I usually took in my independence, the relief I felt on shutting the door of my apartment at the end of a long day of being sociable, had evaporated. I came to the sudden realisation that I didn't want to go through life alone, and that the most important things in the short time we spend on this earth were *relationships*, not building a career or having a beautiful home. I think Charles sensed my change of heart and when he popped the question as we celebrated my twenty-seventh birthday with a group of friends, I didn't hesitate to say yes. In that moment, it was as if I'd found the missing piece of a jigsaw puzzle that had been there in the box all the time.

My parents were somewhat taken aback when I told them Charles and I were engaged. I come from an unashamedly upper-middle-class family; Mum's a dentist and Dad is CEO of a pharmaceuticals company. Although they like him enormously, I think Charles, with his lower second-class degree and his job as a construction manager for a national firm of builders, wasn't quite the high-achieving husband they had in mind for me. Even so, when they saw how happy I was, they soon got on board.

Charles and I didn't anticipate tying the knot quite so quickly, not least because all the nicest wedding venues are booked up years in advance. But then we learned of a last-minute cancellation at a stunning historic home in the Wiltshire village where I grew up and where my parents still live. I was hesitant at first, fearing it might be bad luck to step into another couple's shoes, but Charles convinced me it was too good an opportunity to miss.

He was right. I know *everyone* says this, but our wedding really was perfect. As the shadows pooled on the Valentine's Day ceremony, I was flushed with pride in my new husband and brimming with excitement about our shared future. And now here we are, forty-eight hours later, heading for our honeymoon in Cornwall.

Things were quite frenetic in the run-up to the wedding and these two weeks of pure relaxation are just what I need. With any luck, I think to myself as the train emerges from a tunnel, we'll arrive at our hotel just in time for pre-dinner drinks.

Suddenly, a huge fork of lightning illuminates the sky and the woman on the other side of the aisle gives a loud gasp. 'I hope we're safe inside here,' she says to no one in particular.

Charles leans over to her. 'It's okay, you can relax. A train is actually a pretty good place to be during an electrical storm.'

The woman's eyebrows shoot up. 'Really?'

Charles nods. 'In the unlikely event of a direct strike, the electricity will be routed safely through the metal structure of the carriage. It'll totally fry the train's electrics, of course, but that's not our problem.' He points to the laptop resting on her knees. 'Unless of course you've got that thing plugged in.'

Without a moment's hesitation, the woman reaches down and yanks the plug out of the power point. 'Thanks for the heads up,' she says, beaming at Charles.

I give my husband a playful nudge with my elbow. 'You're such a geek, hon. How do you even know all that stuff?'

The words are hardly out of my mouth when there's a long, loud screech as the train driver brakes hard. *Very* hard. I stare wide-eyed at Charles and we both grip the armrests, bracing for a possible impact.

'What the hell ...' Charles mouths at me.

The braking seems to go on for ever, but finally the train comes to a juddering halt. For a moment, there's stunned silence in the carriage; then a child starts crying.

'Was that an emergency stop?' I ask Charles.

'It certainly felt like it,' he replies with a grimace.

'You don't think we've hit something, do you?' someone behind me says. Suppressing a shudder, I cast around for the nearest speaker, expecting the PA system to burst into life at any moment. When it doesn't, a susurrus of anxious murmurs breaks out in the carriage. A few minutes later the automatic doors slide open and the guard appears. He makes his way through the carriage, the muscles between his eyebrows tightly contracted.

'What's going on, buddy?' Charles asks as he strides past.

The guard's frown deepens. 'Your guess is as good as mine; I'm on my way to speak to the driver now. I'll make an announcement as soon as I have an update, so if everyone could just bear with me.'

'Sure, no problem,' Charles tells the guard's departing back.

Glowering, I press my face to the window, cupping my hands around my face to block out the glare of the fluorescent lights. All I can see in the gathering gloom is a field with a group of cows huddled in one corner.

'I hope we're not going to be here for long,' I mutter. 'Our hotel stops serving dinner at eight.'

Charles gives my thigh a quick squeeze. 'Don't worry, there's always room service – and if all else fails, I've packed loads of protein bars in the suitcase.'

My eyebrows knit together. 'It bloody well better not come to that.'

When there's still no announcement after fifteen minutes, people begin to get restless. A red-faced man with dandruffy shoulders starts pacing up and down, talking loudly into his mobile phone. Further down the carriage, a queue has begun to form for the loo. The boy who had been crying earlier has stopped and is now complaining that he's thirsty.

Now that the train's engine is dead, the storm outside is clearly audible. There are frequent rumbles of thunder, interspersed with the occasional flash and crackle of lightning in the distance. The temperature in the carriage has dropped dramatically. As I pull a scarf out of the backpack on my knee, the guard's voice comes over the PA.

'Sorry, everyone, I'm afraid we're going nowhere tonight; there's a tree on the line up ahead of us. Unfortunately, we have no alternative but to evacuate the train. Can I please ask all passengers to remain in their seats and await further instructions.'

2

CHARLES

This isn't the start to our honeymoon I'd been hoping for. I thought we would be sipping champagne from the trolley service by now, not dragging a suitcase over a slippery railway track in a Force 10 gale. We've given up with the umbrella, it's no match for the wind, but thankfully we had the foresight to pack our waterproof trousers and Gore-Tex jackets. Compared to some of our fellow passengers, who look soaked to the skin already, we're relatively well off.

After everything that has happened, I hate putting Grace through this – not that the storm's *my* fault, of course, but I still feel bad about it. She only came off her crutches a few weeks ago and the physio says it will be a couple more months before she's built her strength up and is walking normally again. She's incredibly self-conscious about her limp, even though it's not that bad. In any case, nobody's paying attention to her, they've all got their heads down against the wind and rain.

Fortunately, we were only a couple of hundred yards from the nearest station when our journey came to an abrupt end. They've turned the live rail off, so we're perfectly safe. Grace can't walk very fast, so it's no surprise that we're among the last to reach the safety of the station. The tree – a massive oak, by the look of it – has come down just beyond the station platform and it isn't just blocking the line; it's brought down the power cables too.

I must admit I hadn't been paying too much attention to our progress while we were on the train; I was too focused on my beautiful wife. Consequently, it came as quite a surprise to find out we were in Saltwater. I know it, you see, this quaint fishing village with its sheltered sandy beach. Grace can't believe it when I tell her I've been here before. 'What are the chances of that?' she says incredulously.

When I was a kid, I spent several summers in Saltwater with my family. It's not as fashionable as some of the tourist magnets on the north coast, but I think it's fair to say it has its own unique charm. I didn't think I'd ever come back – and to be honest I'm not quite sure how I feel about being here.

A staycation honeymoon was Grace's idea. Her parents offered to pay for a fortnight in the Maldives or some other exotic destination of our choice, but Grace couldn't face the thought of being stuck in the cramped cabin of a 747 for hours on end, even though it's never been an issue in the past. Lots of things about her have changed since the accident. Not that I love her any less because of it. Sometimes, I think I prefer the new, softer, more vulnerable Grace; the Grace who isn't afraid to ask for help, instead of always thinking she can do everything on her own.

All credit to her, she showed amazing bravery that day in Turkey; I'm so proud of her. In her position, most people would have been freaking out but, even though she was scared out of her mind, she managed to hold it together. I'm all too aware that it could have had a very different – and not so happy – ending. Just thinking about it sends a shiver up my spine.

I could have lost her that day. I beat myself up about it for ages afterwards. I should have done things differently; my reactions should have been quicker. Still, looking on the bright side, an experience like that does help you put things in perspective; it helps you figure out what really matters in life. That's why

I'm not that bothered about a silly little storm. Or the fact we're probably going to be stuck in Saltwater for a day or two while they drag the tree off the line and fix the power cable. So long as I'm with Grace, that's all that matters.

When we arrive at the station, rail staff are waiting for us with cups of hot tea. They hand out maps of the village and a list of half a dozen guest houses where most of us will be sleeping tonight – unless, of course, we want to take our chances by road, which Grace and I most definitely do not. In any case, it's more than an hour's drive to St Ives from here. A cab will cost an arm and a leg and I'm not convinced it's safe to be on the roads in these conditions. By the look of it, this storm is only set to get worse.

While Grace nips to the ladies, I try to steal a march on the other passengers by phoning the only four-star accommodation on the list, hoping to get us booked into the best room they have available. Unfortunately, I can't get a signal on my phone; one of the station staff tells me the mobile reception in the village is hit and miss, even when it's not blowing a hoolie.

'As long as the roof isn't leaking, I really don't care where we stay,' Grace says, trooper that she is.

What with one thing and another, we're the last ones to leave the station. We set off towards the nearest B&B, which is only two streets away according to the map. Saltwater is deserted; on an evening like this, everyone has battened down the hatches, but despite the weather, the village is just as pretty as I remember, with its cobbled streets and rows of candy-coloured houses.

When we get to the guest house, the young woman on duty tells us apologetically that they're fully booked. The next three places, including the four-star option I'd earmarked for us, are all displaying *No Vacancies* signs, so we don't even bother enquiring. Meanwhile, our faces are caked with salt from the wind blowing off the sea and the rain is starting to leach through our jackets. We're hungry too, neither of us has eaten a thing since lunch.

'How many more places to go?' Grace asks.

I pull the list out of my pocket. The paper's so wet, the print is barely legible and if I'm not careful the whole thing will disintegrate in my hands. 'Just one, a pub called The Boathouse,' I reply, squinting to make out the words.

Grace smiles wanly. 'Let's hope we get lucky this time.' I can hear the optimism in her voice beginning to fade.

Unfortunately, it's more bad news; one of our fellow train passengers has just bagged the last available room. I'm feeling pretty frustrated at this point, but trying not to show it. No doubt the hostelries of Saltwater would usually be half empty at this time of year, out of season, questionable weather, but now they're packed to the rafters, thanks to that damn tree on the line.

'What are we going to do?' Grace asks forlornly. 'I suppose we could always go back to the station.'

I need to get my wife somewhere warm and dry, and there's no way we're spending the night in a station waiting room. An idea is forming in my mind; I just hope it's the right one.

'Follow me,' I say, taking an abrupt left turn and walking up a street that leads away from the sea, our wheeled suitcase bouncing along behind me.

Grace starts limping after me. 'Where are we going? I thought we'd tried everywhere on the list.'

'Ah, but I know a place that isn't on the list,' I tell her.

As soon as I spot the antiques shop where my mother loved to browse, I know I'm on the right track. Sure enough, we turn the next corner and The Anchorage looms into view. Even as a child, I remember thinking how different it was from the other houses in Saltwater – this grey stone monolith, standing alone on a bluff above the lifeboat station. I remember the owners telling my parents that it had been built by a Victorian sea captain who'd lost several members of his family in tragic circumstances. I forget the details, and in any case I suspect it wasn't even true, just a yarn they liked to spin for the amusement of guests, especially impressionable pubescent boys. Some of the locals used to joke that the place was haunted, but that didn't stop it being one of the most popular tourist hangouts in town. Now, in the rapidly gathering gloom with the waves crashing against the sea wall below, The Anchorage is every bit as imposing as I remember.

Despite its austere appearance, I remember the guest house being wonderfully cosy inside, and very well maintained by its owners. However, as we get nearer, it's clear that standards have slipped. The paint on the windowsills is peeling and there's a big crack on the stained-glass fanlight above the front door. It occurs to me, belatedly, that it might not even be operating as a B&B any more; it must be twelve or thirteen years since I was last here after all. But then I spot a sign, rusted at the edges, hanging from the gatepost: *Welcome to The Anchorage Guest House, All Major Credit Cards Accepted.*

As I open the gate, I'm pricked by a sudden, vivid memory of myself at the age of fourteen, bursting through the front door of the guest house and running down the steps, hewn out of the rock face, that led to the beach. That summer was a real turning point for me. It was the last time I felt like a child – mucking around in the sea, eating ice cream sundaes in the Italian cafe, chatting to the volunteers at the lifeboat station – happy and innocent and utterly carefree. By the time I returned to school in September, it was an entirely different world: GCSE coursework, smoking behind the bike sheds, trying to chat up my lab partner in chemistry, a petite redhead with an endearing lisp and endless legs (needless to say, I was punching well above my weight). All that seems a lifetime ago now.

'What is this place?' Grace asks, shouting to be heard above the howling wind.

'It's where we used to stay when I was a boy. What do you think?'

Grace has got one of those faces that can't hide what she's feeling. Her expression right now tells me she's not very impressed. 'I think it's fair to say The Anchorage is past its heyday,' she hollers. 'Do we really want to try our luck here?'

I gesture hopelessly at the gunpowder sky. 'I think we need to take refuge wherever we can. The storm's getting worse. This might be our only option.'

Grace wipes away the raindrops that are streaming off the end of her nose. 'In that case, what are we waiting for?'

3

GRACE

The woman who comes to the door is in her mid-fifties or there-abouts, and rather striking. Her eyes are a bright, gas-jet blue and she has dark hair, tigered with grey, that hangs loose about her shoulders.

She appears surprised – *shocked*, almost – to see us huddled there on the doorstep. I guess we must look pretty awful. I'm pretty sure I have mascara running down my cheeks; meanwhile Charles's curly hair is plastered unattractively to his head like a helmet. The woman looks us up and down, her shoulders drawn up to her ears, like a cobra ready to strike.

'Good evening,' she says, a faint question mark hanging over the greeting.

Charles clears his throat; he seems nervous all of a sudden. 'Hello there, we're, er ... we're looking for a room for the night. I don't suppose there's any chance you can accommodate us?'

A smile stretches tightly across the woman's angular face. 'But of course,' she says unexpectedly.

Charles looks at me triumphantly. 'That's the best news we've had all day, isn't it, Grace?'

The woman opens the door wide and beckons us in. 'Welcome to The Anchorage,' she says in a stiff, museum-guide voice.

We find ourselves in a long hallway that smells faintly musty, like mildew or sour milk. The walls are painted a nondescript greyish-green – the sort of shade that Farrow & Ball might call 'Exhumed' – and a vase of chrysanthemums are wilting on the console table. As first impressions go, it's not a great one, but I'm glad to be out of the wind and rain. Our hostess shows us where we can hang our dripping waterproofs and instructs us to leave our luggage at the foot of the stairs.

'I expect you'd like to warm up before I show you to your room,' she says. 'Why don't you come through to the guest lounge?'

The only thing I want to do right now is change into some dry clothes and settle into the room, but when I glance at Charles he's already nodding in agreement.

My spirits rise when the woman leads us into a generously proportioned sitting room. An open fire is blazing in the hearth and several high-backed armchairs are grouped cosily around it. I make a beeline for the fire, arms outstretched, hungry for its warmth. It isn't until I get closer that I realise one of the armchairs is occupied, by a man with a peppery beard and a hairline in rapid retreat.

He stands up and gives a quick shake of his head, as though trying to rouse himself from sleep.

'I do hope we're not disturbing you,' I say, as he bends down to pick up the newspaper that's fallen from his lap.

'Not at all,' he replies, tossing the newspaper onto the chair. He holds out his hand for me to shake. 'I'm Michael; it's a pleasure to meet you.' His gaze drifts over my shoulder. 'Is this your husband?'

'It certainly is,' says Charles, reaching past me to pump the man's hand blokeishly. 'I'm Charles, nice to meet you.'

Just then, the sash windows rattle in a sudden gust, making me jump. 'Looks like you got here just in time,' Michael remarks. 'From what I hear, this accursed storm's only set to get worse; people are being advised not to travel unless absolutely necessary.'

I turn to look out through the window. The curtains are open and in the glow of the street lamp, I can just about make out the unkempt front lawn, now a restless sea of trembling grass. I give a little shiver and fold my arms tightly across my chest. 'I'm so relieved we've finally found somewhere to stay. Every other B&B in the village is fully booked.'

The tip of Michael's tongue glosses his lips. 'Lucky them.'

'How long are you staying here?' Charles asks him pleasantly.

'Oh, sorry, I should have said. I'm the owner; I live here.'

'Ah,' Charles says, crooking one side of his mouth into a smile. 'When I saw you relaxing there in front of the fire, I assumed you were a fellow guest. I don't blame you for taking a break. You must be rushed off your feet, with all the unexpected arrivals.'

Michael's forehead crinkles in confusion; I can see he hasn't got the faintest idea what Charles is talking about.

'There's a tree on the railway line at Saltwater,' I explain. 'They had to evacuate our train; that's why the village is suddenly over-run with people looking for beds for the night.'

'Goodness, I had no idea, how awful for you,' he says. 'But we haven't had any other new visitors this evening; you're the first ones to try your luck here.'

'I expect that's because you weren't on the list of guest houses that the rail staff gave us,' Charles says. 'We're really grateful you managed to squeeze us in. It's pretty hairy out there; I wouldn't be at all surprised if more trees come down tonight.'

Michael gives a little shake of his shoulders. 'We've had bad storms before but nothing on this scale. I do hope there won't be any fatalities.'

There's a brief, awkward silence that's broken by the sound of our hostess coughing into her fist. I'd almost forgotten she was there. 'I'm Pamela Jeffrey,' she says tersely. 'Michael's wife.'

Charles starts to say something, then stops, his eyes ping-ponging between husband and wife. 'Oh my God, I don't believe it,' he says, clapping his hands together. 'You two are still running this place, after all this time.'

Pamela gives him a questioning look. 'Have we met before?'

'Yes,' Charles says, nodding vigorously. 'I stayed here with my family several times when I was a child.'

Pamela frowns. 'What did you say your surname was?'

'I didn't, but it's McKenna, *Charlie* McKenna, as I was then. You probably don't remember me.' He gives a self-effacing smile. 'It was a long time ago and I've changed quite a bit since then.'

There's a ripple of recognition on Pamela's face. 'Hang on a minute,' she says slowly. 'I think I do remember your family.'

'Seriously?'

'Yes, yes, I'm sure I do. You had an older sister … what was her name … Annie? Abby?'

'Ally.'

'Ally!' Pamela laughs self-consciously. She turns to her husband. 'You remember the McKennas, don't you?'

Michael thinks for a moment and then his eyes widen. 'Yes, of course I do,' he says, although I think he might be pretending. He smiles. 'Little Charlie McKenna, eh? And now look at you – all grown up and married.'

'Only just,' Charles replies. 'We're actually on our honeymoon – or at least we *were* until that wretched tree came down.'

'I'm so sorry, I've just realised I haven't introduced myself,' I say, glancing first at Michael and then Pamela. 'I'm Grace.'

Pamela gives me a long, cold stare. She has a penetrating gaze that makes me feel as if she is unpeeling layers off me, seeing deeper than other people can. I can't think what I've done to upset her, but her hostility is palpable.

She waits for several seconds too long before finally responding in a flat voice. 'Newlyweds - well, how about that? Congratulations to you both.'

'Yes, congratulations,' Michael says, clamping a firm hand on Charles's shoulder. 'I think that calls for a celebratory drink. We can't run to champagne, I'm afraid, but I've got a pretty decent Prosecco.'

'A glass of Prosecco would be lovely,' I say gratefully. A drink is *exactly* what I need.

'And what about something to eat?' Pamela asks. 'We don't serve an evening meal as such, but I can rustle up some toasted cheese sandwiches and a bit of salad if you like.'

I feel myself begin to relax. She sounds a bit more welcoming now.

Charles smiles. 'That would hit the spot nicely – but only if it's not too much trouble.'

'It's no trouble at all.'

Charles reaches into his jeans pocket and pulls out his phone, frowning when he sees the screen.

'I don't want to take advantage of your hospitality, but would it be possible to use your landline very quickly? I've got no signal and I need to call our hotel in St Ives to let them know we've been delayed.'

'I'm afraid not,' Pamela says with a brisk shake of her head. 'The storm seems to have interfered with the landline; it hasn't been working since lunchtime and neither is the Wi-Fi.'

On hearing this, I feel tears catch behind my eyes. I know I'm being utterly pathetic, but I was so looking forward to arriving at our hotel in St Ives. I can't believe we'll be spending the first night of our honeymoon in this sad little place, with no means of communicating with the outside world. 'That's a shame,' I say, biting my lip. I turn to Charles. 'I hope the hotel won't cancel our booking when we don't show up tonight.'

'Don't worry, darling,' Charles tells me. 'Let's relax for now and we'll figure something out in the morning.'

'Good idea,' Pamela says. 'You two make yourselves at home in front of the fire and I'll see to those sandwiches.'

Michael rubs his palms together. 'And I'll fetch the Prosecco.' He follows his wife to the door, then he stops and looks back over his shoulder. For a moment, his expression of bland geniality is dislodged by a flash of emotion. He gives a small, tight smile. 'I'm so glad you came back, Charlie.'

Now that we're alone, I have a proper look around the room. It's clean enough and the furniture is clearly good quality, but it's a million miles away from the minimalist chic of our hotel in St Ives. Still, I tell myself, we're lucky to find a room at all and it will only be for one night, two at most.

'I can't believe there's no phone or Wi-Fi,' I mutter, as I study the uncurated jumble of ornaments that are ranged behind the smoked-glass doors of a deeply unfashionable dresser. 'I didn't think such a thing was even possible in the twenty-first century.'

Charles comes up behind me and peers over my shoulder at a grotesque Toby jug. 'I dunno, modern life can be so stressful at times. I quite like the idea of being cut off from the outside world for a while.' He drapes his arms loosely around my shoulders. 'I know you'd much rather be in St Ives, but it's still wonderful to be on honeymoon with you, Mrs McKenna.'

'Likewise, *Mr* McKenna.' I lean back, resting my head against his muscular chest. 'Aren't you amazed the Jeffreys still remember you after all this time? They must have had hundreds of guests staying here over the years.'

Charles kisses the top of my head. 'What can I say? I'm obviously an unforgettable kind of guy.'

'I can't disagree with that,' I say, smiling. 'But don't you think they're a bit ...' I hesitate and add in a stage whisper, '*Odd*?'

Charles releases me and goes over to the fireplace. 'Not really, I think we just caught them unawares. I doubt they get much passing trade up here on the bluff, especially in the middle of a storm.' He exhales noisily as he sinks into an armchair. 'They were certainly very kind to my family all those years ago. Pamela used to make me an omelette every morning because she knew I liked them, even though it wasn't on the breakfast menu. And she was very kind to my sister the time she tripped over a rug in the dining room and bashed her face on the edge of a table. Ally's nose bled all over the white tablecloth and Pamela didn't bat an eyelid.'

I roll my eyes. 'I think that says more about the perils of having an unsecured rug in a public place than any kindness on Pamela's part.'

'Aw, don't be like that, Grace. They mean well and that's the most important thing.'

'Hmm,' I say, not convinced. There's just something about the Jeffreys that makes me feel on edge.

It's ten o'clock before we reluctantly tear ourselves away from the fire and follow Michael up two flights of stairs to the top floor. He leads us into a spacious double room where our suitcase is already waiting on the luggage rack. The room has a sloping ceiling and the walls are covered with a pink sprigged paper that's reminiscent of vintage Laura Ashley. It's well furnished with a chest of drawers, an armchair and a large wardrobe. There's even an old-fashioned valet stand. There's no sign of a TV, however; I noticed that there wasn't one in the sitting room either.

'The bathroom's at the end of the corridor,' Michael tells us before he leaves us to it. 'You're the only guests on this floor, so you'll have it to yourselves. Breakfast is served from seven-thirty to nine-thirty, so join us in the dining room whenever you're ready.'

Once he's gone, I leave Charles alone in the room while I head to the bathroom for a quick shower. The pressure's not great, but the water's piping hot and plentiful; there's even a full-sized bottle of complimentary body wash. As I dry myself on one of the thin towels, I'm conscious of a tension behind my forehead. I press my fingertips to the sides of my head, massaging my temples. It's probably just a dehydration headache. I haven't drunk nearly enough water today and the two glasses of Prosecco I had downstairs won't have helped matters.

On the way back to the room, I stop to admire a large heron sculpture that's sitting on a low table, halfway along the corridor. It's made of painted metal and looks very rustic, the sort of thing you'd find at a craft market. Its elongated beak seems too big for its body and it's slightly bent at the end, as if it's been knocked over at some point. Above it, on the wall, is a collection of framed photographs. There are black and white shots from a bygone era – fisherman working on their boats, a church fete with children dancing round a maypole, the local cricket team proudly showing off a trophy – all rather charming. There are some more recent colour shots too, family pictures by the look of them, taken mostly at the seaside. I only give them a cursory glance; other people's family albums are never as interesting as one's own. I remember what Charles has told me, about the couple and their kindness, and try my best to shake off the uneasy feeling I have about them. I shouldn't judge the Jeffreys before I get to know them, but something tells me there's a reason this place wasn't on the list the train station staff gave us.

When I get back to our room, Charles is already in bed, so I peel off the pyjamas I changed into after my shower and climb in beside him, eager to feel the press of his warm body against mine. He responds immediately, but our love-making is more restrained than usual. I think we're both conscious that we might be overheard by guests in the rooms below.

Afterwards, Charles falls asleep straight away. Tiredness burns behind my eyes, but still I can't sleep and none of my usual techniques – counting, listing, deep-breathing – will calm my racing mind. I curl into Charles and press my face into his back, inhaling the scent of lavender detergent on his T-shirt. Above our heads, the wind continues to rage, a low, angry snarl that rattles the gutters. Adding to the cacophony is the distant sound of waves collapsing and exploding on the shoreline, one after the other, again and again.

I think back to what Charles said, about a train carriage being a safe haven in a storm. How safe are we here, up in the attic? There's probably a TV aerial attached to the chimney and if that gets struck by lightning, the whole roof will go up in flames. I close my eyes tighter and try to distract my racing mind with nicer thoughts – the 400-thread-count sheets at our hotel in St Ives and our planned trip to the Barbara Hepworth Sculpture Garden, which has been on my bucket list for ages. Hopefully it won't be too long before we're there, and this place, The Anchorage, will just become an awkward evening to tell our friends about.

Eventually, when exhaustion catches up with me, I drift off to sleep.

In the breathless darkness of the night, I'm suddenly awake. At first, I'm not sure what's roused me. I have a clear memory of a sound, something sharp and high-pitched, but I can't tell whether it was just a dream. The only light in the room comes from the moon filtering through the gap in the curtains. I lie very still, my eyes shut, the remnants of the dream still cobwebbing my mind. Outside, the wind continues to hammer away, almost drowning out Charles's intermittent snores. Then I hear the sound again and my eyes snap open. It's the voice of a young child. I can't make out what they're saying, but judging by the tone they're upset.

The child's voice is getting louder, it sounds as if they're in the next room, but Michael told us we're the only guests on this floor. The noise must be drifting up through the floorboards.

After a few minutes, I realise I'm never going to get back to sleep until I've stretched my restless legs. I feel wired. Anxious. I need to stop my mind running at a million miles an hour, the way it always does when I spend the night in an unfamiliar place. Sighing, I fold back the duvet and climb out of bed. I've no idea what the time is, but the house is very cold. It's dark too, so I pick up my phone from the bedside table and switch the torch on. By the time I reach the bedroom door, the child has gone quiet.

Gingerly, I make my way down the corridor, wincing as a floorboard creaks beneath my bare feet. As I approach the collection of photos I spotted earlier, the light from my torch catches the cluster of family snaps. My eye is caught by one photograph in particular and I experience a flutter of dislocation, a sense that something has shifted.

It's a picture of a man and a woman on a beach and they're holding the hand of a little girl, aged around six or seven. The couple are both dressed in shorts and T-shirts and the little girl is wearing a red swimsuit. She's holding a huge pink inflatable, a hideous thing, some sort of bird with a distended S-shaped neck. But that's not why I'm staring at the picture in horror; it's the fact that the face of the little girl is missing. I hold my torch up against the picture frame and lean in for a closer look.

Where the little girl's smiling face should be is an ugly grey smudge. I think at first the damage might be accidental but no, the little girl's face has been deliberately scratched out. There's a twisting feeling in my stomach. Who on earth would do such a thing? A previous guest, perhaps, some bored teenager thinking it would be a laugh. And then another thought occurs me – why didn't I notice the defaced image when I was looking at the photos earlier on? Has this just been done?

No, that's a ridiculous idea.

With a bemused shake of my head, I continue on to the bathroom. I don't really need the loo, but I might as well go while I'm up. As I make my way back to the room, I keep my gaze fixed firmly ahead. I have no desire to see that faceless little girl again.

Soon, I'm back in bed and burrowing under the warm duvet. Before I even close my eyes there's a crack of thunder that's loud enough to wake the dead. I look over at Charles, but amazingly he doesn't stir. I watch him for a few moments, the twitch of his eyelids, the rise and fall of his chest. I have a very real sense that right now I am alone with my dark thoughts in this strange place.

Just then, I hear the child again, not talking this time, but crying – thick, clotted sobs that make me grimace in empathy. Storms used to terrify me too when I was little. I make a mental note to look out for the child at breakfast; perhaps I can offer some words of comfort. The crying goes on for several minutes and eventually dies away. Only then do I feel myself begin to relax. I try to go back to sleep, but my mind won't let me. Eventually I give up and lie on my back, listening to the wind and waiting for the dawn.

4

I'm not myself today. I haven't been for ages; I just feel so anxious all the time. It's a horrid feeling, like a ring of steel tight around my skull. Sometimes, I don't even feel like getting up in the morning. I'm too scared about what the day has in store for me.

I've been putting on a brave face, but he knows something's wrong. Of course he does. Nothing gets past him.

He thinks I don't have anything to be anxious about. That I – that we – have a lot to be grateful for. He keeps saying we should count our blessings and look to the future. I know he means well, but his tired clichés and unsubstantiated optimism are beginning to get on my nerves.

I don't mean it as a criticism, but he's less insightful than me, less observant. Sometimes he can't see what's going on right under his nose.

I keep trying to tell him that strange things are happening here. Things that defy common sense or logic. But he won't listen; he says I'm just imagining it.

His words are like little needles, jabbing at my skin. He says them so often that it feels like a line in a play, spoken with perfect conviction every night but, in the end, they are his thoughts, not mine.

I tell myself in the small hours when my nerves are stretched their thinnest that my fear is irrational. But I know it's not. There is an evil force at work in Saltwater.

5

GRACE

I clap a hand over my mouth, smothering a yawn. It's not surprising I feel like shit – I've barely slept. My left leg is sore and stiff. I'm usually pathological about performing the daily exercise regimen the physio taught me, but with all the drama of yesterday, exercising was the last thing on my mind.

Charles, needless to say, barely moved the entire night. As a result, my husband who sits across the breakfast table from me is annoyingly fresh-faced and chipper. I do my best to look interested while he starts telling me about Saltwater's history as the gin-smuggling capital of Cornwall, but right now all I can think about is how quickly the coffee we ordered is going to arrive.

I'm a little surprised to see we're the only people in the dining room. There is no evidence – crumpled napkins, dirty teacups and the like – that our fellow guests have already breakfasted. Perhaps, like me, they were kept awake by the storm and are now enjoying a lie-in.

'Once upon a time, smuggling would have been the main source of employment in these parts; everyone was in on it, even the local magistrates,' Charles is saying, in an animated voice. 'Rumour has it that illegally-imported gin was so plentiful back then, the locals used it to clean their windows.'

I smile, but my mind is elsewhere. I'm thinking of the child I heard crying in the night and wondering how they're doing today.

When Charles finishes his monologue, I ask him when he thinks the trains will be up and running again.

Frowning, he turns over his shoulder to look out of the window, which overlooks The Anchorage's sprawling back garden. Although the storm seems to have eased a little, a gusty wind buffets the holly hedge and sends a plastic plant pot careening across the lawn.

'Not yet,' he replies. 'It wouldn't have been safe for the engineers to work on the line overnight.'

I don't bother to hide my disappointment. 'Jesus, I hope we're not going to be stuck here another night.'

'Come on, Grace, it could be worse,' he says gently. 'To be honest, I'm quite enjoying being back in Saltwater. There's a few things I wouldn't mind showing you before we leave … places I used to go as a kid.'

I feel myself soften. 'I'd like that,' I tell him – and I mean it. I love hearing stories from Charles's childhood, the way you do when you care deeply about someone. No matter how well you think you know a person, there's always more to learn.

'Maybe not this morning, though,' he adds. 'It's still pretty rough out there. Have you managed to get a phone signal yet?'

I shake my head.

'Me neither.'

Just then, Michael appears with a laden tray and I'm pleasantly surprised to see it contains a cafetière; I was expecting instant in a place like this.

'I hope you both slept well,' Michael says as he begins offloading his tray. 'I thought you would appreciate the privacy of the top floor, but it occurred to me afterwards that it might have been a bit noisy up there in the eaves with the wind whistling round your ears.'

'It was fine, thank you,' Charles replies. 'The room's very comfortable.'

Michael sets down a milk jug next to the sugar bowl. 'Good, good, that's what we like to hear.' He turns away from our table and goes over to a pine sideboard.

'How many guest rooms do you have?' I ask, helping myself to coffee.

'Nine,' he replies, as he rummages in a drawer. 'Six doubles and three twins.'

'What's your occupancy rate like at this time of year?'

He closes the drawer and returns to our table, brandishing a pair of sugar tongs.

'Business is a little slow, to be honest, but we're hoping things will pick up at Easter.'

I look around the empty dining room, noticing for the first time that ours is the only table laid with cutlery and napkins; all the others are bare. 'How many guests do you have at the moment?'

He turns away and begins fussing with the cord of a window blind. 'Actually, it's just you.'

'Really?' Charles says in surprise. 'You've no other bookings at all?'

Michael's lips tighten. 'Unfortunately not.'

I sip the scalding coffee. It's good, *very* good, in fact. I go to take another sip and then a sudden thought strikes me. I set my cup down so hard that coffee slops over the rim into the saucer. 'We can't be the only ones,' I say, rather more sharply than I meant to. 'I heard a child in the night.'

Charles gives an embarrassed laugh. 'Darling, I should think Mr Jeffrey knows better than us how many guests are here.'

Michael goes back over to the sideboard to retrieve the empty tray he left there. 'I expect it was just the wind, whistling down the chimney.' He clears his throat. 'Your breakfasts are on their way; is there anything else I can get you?'

'The landline ... is it working yet?' Charles enquires hopefully. 'We really need to call our hotel in St Ives.'

Our host shakes his head. 'I'm afraid not; I think some telegraph poles must have come down.'

'Wi-Fi?'

Another shake of the head. 'There is a payphone in the village; it might be worth trying your luck there.' He speaks hesitantly, as if this is information he shouldn't be sharing with us. 'You'll find it on the high street, just outside the post office.'

'Thanks, we'll check it out,' Charles says.

'I'll leave you to it then,' Michael says, stroking his beard absent-mindedly. 'And please, don't hesitate to let us know if there's anything we can do to make your stay more comfortable.'

As I watch him go, I can't help thinking that my first impressions were right – there's something odd about Michael Jeffrey. He says all the right things; it's the delivery that's off. His voice is eerily flat, stripped of tone or nuance, and there's no real conviction behind his words; it's as if he's going through the motions. It *is* possible of course that he and Pamela view our arrival as something of an inconvenience. Perhaps they were enjoying the post-Christmas downtime and the chance to regroup before spring heralds the next influx of guests. It does strike me as rather peculiar that we've been housed in the eaves for 'privacy', when the whole damn house is empty anyway.

Before I can mull it over any further, Pamela appears with our cooked breakfasts, which look, and smell, delicious. As she sets the plates down, I notice signs of stress in her face: the pronounced vein snaking from her forehead into her hairline, the downward pull at the corners of her mouth, the wrinkles like spokes around her eyes. I guess working in the hospitality industry is a tough gig.

After yesterday's meagre rations, Charles and I can't wait to tuck in and I'm relieved when Pamela disappears back to the kitchen without engaging in any unnecessary pleasantries.

*

Once we've eaten, Charles and I retire to the sitting room. The fire's been lit and it's lovely and snug in there. We spend some time discussing our plans for getting to St Ives but, with no phone or internet to check the latest situation with the trains, or make alternative arrangements, our options are somewhat limited. After a brief respite, the storm seems to be gathering strength; the sky has turned an ominous shade of indigo and it's started to rain.

'The first thing we need to do is speak to the staff at the train station and see if they can give us some idea when the line will be cleared,' Charles says. 'Then, once we know our ETA in St Ives, we can try and make contact with the hotel. Even if the phone box isn't working, we might be able to find a place in the village where we can get a mobile signal.'

I nod my agreement. 'We should call my parents too, to let them know we're safe. The train evacuation might have made the local news and if Mum and Dad have seen the coverage, they'll be worried.'

A shadow crosses Charles's face. He's seen me surreptitiously rubbing the knuckles of my fist up and down my left calf as I try to release the tension in the ligaments.

'Is your leg hurting?'

'A bit; I forgot to do my exercises yesterday.'

'In that case, you'd better stay here. I don't want you trudging all over the village; you'll only make it worse.'

I give a little groan of protest. 'But it's really not that far to the station.'

'Maybe not, but who knows how far we'll have to walk to get a signal. Honestly, Grace, it's not worth the risk. I'd feel much better if you stayed here and rested up.'

'Fair enough, have it your way,' I say, showing him my palms in a gesture of defeat.

I follow him out into the hallway and watch as he dons his waterproof jacket and begins lacing up his walking boots. It's cold away from the fire and I can feel a draught seeping through the gap at the bottom of the front door.

'You will be careful out there, won't you?' I say, drawing the two sides of my cardigan tightly around my throat.

'Of course; I'll be back just as soon as I've made those phone calls.'

'Heading out somewhere?'

The voice makes me jump. Pamela is standing in the shadows at the other end of the hall; I didn't even hear her approach.

'Michael and I are going to the cash and carry to get some supplies,' she continues. 'We can give you a lift if you like.'

Charles straightens up. 'That's kind of you to offer, would you mind dropping me at the station? We need to find out what's happening with the trains.'

Michael emerges from the door that leads to the dining room. 'Of course we can. Are you coming too, Grace?'

I pull at the flesh of my neck. 'No, I think I'm just going to hang out here and relax.'

'Are you sure you'll be all right on your own?'

'Quite sure,' I reply, feeling slightly irritated that he's talking to me as if I was a child and not a full-grown adult.

'Oh well, we won't be long, an hour at most.'

I look through the sitting-room window as Charles and the Jeffreys climb into the ancient four-wheel drive that's parked outside the house. The car reverses out of the driveway and sets off down the road towards the village. I watch it until it disappears out of sight.

I spend half an hour or so painstakingly going through my exercise routine, even though I find it desperately boring. Muscle stretches, ankle rotations, gait training, each and every move performed slowly and methodically, precisely the way I've been taught. When I'm done, I roll up the left leg of my sweatpants and inspect the scar that runs almost the full length of my lower leg, evidence of the open surgery that was needed to mend my shattered fibula. It's not pretty, but it's healing well and I wear it like a badge of honour, irrefutable proof that I'm a survivor.

Afterwards, I pick up the book I brought down to breakfast with me and settle in an armchair. I love reading, I have done since I was a child and this novel – an old-fashioned whodunnit, set on a remote Scottish island – is one of several I've been saving up for my honeymoon.

Usually, I have no trouble disappearing between the pages of a good book, so much so that I almost forget the world around me, but not today. Today I can't concentrate; my mind is full of confused thoughts that flutter around my head like dusty moths seeking the light. The voice I heard last night seems like a dream now. It is entirely possible that what I heard was not a voice, but the wind, as Michael suggested. Even so, there's a nagging doubt at the back of my mind.

Outside, the wind is still moaning and the rain scratches at the window with its sharp nails. It's so overcast I might need to turn a light on in a minute, even though it's not even midday. I stand up, intending to add another lump of coal from the scuttle to the dwindling fire. Then I hear a noise.

I freeze, ears pricked, my heart drumming against my ribs.

There. There it is again. It's coming from upstairs. It sounds as if something heavy is being dragged across the floor.

I sit back down again. Old houses make noises, I tell myself firmly. A minute goes past and there is silence. I release the breath I've been holding and lean back in the armchair. As I pick up my book, I catch it: the pitter-patter of light footsteps, followed by the soft suck of air as a door is pulled open.

Someone else is in the house.

6

GRACE

I walk to the foot of the stairs and stand very still. All my senses are heightened. I can feel the throb of a vein at my temple, the goose bumps blooming on my arms, the sickly sweet stench of the flowers decaying in their vase on the hall table. I spend a few moments trying to come up with plausible explanations for what I heard.

Could it be mice? Only if it were a supersized breed of vermin, capable of moving a large item. The cleaning lady, come to give the guest rooms a once over? Surely the Jeffreys would have warned me of her imminent arrival; in any case, wouldn't I have heard her enter the property?

All my instincts are telling me to stay put, but instead I grasp the banister and begin climbing the stairs, drawn by an invisible, nameless force. My pulse is jumping in my throat; it feels as if something is straining beneath my skin, a pressure against a suture that is threatening to tear.

When I reach the first-floor landing, I pause. 'Hello?' I say cautiously. No one answers. It's dark up here, so I reach for the nearest switch and a light bulb flickers into life above my head. Its light casts eerie shapes and my shadow stretches along the wall as though trying to detach itself from me.

All the doors to what I presume are the guest rooms are closed. It occurs to me that they might also be locked. I walk over to the nearest one and tentatively try the handle. The door opens with a sigh to reveal a double room, neat and tidy, the window blind set at half-mast. Nothing looks out of place, so I move to the next room. Two single beds with matching duvet covers. A pair of side tables and an attractively découpaged chest of drawers. No sign of any occupant, however.

I continue down the hallway, checking two further rooms, but find nothing to indicate a recent presence. The final bedroom is tucked away next to a shared bathroom. It's smaller than the rest, just big enough for a double bed and a narrow wardrobe. Unlike the other rooms, the bed has been stripped, exposing the stained mattress. I step across the threshold, my curiosity piqued by the old portrait that's prominently displayed on the wall opposite the bed.

Gazing down at me through layers of blackened varnish is a woman about my age, wearing an ankle-length dress in a pretty shade of blue. Her face is in semi-profile, and she is sitting in a high-backed chair, the suspicion of a smile playing on her lips, her hands resting lightly on a book. There's something fiercely independent in the tilt of her head and the intelligent look in her grey eyes. Through a window in the wall behind her, there's a glimpse of the ocean in the distance.

Then my attention turns away from the portrait, caught by something else in the room, something that seems off-kilter. A single white glove, lying on the beige carpet at the foot of the bed, as if the owner had dropped it there and not realised.

I bend down to pick it up. It's a pretty thing, vintage not reproduction, judging by the softness of the leather. A small spray of flowers is embroidered in coloured silks on the back of the hand and there are two tiny buttons at the wrist. I raise the glove to my nostrils. It has a faintly spiced odour of cinnamon and cloves, mixed with the fusty smell of well-thumbed paperbacks. I can't imagine what it's doing here, or what sort of person would wear such an old-fashioned thing.

I turn in a slow circle, scanning the room. There's a strange atmosphere in here, the air suspended like breath, held in anticipation. Shivering, I drop the glove on the mattress. Just then, a tremendous blast of wind hits the house, practically rocking it with the impact. A second later, the light in the hall goes out.

I head for the door, suddenly anxious to get back to the security of the sitting room. As I make my way towards the stairs, walking as quickly as my injured leg will allow, I have the sensation of being followed. My scalp tingles. There is a pressure on my shoulders and an elastic tug at my heels. I half expect to feel a pull on my upper arm at any moment. I know it's only my imagination on overdrive, but it's unsettling just the same.

Back in the sitting room, I retrieve my phone from the depths of the armchair. Rapidly, frantically almost, I scroll through my music collection, selecting a playlist at random. The sound is reedy and unsatisfying, but it's a welcome distraction; something to stop me thinking about the melancholy of this place and the unshakeable feeling that The Anchorage is choked by secrets I can't begin to unpick.

7

GRACE

It's a relief when I hear the Jeffreys' car pull up outside. I emerge into the hall just as Michael is letting himself in. He's laden with shopping bags and his cheeks are rosy from the wind. He seems to sense my agitation because right away he asks if everything's all right.

'There was a power cut,' I tell him, my voice catching on the words. 'All the lights went out.'

He presses the nearest wall switch and we both look up as the chandelier shoots lozenge-shaped fragments of light across the ceiling. He turns to me and smiles. 'Everything seems to be working fine now.'

'That's good,' I say, smiling back. I gesture to the bags. 'Did you manage to get everything you needed?'

'Just about. The cash and carry was heaving, people were stocking up as if we were on the brink of the next global pandemic. I just hope this storm blows over soon, if you'll pardon the pun, and then we can all get back to normal.'

'What's it like out there?'

Michael makes a sucking noise with his teeth. 'Pretty nasty. There's debris all over the roads and a tree came down on the village school overnight.'

'Surely the worst is over now though, isn't it?'

'I wouldn't count on it. We heard on the car radio that the winds are set to pick up again this afternoon – eighty miles per hour gusts along the coastline, they reckon.'

I groan. 'Did they say anything about when the trains would be up and running?'

'No, but the ticket office was open when we dropped Charlie off, so I'm sure he'll have found out the latest. I take it he's not back yet.'

'No, I hope he's all right.'

'I'm sure he will be, he's a resourceful lad.'

I raise my eyebrows. 'I didn't realise you two knew each other that well.'

'We don't, it's just an instinct I have about him.' Michael bends down and sets the shopping bags on the floor. 'Are you sure you're all right?'

I wonder if I should tell him about the noises I heard, but decide against it. I don't want to sound foolish. Or neurotic. Or both.

'I'm just a bit tired, that's all. I didn't sleep very well last night.'

He looks disappointed. 'I'm sorry to hear that. Do let us know if you need more pillows or blankets.'

'I will, thank you.'

I hear the slam of the car boot through the open front door. A second later Pamela appears with more bags of shopping. She barges straight past Michael and comes towards me.

'Sorry, do you mind?' she says abruptly.

Realising I'm blocking her way, I apologise and flatten myself against the wall.

'I don't suppose you could rustle up some tea and biscuits, could you?' I say, as she passes me.

She stops dead and swivels her head, like a hawk sizing up a field mouse. 'Breakfast service ended two hours ago.'

'I appreciate that.'

She sighs as if I've just asked her for Beluga caviar on a silver platter. 'I'll see what I can do.'

I leave the Jeffreys to unpack their shopping and retreat to the sitting room. I can't settle; instead, I stand at the window, my gaze trained on the road. Waiting for my husband. My heart gives a little leap when he finally appears in the distance, long arms swinging by his sides. I run to the door and wait for him under the sagging roof of the porch. Seeing me standing there, Charles begins a series of frantic hand gestures, indicating that I should go back inside. I ignore them and when he finally reaches me, I pull him close, holding on to him with a drowning grip.

'What's happened?' he says huskily into my hair.

'Nothing,' I reply. 'I missed you; that's all.'

As Charles warms up in front of the fire, he shares with me what he's learned. Weather permitting, the tree should be off the railway line by tomorrow afternoon at the latest. More problematic, apparently, is the damage to the overhead power cable. It requires specialist engineers from Plymouth and that could take another forty-eight hours.

There's more bad news when I hear that the phone box in the village isn't working. Charles said it looked as if it had already been vandalised and was probably out of service even before the storm struck. At least he managed to get a signal on his phone by walking to the highest point in the village. Just a single bar, but it was enough to make contact with our hotel in St Ives.

'They assumed we'd been delayed by the storm,' he tells me. 'The receptionist said we shouldn't worry; they won't give our room away. We just need to get there as soon as we can.'

I exhale a relieved breath. That's one weight off my mind. 'Did you call my parents?'

'I tried to, but the signal was so patchy, I ended up sending a text instead.'

'So they know we're stuck in Saltwater?'

'Yep, I told them where we were staying. I said we'd call them once we got to St Ives.'

Two weights off my mind. I flop back in the armchair, cradling the back of my head in my hands. 'So what do we do now?'

Charles gives a one-shouldered shrug. 'What choice do we have? All we can do is sit tight and wait for the engineers to fix the power.'

'But that means spending two more nights here.'

'That's not so bad, is it?'

I purse my lips. 'I can't believe there isn't some other way of getting to St Ives. We're only talking about the north coast of Cornwall, not the Outer Hebrides.'

'I've already explored the other public transport options,' Charles says, talking slowly and patiently, the way you would explain something to a child. 'The bus service in the village is very limited and none of the routes goes anywhere near St Ives. We're just going to have to stay here for a little while longer.'

I fight a wild, nervous urge to scream. 'Honestly, anyone would think you didn't want to go to St Ives.'

'Don't be silly, of course I do. It's just that being in Saltwater again brings back so many happy memories of Mum.'

I feel a stab of guilt. Charles's mum died of leukaemia a few months before we met. They were very close and her death hit him hard. She sounds like a wonderful woman – clever and funny, with a lovely, expansive capacity for happiness. I deeply regret the fact I never had the chance to meet her.

'I'm sorry, darling,' I say gently, reaching out to cup the side of his face with my hand. 'I'm just impatient to start our honeymoon, that's all. I don't know what it is about this place; I just can't relax properly. It's comfortable enough, it's just ...' I pause, grasping for the right words.

Charles gives me a quick, appeasing smile. 'Not the five-star luxury you were looking forward to.'

Actually, that isn't what I was trying to say, but it's easier to nod. 'You know, we could always hire a car and *drive* to St Ives.'

He looks doubtful. 'I'm pretty sure there are no car hire companies in the village.'

'No, but there's bound to be one somewhere around here. The Jeffreys might be able to recommend someone – and if not, we can ask them to lend us a phone directory and we'll make our own enquiries. You've already found a spot in the village where we can get a mobile signal, it'll be easy enough to put in a few calls.'

'How will we pick up the car?'

'We can get a taxi, or we might even find a firm who'll be willing to deliver the car to The Anchorage.'

Charles's eyes dart off to the side, as if he's thinking about the practicalities. 'I suppose it's worth considering.'

'Great, that's settled then. We'll stay one more night here and tomorrow we'll sort out the car hire.'

I smile to myself, certain that this time tomorrow we'll be on our way to St Ives.

I am wearing a white dress with a high neckline and a stiff petticoat. When I look down, I can see the hem skimming the tops of my bare feet. All around me are spectacular views, sea and sky merging in a shimmer of silver grey. The gentle breeze is warm and fragrant. I can smell jasmine and rosemary and another plant I recognise but can't quite identify. I feel something inside me rising, reaching for air, filling me with all sorts of glorious possibilities. But then the landscape seems to shiver, the edges of my vision turn monochrome and my legs begin to shake.

The next moment I'm trying to claw my way out of the dream quickly, in a panic, as if I were climbing a ladder and something nasty was snapping at my heels. My eyes flutter open. Just like last night, I don't know what it was that woke me. There's a thickness in my throat and I can feel sweat clinging to the back of my head, dampening my hair. Carefully, so as not to wake Charles, I push back the smothering duvet.

I hate the fact that I'm wide awake in the middle of the night. Again. I'm all too aware of the disruptive effect insomnia has on one's mental capacity. After my accident, I struggled to sleep for weeks and I know that without sufficient sleep, my reaction times will be slower, my mood irritable. Above my head, I can hear the insistent drum roll of rain. Why is it that weather always sounds so much louder at night? I wish it would stop; it feels as though it's been raining forever.

Sighing, I roll onto my back. That's when I notice that the door to our room is slightly ajar, even though I'm certain Charles shut it before he came to bed.

There's a watery light filtering through the gap. I can't think where it's coming from; I distinctly remember turning off the light in the hall after I'd brushed my teeth. And then, while my eyes are still struggling to focus in the semi-darkness, I see a shadow flit across the doorway. It's very quick, more of an impression than anything tangible. I feel something ugly crawl along my veins, put its fingers tightly around my heart.

'Charles,' I hiss, not taking my eyes off the door. 'Charles, wake up.'

When he doesn't respond, I turn my head to look at him. Snores catch in his throat and whistle out between his parted lips. He's out for the count. It would be selfish of me to wake him up over something and nothing.

I raise myself up onto my elbows. I want to get out of bed and investigate, but already I can feel my courage slipping away, slithering down between the cracks in the wall and the gaps in the skirting boards. I tell myself it's nothing; there is no one there, it's just my eyes playing tricks. I lie back down again and squeeze my eyes tight shut, but still the questions press in, blocking my nostrils and flooding my mouth with their acid tang.

8

This morning, I received a poison pen letter. Written in purple ink and slipped under the door. Anonymous, of course. The handwriting was terribly old-fashioned, all loops and swirls. I didn't know anyone still wrote like that these days.

Although the penmanship was beautiful, the words were cruel. They sprung at me like sharpened claws, cutting so deep I almost forgot to breathe as I read them.

Whoever the author is, he or she seems to know a lot about me. It's almost as if they've had me under surveillance. The thought that someone has been paying such close attention to my comings and goings chills me to the bone.

I read the letter twice and then I threw it in the fire. With hindsight, perhaps that was a mistake. I might well need it as evidence one day.

I don't know what they are hoping to achieve. But if their intention was to scare the living daylights out of me, then their mission has succeeded.

My head was so clear at the start of the day, but now it feels as if my mind has been taken over by someone else. I can't tell which thoughts are mine and which are theirs, which ones are true and which ones are lies.

9

CHARLES

I'm shocked at how much they've changed; no wonder I didn't recognise them at first. I know I haven't seen them for more than a decade, but even so.

For starters, they both look exhausted. I guess that's not surprising – running a guest house for all these years must take it out of you – but I can't help thinking it's something more than that.

When I was a kid, Michael always seemed such a strong, competent sort of man. I used to think there was something rather debonair about him, with his immaculately pressed chinos and open-necked shirts. Now he just looks scruffy and faintly bewildered, like a creature emerging from an unscheduled hibernation.

It's the same with Pamela. The pretty, low-cut dresses, which brought a smile to many a male guest (my dad included), have been replaced with sludge-coloured skirts and shapeless sweaters. She used to be colourful and chatty and full of stories, but now she seems like such a sad, drooping, willow of a woman.

They moved to Saltwater from London, if memory serves me right. My family's first visit to The Anchorage came during their inaugural summer season. I remember Michael telling my parents that neither he nor Pamela had worked in the hospitality industry before, so setting up a guest house had been a bit of an experiment – and one that they seemed to take to like ducks to water.

Back then, The Anchorage was such a happy place, a real home from home. My family loved its proximity to the beach, the comfy communal areas and Pamela's hearty breakfasts. Other folk clearly felt the same way, because there was never any shortage of clientele and many of them seemed to be repeat customers. I wonder what's changed since then? A downturn in the local economy, perhaps? Bigger, buzzier towns with upscale restaurants and better tourist attractions luring the holidaymakers away? Whatever the reason, I think I made the right decision in bringing Grace here. It's good to touch base with one's past every now and then.

I know she isn't impressed with what she's seen of the village so far, but all things considered, I'm glad to be back. I'd forgotten how much I love it here. Saltwater is one of those unassuming places that creeps up on you and steals your heart when you're not looking. I think if Grace stayed here a bit longer, she'd feel the same way too.

I had a good wander round after I'd been to the train station. The dramatic weather conditions made the experience even more enjoyable. The waves were immense and the fishing boats in the harbour were bobbing up and down like tin cans. I walked to the end of the lifeboat slip, even though I knew it was a dangerous place to be. What can I say? Storms have that effect on me. It's like a sound in the middle of the night that you go downstairs to investigate, or a mysterious, shining light you follow deep into the woods, not knowing where it will lead.

As I stood there, hands shoved deep in my pockets, listening to the waves crash against the sea wall, my stomach buckled with a memory I couldn't quite grasp. And then, just as suddenly as it appeared, it melted away.

Afterwards, I went to the antiques shop and spent a while looking at all the weird and wonderful things in the window. That place has always been such an Aladdin's cave. I used to love going there with my mother and poking around to see what treasures I could find. Being there again brought back such happy memories that I was tempted to go in, but then I remembered I was supposed to be hunting for a phone signal.

I headed straight for the war memorial because it's the highest point in the village. After a bit of trial and error, I eventually got a single bar and put in a call to our hotel in St Ives. Then I tried to phone Grace's parents, but the call kept being disconnected, so I sent them a text instead. It was only when I was on my way back to The Anchorage that I received the 'failed' notification. The signal must have dropped out just as I hit send. I haven't told Grace; her anxiety levels are high enough as it is and knowing I haven't been able to make contact with her parents would only make things worse.

I suppose I should feel bad about lying to her, but I don't. I've learned over the years that truth is malleable, and that white lies can sometimes help shade in the less palatable areas of truth. That knowledge has occasionally caused me to misjudge situations, to make the wrong decisions, to bend a fact so far that it won't bounce back to its original shape, but generally speaking, it's served me well.

I have to confess that I'm a little concerned about Grace. Ever since we arrived in Saltwater, she's been on edge. She keeps imagining things – like the child she said she heard crying on the first night, when as we now know there are no children staying at the guest house. Then she claimed to have heard someone moving around upstairs while the Jeffreys and I were out.

As I was at pains to explain to her, the building is the best part of a hundred and fifty years old, so the joists *will* creak and the roof trusses *will* groan. It's called thermal expansion and it's a perfectly normal phenomenon, even in new builds. I think I succeeded in putting her mind at rest. At least I hope I did.

I don't mind dealing with Grace's insecurities; she's the most important thing in the world to me and I would do anything for her. From the moment we met, I knew she was different to any of the women I'd been involved with before. My previous relationships followed a similar pattern: the initial spark of attraction, followed by conversation and then, when the time was right, sex. But I realised later that what I looked forward to most was breaking up with them, the look on their faces when I asked them to delete my number from their phone, the light going out of their eyes. The thrill of the chase was what I really enjoyed and the minute I knew a woman had fallen for me, I tended to lose interest. Not that I'm proud of any of it. Thinking about it now makes my insides crawl with shame.

I don't know what I'd do if Grace ever left me. I want us to grow old together. I want to be there when she has grey hair and crow's feet around her eyes. I want to hear her voice when it's slow and croaky. I want to reassure her when she can't remember the name of someone she's always known. I want all of it. Not because I need to *own* her, but because I love her. I love her more than words can describe.

IO

GRACE

Despite another restless night, I'm in a good mood when I wake up. In just a few short hours, Charles and I will be unpacking our suitcase again, only this time in St Ives. Then, at last, our honeymoon can begin.

I feel a bit embarrassed about my behaviour over the past couple of days. I've been acting like a sulky kid, criticising the Jeffreys (quite unfairly) and picking holes in The Anchorage whenever I've had the chance. Meanwhile, my wonderful, kind, endlessly upbeat husband has been trying to make the best of a bad situation. As for my absurd *fantasies* ... let's just say I've always had an overactive imagination and this creepy, creaking old house, plus the appalling weather, have conspired to send it spinning out of control. Anyway, now I know that Saltwater will soon be nothing but a distant memory, I'm beginning to feel more like my normal, sensible self.

Unusually, Charles has woken up before me and when I open the bedroom door, I can hear the sound of the shower running. When he returns he's wearing a towel around his waist and another one around his neck. He comes over to where I'm standing at the window and gives me a kiss, the way he does every morning.

'Hello, Mrs McKenna, how's it looking out there today?' he says.

'It's still raining, but it's definitely less windy than yesterday,' I say eagerly, excited by the thought of our departure. 'Hopefully there won't be much debris on the roads and we'll have a clear run to St Ives.'

He takes the towel from his neck and begins drying his hair with it.

'Are you sure you want to leave today?'

I stare at him, incredulous. I would have thought the answer was obvious.

'A hundred per cent sure. I think we should sort out the car hire as soon as we've had breakfast. I just checked my phone and the Wi-Fi's still down by the look of it, but maybe the Jeffreys' landline is working.'

He pulls thoughtfully on his bottom lip. 'It's just that I was looking forward to showing you round the village.'

'And you still can,' I tell him. 'Just as soon as we've booked the car.'

He makes a resigned face. 'Sounds like a plan.'

Down in the dining room, it quickly transpires that the landline *isn't* working, which immediately strikes me as highly improbable. Whoever heard of a phone line being out of service for thirty-six hours straight? But surely the Jeffreys wouldn't lie to us ... or *would* they? When all's said and done they are desperate for business. But anyway, who cares? We know we can get a signal up by the war memorial; we don't need their shitty landline. At least Pamela has had the good grace to jot down the names and phone numbers of two car hire firms in the nearest town, one of which is bound to have a vehicle available at short notice.

After breakfast, Charles suggests waiting to see if there's a let-up in the rain before we head out. He doesn't say it, because he knows I hate being fussed over, but he's worried about me slipping in the wet because of my leg. Keen to get going, I brush aside his concerns.

I assumed we'd be going to the war memorial first, but Charles wants to go the long way round via the seafront. I open my mouth to protest, but when I see the look of bright expectation on his face, I shut it again.

I follow him out of the front door and across the road to a large open green, dotted with picnic benches. There's a small bandstand in the middle with a handsome domed roof, looking out towards the sea.

As we pick our way across the sodden grass, we see a lone man with a dog coming towards us, his broad shoulders hunched against the wind. As we pass each other, Charles calls out a greeting. The man gives us a sharp look, almost as if we're trespassing. His eyes ricochet between The Anchorage and us, then he presses his thin lips together and walks away quickly without so much as a *hello*. Charles doesn't seem to have noticed his rudeness; he's too busy making for a row of metal railings. Standing chest high, they're clearly functioning as some sort of guardrail because, on the other side of them, the land just falls away.

At first I think Charles wants to show me the view, but then I spy a gate about halfway along. It's rusted from the salt air and when Charles touches it, it opens with a loud shriek. He turns to me and gives a little bow. 'After you, madam.'

As I take a step forward, something sways and lurches in my gut. I hesitate for a second, and then I see the stone steps, carved out of the limestone, leading down the cliff face to the road below. It's quite a feat of engineering; there's even a sturdy handrail, attached to the rock with metal bolts.

Once upon a time I would have bounded down the steps without a second thought; now I find the prospect quite daunting. *Breathe, Grace*, I tell myself, *you can do this.*

All at once I feel Charles's hand on my shoulder. 'Grace? Are you okay?'

'It's nothing, I just feel a bit light-headed all of a sudden.'

As realisation dawns on him, Charles's face folds. 'Sorry darling, I wasn't thinking. We don't have to take this route; we can get to the beach via the high street.'

'No, no, I'm fine,' I say quickly. 'Let's go this way.'

'Well, all right then, but let me go first – and keep hold of the handrail.'

I feel silly for making a fuss, because the steps aren't half as steep, or as narrow, as I thought.

'That was fun,' I say, when we reach the bottom. 'How long have those steps been there?'

'I'm not sure, a couple of hundred years I should think. They were originally made by smugglers, although various safety improvements have been made since then. Ally and I used to be up and down those steps all day long when we were kids; it's the quickest way to the beach.'

He takes my hand and together we cross a narrow road that hugs the coastline. A little further along, a gap in the sea wall leads us onto a corrugated expanse of sand, scattered with pebbles and ribbons of kelp. Beyond it is the vast and roiling sea. The rain's getting heavier now, sharp needles pricking our faces, so we don't hang around to admire the view. Instead, we keep on walking, hoods up, heads down.

We pass a newsagent and an old-fashioned butcher's shop, with an appetising selection of homemade pies in the window. It's not even ten o'clock, but both seem to be doing a brisk trade – no doubt some of their customers are fellow train evacuees, desperate to get out and stretch their legs. A short distance away is a small gift shop. The door's open and I can see a couple inside choosing postcards from a revolving stand. Next to the gift shop, at the end of the terrace, lies a small cafe, its exterior walls painted a pleasing, seaside-y shade of pale blue. The name Rosario's is emblazoned in a looping script across the window. It too appears to be popular, with more than half the tables already occupied.

'They used to do the best ice-cream sundaes here when I was a boy,' says Charles. 'I wouldn't mind grabbing a quick coffee – for old time's sake.'

'Good idea,' I say.

We've only just had breakfast, but the chance to delay our return to The Anchorage is too good to miss. Furthermore, if we ask nicely and leave a generous tip, the owner might be kind enough to let us use their phone, saving us a trip to the war memorial.

Pretty soon, we're ensconced at a cosy corner table with two steaming lattes. The cakes ranged on the counter under their glass domes looked delicious, so we've treated ourselves to a slice of lemon drizzle to share. Soul music plays from a vintage jukebox, adding to the warm and relaxed vibe. I can see why this place is popular. It certainly makes a welcome change from the chilly atmosphere at The Anchorage.

'It's a shame it's such a vile day,' Charles says, raising the tall coffee mug to his lips. 'You're really not seeing Saltwater at its best.'

'I know what you mean,' I reply. 'I don't think it's stopped raining since we got here.' As I twist my head towards the window to check the latest weather conditions, I make eye contact with a smartly dressed woman at a nearby table. She's sitting alone and a book is lying open on the table in front of her.

'Nasty out there, isn't it?' she says chattily. 'A tree fell on the primary school the night before last, you know.'

I smile at her. 'We heard. I do hope no one was hurt.'

'No, it happened in the middle of the night so the school was empty.'

'That was lucky.' I push what's left of the cake towards Charles. 'Do you live here?'

She nods proudly. 'I was born in Saltwater. I love this place; it has such a wonderful community spirit. I lived in London for a while after I got married, but my husband and I kept a holiday home here. We moved back full time when we retired and now we can't imagine living anywhere else.'

'Wow, that's amazing, I guess you must know everyone in the village then.'

She gives a little laugh. 'I wouldn't go that far, but I'm probably on first-name terms with at least half of them.'

'Do you know the Jeffreys? They own The Anchorage; that's where we're staying.'

I hear the draw of air into her lungs, quick and low. At the same time, a curious look flashes across her face, surprise fused with pity. A moment later, her smile is back in place. 'You two are on holiday then?'

Charles reaches across the table and squeezes my hand. 'Honeymoon, actually.'

The woman beams at us. 'Ah, how lovely, congratulations!'

'We're not supposed to be in Saltwater,' I tell her. 'We were on our way to St Ives when a tree came down on the railway line and our train had to be evacuated. We're just staying here for a few days until it gets sorted.'

'That's a pain,' the woman replies, grimacing in sympathy.

'Oh, it's not so bad,' Charles tells her. 'We're being very well looked after at The Anchorage.'

'So do you know the Jeffreys then?' I ask, realising the woman still hasn't answered my question.

She snaps her book shut, as if she's already planning her getaway. 'Not really, but I know The Anchorage; everybody round here does. It's a local landmark.'

'Is it true that it was built by a Victorian sea captain?' Charles asks her.

'That's right, John Murrish. Back in the day, he was something of a celebrity in Saltwater. He built The Anchorage soon after he married his wife Emma, who was a scientist. She's famous for being the first woman to be elected to the Royal Geological Society of Cornwall.'

I break into a smile. 'I had no idea the property's original occupants were so illustrious.'

'Yes, they were great philanthropists too. They used to give all the poorest children in the village a new pair of shoes at Christmas.'

'What a lovely gesture. Did they have children of their own?'

'Two, a boy and a girl. Sadly, they died with their mother in very tragic circumstances.'

'Really?' I say, leaning forward across the table. 'What happened to them?'

'It's a pretty grim tale and probably not the sort of thing you want to hear about on your honeymoon.'

It's too late; a worm of curiosity has hatched inside me. 'Oh no, please, I'd like to know.'

The woman grins and wags her finger at me playfully. 'Well, all right then, but don't blame me if this gives you nightmares.'

I glance at Charles, but he doesn't seem to be listening, his gaze fixed instead on the laminated menu that's lying open on the table.

When the woman starts speaking again, her voice is low slung, husky almost; it's as if she doesn't want anyone else but us to hear.

'One winter's day, in 1876, a merchant steam ship called the SS *Albion* set off from Falmouth, bound for Liverpool with a valuable cargo of tin. At the helm was Captain John Murrish.

Also on board were his wife and two young children, who were planning to do some shopping during the two-day stopover in Liverpool.

'By all accounts it was a filthy day and the sea was swathed in fog. Less than an hour into her journey, the *Albion* struck the Seven Stones, a notoriously dangerous reef off the north coast of Cornwall. When the ship began to list and take on water, the crew tried to launch the lifeboats, but the ship was sinking so fast they didn't have time.'

The woman pauses and takes a fierce gulp of tea, the tendons in her throat standing out as she swallows. 'Of the eighty or so souls on board, only a handful survived, plucked from the freezing sea by a passing liner who saw the rocket flares launched from the *Albion*'s deck. Captain Murrish was one of the lucky few who survived.'

'Emma and the children?' I ask, even though I already know the answer.

'Their bodies were recovered in the days and weeks that followed.'

I gasp softly. 'Poor Captain Murrish; imagine losing your entire family in one fell swoop – and to know on top of that all those other people died as well.'

The woman nods. 'He was called to give evidence at some sort of official enquiry, but the consensus seems to have been that he simply lost his bearings in the fog. I don't expect he ever forgave himself for what happened; certainly he never went to sea again. Legend has it that for ever after, when weather conditions were bad, he would stand outside The Anchorage on the bluff, looking through his telescope for any sign of a ship in trouble.'

'I think that's one of the saddest stories I've ever heard.' I turn to Charles, but he's still engrossed in the menu.

'I know ... dreadful, isn't it?' The woman picks up her book and stuffs it into her handbag. 'I'm afraid I've got to get going now; I have to take my husband to a doctor's appointment. Enjoy the rest of your honeymoon – and be careful, won't you?'

'Of the storm?' I ask.

She fixes me with a stare so intense it causes my insides to knot. 'Of The Anchorage. It's a funny old place ... things have happened there.'

A flash of anxiety, sticky and hot, crawls into my throat. I remember the photo with the girl's face scratched out and the weeping child I thought I heard in the night. 'What sort of things?'

To my dismay, the woman is already on her feet and halfway to the door. 'Just get to St Ives as soon as you can, okay?' she says, throwing a quick look over her shoulder.

II

GRACE

I turn to my husband. 'What the fuck was that all about?'

Charles looks up from the menu. 'All what?'

'The warning that woman just gave us. What do you think she meant?'

He frowns. '*Warning's* a bit strong, isn't it?'

'What else would you call it?' I say shrilly. 'She told us to be careful. If that isn't a warning, I don't know what is.'

He shrugs non-committally. 'Maybe The Anchorage's health and safety isn't up to scratch. The place does look as if it could do with updating.'

'Oh don't be so ridiculous,' I snap.

Charles sighs. 'To be honest with you, Grace, I wasn't paying much attention; I was too busy eyeing up the ice cream.' He jabs a finger at the menu. 'Have you seen the salted caramel sundae? They've definitely upped their game since the last time I was here.'

I bite my lip and draw my coffee mug towards me. Thoughts are bubbling through my mind at a furious rate. I don't understand why Charles isn't taking this more seriously. Or is it me? Am I overreacting?

I stare into my half-drunk coffee, thinking about Emma Murrish and her dead children. Is it possible that Charles and I are not the only guests at The Anchorage after all?

Charles seems to know what I'm thinking. He's good at that; he can read me like a book. 'You don't think The Anchorage is haunted, do you?' he says, his tone implying a roll of the eyes. 'That story about the Murrish family has been doing the rounds since I was a kid. It's probably not even true, just a folk tale the locals tell to make the village sound more intriguing to tourists.'

I lift my head to look at him. 'So you haven't seen or heard anything out of the ordinary since we've been staying at the guest house?'

'Nope.'

'How about when you stayed there as a boy?'

He reaches for my hand across the table. His eyes look so dark in the dim lighting of the cafe, I can scarcely discern pupil from iris.

'No, Grace, because The Anchorage isn't haunted. We're perfectly safe there, so please stop worrying.'

I grip his fingers tightly. 'Do you think there's something wrong with me? These things I keep hearing ...'

He shakes his head. 'I believe that even the most rational mind can conjure up ghosts, given the right set of circumstances. Consider the facts: you're stressed because our travel plans have gone tits up; you're not sleeping well; your leg's giving you grief. Is it any wonder you're losing perspective?'

I let go of his hand and lean back in my chair. Everything he says is true; Charles can always be relied on to provide an objective analysis of any situation. Then another possibility presents itself to me.

'Maybe she was warning us about the Jeffreys.'

He gives a gruff laugh. 'You seem to be forgetting that I know these people, Grace. They might be a little eccentric, but I'm quite sure they don't pose a danger to us – or anyone else, for that matter.'

'But you must admit it is weird ... us being the only guests.'

'It's out of season, you can't expect the place to be packed.'

'Granted, but you'd think they'd have one or two other book-ings – or at least some refugees from the train. Judging by what I've seen so far, everyone else in Saltwater seems to be doing all right for themselves. There's clearly a thriving tourist industry here, so why are the Jeffreys the only people who are crying out for business?'

Unusually for him, Charles doesn't seem to have a ready answer. 'You're right,' he admits finally. 'It is a little surprising. The Anchorage was certainly a different place when I used to come here with my family.'

'So what's changed since then?'

Another shrug. 'I've been asking myself the same question. Anyway, look, it doesn't matter now. We'll be leaving soon, won't we?' He glances at his phone. 'Still no reception, damn it. Let's finish our coffee and then we can go up to the war memorial.'

'Good idea, but first let's see if they've got a landline here we can use; we'll say it's urgent.' I catch the eye of a passing waitress and put our request to her.

'Sorry,' she says, scooping up our empty cake plate. 'The phone lines are down, they have been since Monday. From what I've heard, the whole of Saltwater's affected.'

My lips compress. So the Jeffreys weren't lying. I was wrong to suspect them of that. What else am I wrong about?

Ten minutes later, we're walking up a grassy mound in the rain to the war memorial. The whole time, I'm checking my phone, searching for the solitary bar that represents our ticket out of here.

'Where was it you got a signal last time?' I ask Charles when we reach the top.

He scans the landscape. 'Uh, just over there, I think,' he says, pointing to a wooden bench.

I walk over to it and look at my phone. Nothing. Ignoring Charles's request for me to be careful, I climb on top of the bench and hold my phone up to the sky. Still nothing.

Fifteen minutes later, neither of us has managed to get a signal. I flop down on the bench, not caring that it's soaking wet. I feel a rising helplessness, a mounting urge to cry; all our options seem to have run out. And then my pathetic self-pity morphs into a fury that propels me to my feet.

'Come on,' I say to Charles, as I start limping back down the hill.

'Where are we going now – back to the guest house?' I'm sure I can detect an undercurrent of glee in his voice.

'No, we are *not*!' I call out over my shoulder. 'We're going to keep walking until we find a signal. How far do you think it is to the nearest town?'

His words drift back to me on the wind. 'Three or four miles, I should think. But we can't walk that far. What about your leg?'

'My leg's fine, thank you – and if you don't want to come, I shall go on my own.'

The road that leads out of the village is narrow and winding. On one side is the sea wall, on the other a towering limestone cliff. The wind coming off the ocean is fierce. I can feel its icy fingers reaching underneath the three layers of clothing I'm wearing.

'Isn't there a less exposed route we can take?' I ask Charles, as I pump my arms like pistons in an effort to increase the blood flow around my body.

'No, unfortunately. Saltwater has a unique geography; it's bounded on three sides by water. There's only one road in or out; I used to think that was really cool when I was a kid.'

'I bet you did,' I mumble through lips that are growing numb.

We walk for half a mile or so. The pavement is barely wide enough for two abreast, which leads me to suspect there isn't much pedestrian traffic. There aren't many cars, either. On a day like this, any sensible person is safely tucked up indoors.

I haven't walked this far since the accident and a gnawing ache is developing in my left calf. I'm getting hungry too; it must be getting near to lunchtime. I'm just about to ask Charles if he knows of any petrol stations en route where we can grab a sandwich when I hear a deep, resonant rumble. At first, I think it must be thunder. But the next instant, there's a loud boom that seems to shake the very ground we're standing on.

Charles and I stop dead in our tracks.

'That sounded like an explosion,' I say.

'It did, didn't it?'

'Why would anybody round here be blowing stuff up?'

Charles rubs his jaw with the back of his hand. 'There used to be a quarry not far from here, but as far as I know it closed in the 1980s.'

We walk a bit further. The pain in my leg is getting worse. I don't know if I can make it as far as the town; surely there's a phone mast somewhere round here. Suddenly, a police car races by, lights flashing. It's quickly followed by another. Then a fire engine speeds past, its backdraft nearly knocking me off my feet.

Charles is starting to look worried. 'I've got a bad feeling about this. Do you think we should turn back?'

I waggle the phone that's gripped in my gloved hand. 'Absolutely not. We keep going till we get a signal; that's what we agreed.'

Charles knows what I'm like once I've made my mind up about something, and I'm pleased when he doesn't demur.

We continue to speculate about the possible source of the explosion but as we round the next corner, the nature of the emergency becomes frighteningly apparent.

A huge chunk of the cliff face has come down and the road up ahead is now unrecognisable, buried under a mass of mud and rocks. Some of the boulders are the size of tanks and anybody who happened to be on the road when they fell would have been crushed in an instant. My breath tugs painfully inside my chest; a few minutes later and we would have been right in the landslide's path.

Above the fallen rocks, a mushroom cloud of dust is billowing in the wind. As it drifts towards us, I instinctively pull my scarf up over my mouth and nose.

'Why do you think the cliff gave way like that?' I say, incredulous.

Charles's face is ashen. 'I don't know. It could be the cumulative effect of all the rain we've had. Or maybe it's something to do with the quarry. These cliffs must be riddled with old mine workings.'

In the distance, we can see two police officers setting up a cordon with traffic cones and crime scene tape. I can just make out the frantic crackle of their radios. Behind them, a firefighter is picking his way through the rocks, while his colleagues offload cutting gear from their vehicle.

The whole scene is like something out of a Hollywood disaster movie. It's chilling to watch and it triggers something inside me, the stirrings of something big and dark and scary that I want to shove in a drawer and forget about. I'm only twenty-seven, but I've already had enough drama to last me a lifetime. I know what it's like to be caught up in a crisis situation; to see your life flash before your eyes; to wonder if you're ever going to see your loved ones again. It's not an experience I want to repeat.

Charles nervously surveys the rugged expanse of cliff nearest to us. Then he grabs my hand. 'Come on, let's get back to the guest house. For all we know, this whole lot could come down at any moment.'

As we hurry away from the scene, my thoughts are plunging like a bad rollercoaster ride. The one road out of the village is completely impassable. What are supposed to do now? Are we ever going to get out of here? If I didn't know better, I'd say that Saltwater doesn't want to let us go.

12

The weather here is so changeable. It can be foul one moment, beautiful the next. It's one of the many things I find confusing about this place.

I managed to get out for a walk earlier. I was actually in a good mood for once. It was a typical February day: sharp and blustery, one of those unpredictable mornings, randomly bright and dark. A day when your eyes water in the wind and you keep your coat zipped up right to the neck.

I walked across the cliff tops and stood for a while looking out across the sea, entirely emptied of thought or even the slightest awareness of myself. It was such a beautiful moment.

But then, when I returned to the house, I saw a seagull lying in the road. It wasn't moving and I wondered if it had broken its wing.

I nudged it with my foot and gently turned it over. Its claws were curling inwards, grotesquely, the flesh of its breast eaten away. All that was left was a gaping cavity filled with worms. Fat, squirming worms.

It was so shocking, so repulsive that I retched and was almost sick. I think it might be a portent, a warning of what's to come.

13

GRACE

Neither of us says very much on the way back; we're both too shocked by what we've just witnessed. It's not like Charles to be so quiet. He seems lost in his own private world; it's clear that this has affected him deeply. As we walk, I thread my arm through his, and rest my head against his upper arm, drawing comfort from his bulk. I feel so helpless; all we can do now is hope and pray that no vehicles were travelling along that stretch of road at the precise moment the landslide struck.

By the time we reach the high street, the daylight is already fading, even though it's only mid-afternoon. A wave of depression washes over me as The Anchorage looms into view. Its tall sash windows seem to gaze beyond me, looking towards the sea with a disdainful expression that reinforces my sense that I am troublesome, temporary, that this old building has dealt with worthier adversaries than me in its time.

Inside, there's no sign of life, no warm welcome or offer of hot tea and buttered scones. When we peel off our waterproofs, the air in the house feels cold and fragile. The radiators are stone cold; the central heating clearly went off some time ago.

As we enter the sitting room, the edges of the furniture seem to leap out of the gloom in a way I find vaguely threatening. First I'm hearing things, now I'm picking fights with an armchair. The thought's enough to make me smile.

I move quickly around the room, turning on all the lamps. Both of us are starving; I don't know why we didn't think to get some lunch on our way back through the village. As Charles heaps coal on the fire, trying to nurse the dying embers back to life, I volunteer to retrieve some protein bars from our luggage.

Ascending the stairs, I feel a prickle of unease as the house ticks and creaks around me. I force myself to remain calm, reminding myself that this is just a house, an *empty* house at that. There's nothing here that can harm me.

When I reach the first-floor landing, I hesitate. My mind is still working over what I learned at Rosario's. Rather than continuing up the second flight of stairs to our attic room, I set off along the dark, windowless corridor. As before, every door is shut, adding to my growing sense of claustrophobia. When I get to the last room, I stop and cough into my hand, as if to announce my arrival.

Once inside, I go straight to the portrait of the woman in blue. I stand in front of it, my arms folded, staring hard, hunting for clues.

It isn't long before I identify a small detail I overlooked before. The book on the woman's lap – there's a picture on the cover: a spiral-shaped fossil; I think it's called an ammonite. I remember what the woman in the cafe said about the Royal Geological Society. The woman in the portrait is Emma Murrish; I'm certain of it.

I close my eyes, absorbing the atmosphere, letting my senses take over. There's a resistance here, I can feel it bristling like an electrical current and the air smells scorched, the way it does when you leave the iron on for too long. When I open my eyes, I half expect something in the room to have moved, but everything's the same. Am I really experiencing these things or is my brain inventing them? I know what Charles would say.

He's probably wondering where I am, but before I go I let my eyes sweep over the portrait one final time. That's when I pick out another detail. Something small and light-coloured lying on top of the mahogany bureau that's positioned just behind Emma.

The painting has darkened with age, so it's hard at first to see what it is. Squinting hard, I lean forward for a closer look. As the article comes into focus, every cell of my skin tightens. It's a pair of gloves; *white* gloves.

I spin around. It's not there any more. I look beneath the bed and check under the mattress, but the glove I found yesterday has vanished.

My fingers push into the roots of my hair, as my brain sorts through the possibilities. It's like trying to sift through a pile of hundred-year-old papers that are crumbling to dust in my hands. I don't understand what this means; nothing makes any sense. I wish there was someone I could talk to, someone I could trust. I know I can trust Charles, but if I share my suspicions with him, he'll think he's married a madwoman and I couldn't bear that.

By the time I return to the sitting room, the fire is aglow. There's music too, coming from a radio that Charles found in the dresser.

'It's tuned to the local radio station,' he tells me. 'When the news bulletin comes on, they might have a report on the land-slide.'

'Good, I want to find out if anyone's been injured.' I toss him a protein bar and join him on one of the armchairs, wincing at the stiffness in my leg.

'I hope you didn't overdo it today,' Charles says. He leans forward and pulls a cushion from behind his back, then bends down and gently positions it under my left foot. 'I can massage your calf, if you think it would help.'

'Thanks, but maybe later, after I've done my stretches,' I say, grateful for his kindness; I don't know what I'd do without him. I stare into the dancing flames. 'So what do we do now?'

'Well, we're clearly going to be staying in Saltwater for a little while longer. I think we just have to make the best of it. If nothing else, it'll be an amazing story to tell our children.' Charles unwraps the protein bar and breaks off a chunk. 'Seriously, all these near misses we keep having ... first the tree on the railway line, then the landslide. You couldn't make it up.'

I try to smile, but my lips won't press themselves into the right shape. Given what happened in Turkey, his comments seem a little insensitive, but I know he doesn't mean to hurt my feelings. 'Fine, but can't we at least find somewhere else to stay? Somewhere a little less ...' I hesitate. I want to say *dangerous*, but I'm mindful of Charles's affection for this place. 'Basic.'

'You're joking, aren't you?' he says. 'Nowhere will have any vacancies. If *we* haven't managed to make it out of Saltwater, I doubt any of the other train passengers have.'

'It's still worth a try,' I protest. 'Someone might have managed to escape by road before the landslide hit.'

'*Escape*? You make it sound like we're in prison.'

I shrug. 'We might as well be.'

'Fine, if it's really that important to you we'll start looking first thing in the morning, all right?'

My jaw tightens. 'What's wrong with right now?'

Charles jerks his head towards the window. 'Be reasonable, Grace. It's getting dark and the temperature's dropping. Do we really want to be knocking on doors? One more night here isn't going to kill us; the Jeffreys did say we could stay as long as we liked.'

'Of course they did,' I say bitterly. 'Where *are* they anyway? I'd kill for a hot drink. This must be the only guest house in the world without tea- and coffee-making facilities.'

'Their car's outside, so I guess they must be in the annexe.'

I throw him a sharp look. 'What annexe?'

'There's a single-storey extension at the rear of the main building. It's totally self-contained; that's where Michael and Pamela live.'

I take a bite of protein bar, chewing slowly as I digest this new piece of information.

'So the Jeffreys don't sleep here, with us, in the main house?'

'No, I just told you. Their living quarters are in the annexe.'

'Why haven't you mentioned it before now?'

'I didn't think it mattered.' He frowns. '*Does* it matter?'

'Well, yes, actually. It means that at night we're all on our own here.'

'That's a good thing, isn't it? It gives us total privacy.' He grins, suggestively. 'Perhaps we should take advantage of that this evening. This *is* our honeymoon, after all.'

'Don't worry, I hadn't forgotten.' I think of the expensive lingerie that's lying, unworn, in our suitcase. I was saving it for St Ives, but who knows when we're going to get there now? 'But if the Jeffreys live in the annexe, what were they doing here, in the sitting room, the night we arrived? They even had a fire going. Do you think they were expecting us?'

Charles laughs. 'Of course not, how could they?' He looks at me, his face etched with concern. 'Are you all right, Grace? Only you're starting to sound the tiniest bit paranoid.'

I smile. 'Sorry, ignore me. I'm disappointed about today, that's all. I was sure we'd be in St Ives by now.' I cock my head as a jingle on the radio heralds the start of a news bulletin.

The landslide is the lead story. The reporter says that the cause is, as yet, unknown and investigations are ongoing. Meanwhile, a police spokesman reveals that the road is likely to be blocked for several days until heavy lifting gear can be brought to the scene. My heart plummets when I hear that a car, heading towards the village, was struck by falling debris. Its two occupants, a husband and wife, have been airlifted to hospital, where the female is said to be in a critical condition.

'Thank God more people weren't injured,' Charles says, getting up to turn off the radio.

'Yes, but that poor woman. Her family must be so worried.' I think of my own accident, how scared everyone was. My parents were beside themselves; as soon as they heard, they caught the next available flight to Turkey.

Just then, an alarming thought strikes me. 'What if Mum and Dad hear the news and think it was us in that car?' I reach for Charles's phone that's lying on the small coffee table in between our two armchairs. 'Can I see the text you sent? Did you say we were staying in Saltwater?'

'Stop fretting, Grace; your parents will know it wasn't us because the report said the next of kin had already been informed.' He swipes the phone out of my hand and tucks it in the back pocket of his jeans. 'What shall we do about dinner tonight? There's a Chinese takeaway in the village. I'm sure Pamela wouldn't mind if we borrowed a couple of forks and ate it in the dining room.'

I make a face. 'I'd rather get out of here, if it's all the same to you. What about that pub with the rooms, down by the harbour? They'll do food, won't they?'

'The Boathouse? For sure,' he replies. 'That's a great idea.'

14

GRACE

The Boathouse is one of those 'theme' pubs, with lobster pots hanging from the ceiling and mirrors in driftwood frames. It's a little overdone for my taste, but the atmosphere's pleasant enough and the food's not bad.

Having made short work of our main courses, Charles offers to go to the bar for a dessert menu and more drinks. While he's gone, I flick through the pages of a local entertainment guide that someone's left lying on a nearby stool. There's certainly plenty for visitors to do round here, with live music and a regular farmers' market and guided coastal walks. It begs the question, yet again: why is The Anchorage, alone out of all the guest houses, languishing in the doldrums when this is clearly a vibrant community?

Charles takes his time with the drinks and when he still hasn't returned after ten minutes, I look around to see where he's got to. I spot him standing at the bar, talking to an older man in a pink polo shirt that I think must be the landlord. They seem to be having quite a lively conversation, although I'm too far away to hear what they're saying.

Charles has his back to me, but I have a good view of the landlord. His eyes are wide, as if Charles has said something surprising. A moment later, he thumps a beefy fist on the bar – not in an aggressive way, more to emphasise a point. I wonder what it is they're talking about. I'd like to join in, but it's busy in here and if I get up, someone else might take our table. It makes me feel absolutely ancient, but I need to know I can sit down. That's another hangover from the accident – if I stand up for too long, the muscles in my leg start screaming.

As I wait for Charles to return, I consider the prospect of another restless night at The Anchorage. I'm beginning to wish I hadn't turned down the prescription for sleeping pills my GP offered me. The thought of sliding into a deep, dreamless slumber, instead of stitching together the ragged scraps of oblivion that pass as sleep these days, is immensely appealing. Perhaps getting drunk will help and, after two glasses of Pinot, I'm halfway there already.

Charles's face is flushed when he finally returns with our drinks. He's been gone so long that he's already downed half his pint.

'It looks as if you've made a new friend,' I say, as he sets down a glass of wine in front of me. 'What were you two talking about?'

'Oh, this and that,' he responds vaguely. 'I asked him if they had any rooms available.'

'And did he?' I say, my voice rising hopefully.

'Uh-uh. A couple of guests were due to leave tomorrow, but because of the landslide they've had to extend their stay. The landlord reckons the road is going to be closed until the end of the week at least.'

'Just our bloody luck,' I say through gritted teeth. 'Does he know if they've got the tree off the line yet?'

'Yep, it's gone now, but apparently the power cable's proving trickier to fix than they anticipated. The engineers have had to get parts in from a depot in another part of the country – except of course the courier who's bringing the parts won't be able to get here because of the landslide.'

My heart sinks. That settles it, I think as I raise my wineglass to my lips. I'm definitely getting pissed tonight.

*

When we leave The Boathouse just before closing, we're both pretty merry. For the first time since we arrived in Saltwater, it feels like we're on honeymoon. Amazingly, it's stopped raining and the sky is filled with stars, tiny and fierce, a billion grains of sand spilling across the inky darkness.

As we stroll through the village hand in hand, even the thought of another night at The Anchorage doesn't seem so bad. But then, as we turn onto the road that leads to the guest house, I notice something unusual.

'That's odd,' I say to Charles, pointing up ahead. 'Our street lamp isn't working.'

'*Our* street lamp?' he says, slurring his words slightly.

'The one right outside the guest house.'

He squints into the darkness. 'Oh yeah,' he hiccups. 'I guess the storm must have affected the electricity supply.'

'I don't think so.' I turn around and gesture towards the high street, which is bathed prettily in the glow from a dozen or so street lamps. 'See, all the others are working just fine.'

I turn back to Charles, but he's already at The Anchorage's front gate and fumbling in his pocket for the key.

Beyond the front door, the guest house lies quiet and still. At least the Jeffreys have left the hall light on for us, and the radiators have some residual warmth. We go straight upstairs to our room, where Charles immediately peels off his clothes and collapses into bed without even bothering to brush his teeth.

Despite his earlier suggestion, a night of passion is clearly the last thing on his mind, but that's all right; we can make up for it in the morning. I'm pretty tired myself but, keen to maximise my chances of an unbroken night's sleep, I decide to take a relaxing bath before turning in.

I can't find any bubble bath, but there's a fat candle in a glass jar and a box of matches on top of the medicine cabinet.

Humming softly to myself, I light the candle and place it on the edge of the bath, before turning off the overhead light. There's no extractor fan, so I lift the sash window a couple of inches so that the steam can escape.

As I slip into the water, I give a moan of pleasure and allow my eyes to close. I feel happy, relaxed. Even the anomaly of the faulty street lamp can't spoil my good mood. My mind drifts pleasantly for ten minutes or so and then, as I reach for the hot tap to top up the water, I hear it.

It's hallucinatorily faint at first. The sound of singing. A single voice, high and clear. The words drift up to me through the open window and hang in the air like smoke.

I don't pay too much attention at first, dismissing it as a tipsy female making her way home from the pub. But, as the singing gets louder, I realise it's not an adult. It's a child.

My pulse flickers in my throat like a stray heartbeat. What would a child be doing out at this time of night, particularly up here on the bluff?

I lift my head up out of the water, ears straining. The song has a pure and plaintive quality, though it's difficult to make out the words.

Just then, a moth flies in through the window and begins dashing at the candle, rapidly and frantically, as if it's got some sort of death wish. Almost without thinking, I pinch out the flame with my damp fingers. Instantly, I wish I hadn't. Now I'm sitting in complete darkness.

Suddenly, the volume increases. It sounds as if they're right underneath the window. I can hear the words quite clearly now:

> *We'll hoist him up to the mizzen mast*
> *Let him hang till danger's past*
> *We'll drop him down to the depths of the sea*
> *Where the sharks will have his body*

Despite the warmth of the bathwater, it's as if all my blood is draining from my body. My arms feel heavy and cool; my fingertips tingle; I am suddenly incredibly sober.

I don't recognise the song, but I know what it is: a traditional sea shanty, the sort sung by sailors on board merchant ships in days gone by.

Panic spreads along the cartilage between my ribs, tightening, compressing, throttling my natural reserves of courage. Pushing my fears aside, I leap out of the bath, ignoring the tidal wave of water that cascades onto the lino.

The window mechanism is stiff and I waste vital seconds trying to lift the sash higher. By the time I manage to create a gap big enough to get my head and shoulders through, the singing has faded to a whisper.

The moon is covered with clouds and I can't see anything on the bluff, just the shadowy outlines of the bandstand, and beyond it the distant lights of a ship far out at sea.

'Who are you?' I call into the night, my words disappearing into the devouring darkness.

No one answers. The singing has stopped altogether now.

I draw a stiffening breath. 'What do you want?'

Nothing. Only silence. I suddenly feel self-conscious, as if I am a caged animal in an experiment, observed through one-way glass, while the scientists take notes.

There's no point in waking Charles. He's bound to have a ready-made explanation: it wasn't a child singing; it was the wind, the waves, air trapped in the pipework. But I know what I heard. Something's happening to me, *through* me, something dangerous and new. It's taken root, a poison tree; its vines are winding round my gut, my liver, my heart.

Back in the room, I lock the door for the first time since we've been here. I climb into bed beside Charles and pull the covers over my head, but still the words of the shanty pour like spiders from the crevices of my brain until my head swarms with them. I know that tonight any sleep will be a long time coming.

15

CHARLES

There is always a grey area between the person we want to be and the person we actually are. I have a perception of myself as honest, decent, secure in the knowledge of my own moral boundaries. But good and bad can be complicated things. That was something I learned during my first summer in Saltwater.

I was twelve years old and I was walking back to The Anchorage after buying an ice lolly. Ally was supposed to be keeping an eye on me but, as we delved into the newsagent's freezer cabinet, I told her she looked fat in her swimsuit. Not unreasonably, she'd thrown a strop and stalked out of the shop empty-handed.

I was enjoying the unusual freedom of being on my own, so I took my time going back. There was a man walking in front of me along the high street. It was a warm day and he was carrying a denim jacket over his arm. As he walked past the post office, a black leather wallet fell out of the pocket. I thought the man would realise, but he didn't; he just kept on walking.

I bent down to pick up the wallet, but I didn't run after the man as he turned down the side street that led to the car park; I didn't even call out to him. Instead, I opened the wallet, my eyes bulging as I clocked the fat wedge of twenty-pound notes. After looking around to make sure no one was watching, I withdrew one of the crisp notes and tucked it into the elasticated waistband of my shorts. Only then did I hail the man: *Hey, mister! I think you've dropped something.*

Naturally, he was delighted to be reunited with his wallet. He even bunged me a couple of pound coins and told me to buy myself some sweets. I doubled back and bounded up the hill to The Anchorage in high spirits – and considerably richer than when I had set out.

Even though it happened a long time ago, that incident has always stuck in my mind. I know I could have been a lot shittier – I could have taken *all* the money and chucked the wallet away – but I still did a bad thing. Certainly, it was the first time I realised my capacity for deception. Saltwater's like that. It has the power to draw out aspects of one's personality one never knew existed. Don't ask me how it happens; I don't really understand it myself.

It would be easy to look back and pinpoint that day as the beginning of my journey of self-discovery, the moment those things in me that had lain dormant and submerged suddenly stirred and came to life. But I've never been prone to flights of fancy and I'm certainly not going to embark on one now. All I know is that the more time I spend here, the more I learn about myself.

I think my wife is beginning to discover Saltwater's power for herself. She's certainly well out of her comfort zone; that much is obvious. Grace is an only child. I wouldn't say her parents spoiled her, but compared to a lot of people, myself included, she enjoyed a privileged upbringing. Horse-riding lessons, private schooling, lavish family holidays in far-flung destinations. She had all those things, and more besides.

Not surprisingly, she grew up with a taste for the finer things in life. Hence the swish apartment in the heart of the cathedral quarter (Mummy and Daddy coughed up for the deposit, *natch*), the meals out in smart restaurants, the shiny new BMW.

I'm not criticising her for it. Grace works hard and earns good money. Why shouldn't she treat herself? When we first started dating, I was worried I wouldn't be able to keep up with her. Considering the start I had in life, I've done pretty well for myself, but I knew right away that I didn't have the 'breeding' or the 'polish' of most of the people in Grace's social circle.

Grace's parents knew it too. You should have seen the way her mother looked at me the first time we met. She did her best to disguise her disappointment, but I could feel her silently auditing my shortcomings: my chain-store shirt, my chipped front tooth (fair enough, Grace's mother *is* a dentist), the way my accent occasionally slipped, as it tends to do when I'm under pressure. When she asked me about my career in construction, her voice contained a tone of strained brightness, like an actress trying so hard to remember her lines she'd forgotten their meaning.

I might have felt like a fish out of water that first weekend in Grace's parents' home, but I wasn't put off. Their tacit disapproval only made me more determined to win their daughter's heart. And actually, it was a lot easier than I thought it was going to be. I got the impression Grace was hungry for a man like me – someone savvy, someone practical, someone who loved the great outdoors – not like those jumped-up public-school twits she'd been wasting her time on.

Grace was like an addiction for me – an intoxicant rolling through my veins, like that first sip of alcohol coursing through the bloodstream. And once she'd fallen in love with me, I was keen to make it official. That's why I proposed at a time I thought she was most likely to say yes. A cynic would say I exploited her vulnerabilities. A romantic would say I followed my heart. I'll let you make up your own mind.

There are many reasons I love my wife, but one of the things I admire most about her is the fact she's never been content to rest on her laurels. Someone else in her position would have taken an undemanding job in her father's pharmaceutical company, or on the reception desk of a fashionable art gallery, just whiling away the years until the time came to collect her inheritance. Not Grace. She's ambitious, a grafter. She has a desire to grow and improve, to become a better, more successful version of her original self. Just like me.

She's always had good people skills, so it's fitting that she chose a career in HR – and nobody was more proud than me when she landed her dream job at a prestigious technology firm last year. Who knows where she'll end up eventually; I really believe she can achieve anything she sets her mind on. I know she feels that taking all that time off work after the accident has set her back a bit, and maybe it has. But I'm confident that she can get back on track, just so long as she doesn't let her insecurities get the better of her.

To be honest, Grace has changed quite a bit since Turkey. She used to be so carefree, so full of fun, that to see her looking so serious all the time produces a kind of jolt, like a needle skidding off the vinyl. She can't seem to relax and she keeps imagining things that aren't there. I think she's even starting to question her own sanity. That's utter rubbish, of course; Grace is one of the most well-adjusted people I know. Still, she's behaving so erratically it has crossed my mind that maybe she suffered some sort of brain injury in the accident, something that's triggering visual and auditory hallucinations. Sometimes it scares me.

True, she was checked over thoroughly at the hospital in Bodrum – and again after she'd been medevac-ed back to the UK. But doctors aren't infallible, are they? It's always possible they missed something. If there's no improvement when we get back home, I might suggest she seek out a second opinion.

In the meantime, I need to tread carefully. She almost caught me in a lie earlier on, when she asked to see the text I sent her parents. The urge to be honest about that – and a few other things besides – bites at me, but it's too late for regrets. Grace has a certain image of me, an image I've worked hard to cultivate. I don't think it would do either of us any good to shatter that illusion. All I want to do now, all I've ever wanted to do, is to protect her, to make her happy.

That's why I didn't tell her what the landlord of The Boathouse said to me, how he reacted when I mentioned where we were staying.

'The Anchorage?' he'd said with a look of undisguised horror. '*You're* brave. No wonder you're looking for somewhere else to stay.'

Disturbed by his response, I asked him for specifics.

'It's really not my place to say,' he insisted. 'I shouldn't be slagging off my competitors; it's bad form.'

'But you just did,' I told him. 'And now I want to know what's so bad about the Jeffreys' place. Why are we the only guests while everywhere else is fully booked?'

At this, the landlord gave a knowing chuckle. 'Let's just say that quite a few guests have left in a hurry. If you want to know more, just read the reviews on Tripadvisor.'

'Love to,' I said, producing my phone. 'So if you could just give me your Wi-Fi password ...'

He shrugged an apology. 'Sorry, mate, we're offline at the moment; you can blame the storm for that.'

How very convenient.

As I turned away with our drinks, another bloke at the bar, some old-timer in a woolly hat, had the cheek to raise his pint glass to me. 'Good luck at The Anchorage,' he said. 'You're going to need it.'

I wish I knew what was going on. It's like being in a third-rate horror movie. The mere mention of The Anchorage's name is enough to have the locals crossing themselves and sharpening their stakes. What is it with these people and their coded warnings? It's quite pathetic, really. If they've got something to say, they should just come out and say it. I'm sure most of it is nonsense – idle gossip from people with nothing better to do with their time – but I can't deny that there's a strange atmosphere at the guest house. It's hard to put it into words.

The situation isn't helped by Michael and Pamela themselves, with their ponderous looks and strained conversation. Perhaps I should just ask them why the guest house is dead on its feet. It really is none of my business though, and I don't want to make them feel any worse about it than they probably already do. More importantly, I don't want to alarm Grace. No, better to keep a lid on it and then hopefully tomorrow we'll find somewhere else to stay.

It's all a bit awkward really. I can tell the Jeffreys are genuinely pleased to see me again and I get the sense they'd like to spend a bit more time with us. I haven't said anything to Grace, but this morning, as I rescued my phone charger from the sitting room, I bumped into Michael. He suggested we might like to join him and Pamela for dinner in the annexe one evening – 'for old time's sake'. He caught me on the hop and I told him I'd have to speak to Grace, that I wasn't sure what our plans were. But actually, in the circumstances, it might be a good idea to keep the Jeffreys at arm's length. I'm sure they would love the opportunity to relive The Anchorage's glory days with someone who was there, but I've never been a great one for reminiscing. What's more, there are aspects of my previous time in Saltwater I would rather not be reminded of.

Fingers crossed, Michael won't bring up the subject of dinner again. Oh, and I do wish he wouldn't keep calling me *Charlie*. Hearing that name brings back memories I thought I'd buried. The more time I spend at The Anchorage, the more nostalgia creeps over me, the strings of the past tightening around my neck, like a noose.

16

I heard them before I saw them. The relentless clicking and skittering. The sickening crunch beneath my shoes.

Cockroaches. Everywhere. Dozens of them. Too many to count. Crawling over the floor. Scuttling up the walls. Squeezing into the gaps under the skirting boards. I nearly fainted when I saw them.

Disgusting, filthy creatures. Germ-spreaders. Disease-carriers. They eat anything and everything. Food, hair, shit – even each other if push comes to shove. How on earth am I going to get rid of them?

He thinks I've been making stuff up. Letting my imagination run away with me. But this is something real, something he can see with his own eyes. Surely he'll believe me now.

I'm always so careful, I don't understand how they got in. Is it my own negligence – or is it a sign from God? Like a plague of locusts, sent as a punishment. What next? Thunderstorms of hail and fire? The death of my firstborn?

I just wish I knew what I've done wrong. If only I knew, then I could try and make amends. Extend an olive branch. Do whatever it takes.

I can't cope with this when I'm already under so much strain. They don't care about other people's feelings; don't see the pain they're causing. They're still coming at me; still trying to tip me over the edge.

Their hate is like an invasive weed. It forces its tendrils into everything. Spreading. Smothering. Choking. Until finally everything in its path is DEAD.

17

GRACE

When I wake up, the door to our room is wide open and Charles is gone. In the distance, a powerful voice is belting out the chorus of 'Oklahoma'. My husband always sings show tunes in the shower; I love that he does that.

Blinking like a cave-dweller coming into the light, I fumble for my phone on the bedside table. Nine-fifteen; I haven't slept in this late since the accident. My head feels thick and there is a nasty hot feeling souring the back of my throat; I must have drunk a lot more than I realised.

Yawning noisily, I think back to last night. I know that what I heard was real and yet it seems so very far away now, nothing left of it but a ringing in my ears and the feeling that something important has slipped from my grasp and is now lying, unreachable, at the bottom of a crevasse.

As I lie there, staring at the cracks in the ceiling, a theory begins to form in my mind. I've never been an especially spiritual person, but I'm beginning to wonder if my near-death experience in Turkey has left me uniquely sensitive to the souls of places and objects, to the emanations left by time. If perhaps I'm some sort of conduit, that I can hear and see things that other people can't. It's a prospect I find terrifying and yet, at the same time, curiously appealing.

I wonder how my husband would react if I told him about the ghost child's siren song and shared my – admittedly far-fetched –

hypothesis. Although Charles prides himself on being open-minded, he's also fiercely pragmatic and operates on the assumption that there's a rational explanation for everything.

By the time he returns from the bathroom, I've already made up my mind. Tempting as it is to unburden myself, I can't ignore the small but insistent voice calling from my subconscious. It's warning me not to say anything to anyone. Not until I'm sure.

Charles smiles when he sees that I'm awake. 'Hey sleepyhead, how are you feeling?'

'Pretty rough,' I reply, tilting my chin up as he bends down to kiss me.

'Me too; last night was fun though.'

He drops his towel on the floor and starts rummaging for clean underwear in the chest of drawers. I love seeing Charles naked. He takes really good care of himself; he was the first man I ever dated who had an actual six-pack. As I watch him, an uncomplicated flood of desire surfs through me. I think about telling him to get his arse back in bed, but then I remember that breakfast service ends at nine-thirty and in this moment, the thought of hot coffee wins out over sex.

'Sorry I crashed like that last night,' he says, as he pulls a sweater over his head. 'What time did you come to bed?'

I run my tongue around my dry lips. 'Half an hour or so after you; I had a bath first.'

'I noticed that you'd locked the bedroom door. Why did you bother? It's just us here, so no one's going to nick our stuff in the night.'

'I don't know; I guess I just felt like it.'

He picks up the watch I bought him as a wedding present. 'If you want something to eat you'd better get a move on, the kitchen's closing in a minute.'

I throw back the duvet. 'Why don't you go down and order for us? I'll throw on some clothes and join you in a minute.'

By the time I get to the dining room, our coffee has already arrived. I seize on the cafetière greedily, filling my cup to the brim.

'I've ordered the cooked breakfast for you,' Charles says. 'I hope that's what you wanted.'

'Perfect,' I reply, sipping at my coffee. I turn my head and look out of the window. To my surprise, the garden is shrouded in fog. I can barely make out the greenhouse or the sharp outline of the holly hedge.

I tut in irritation. 'Have you seen it outside? Visibility must be down to two metres.'

Charles helps himself to sugar. 'I know. Bad, isn't it? I think it might be raining as well, although it's hard to tell.'

'In Cornwall, we call it *mizzle*.'

I snap my head round to see Pamela standing in the doorway. She's wearing an apron and carrying a plate in each hand. She comes towards our table. 'It's a combination of fine rain and fog; here on the coast it can hang around for days.'

'Oh goodie, a brand-new weather phenomenon, just what we needed,' I say sarcastically.

Charles glares at me reproachfully, but I pretend not to notice.

Pamela lowers one of the plates down in front of me. I can't help noticing the dark circles, like bruises, under her eyes, the taut pull of muscles in her face, as if something angry and pained is lurking within her.

'I've given you an extra grilled tomato, Charlie,' she says as she offloads the second plate. 'I know how much you love them.'

'Thank you, Pamela, that's very kind,' Charles says, rubbing his hands together in anticipation.

I throw him a questioning look before turning my attention back to our hostess. 'Any news on the phone and Wi-Fi?'

'Both still down, sorry. I'm not sure what's going on, the service in the village can be unreliable but this really is unprecedented.'

'Oh well, it's not your fault.' I set down my coffee cup. 'I suppose you've heard about the landslide?'

She gives a small incline of the head. 'Michael and I couldn't believe it when we saw it on the news; what a terrible thing to happen. I believe two people have been quite badly injured.'

'Were they locals, do you know?' Charles asks her.

'No idea, they haven't released the victims' names yet.'

I frown at her. 'So you haven't heard on the village grapevine.'

She shakes her head.

I smile at her. 'As hoteliers, I would've thought you and Michael would be privy to all kinds of interesting gossip.'

'Not really,' she says dismissively, wiping her hands on her apron. 'We tend to keep ourselves to ourselves.'

I take a sip of coffee. 'We were just around the corner when it happened. We heard the rocks fall. Another minute or so and it would have been us underneath them.'

'Somebody must've been looking out for you then,' Pamela says, although I must say she doesn't sound terribly pleased about it. 'What were you two doing all the way out there anyway?'

'Trying to get out of here.'

Charles gives an awkward laugh. 'What Grace means is that we were trying to find some mobile reception, so we could call the car hire company.'

'Well, I'm very sorry the landslide ruined your plans.' Her voice is flat and lifeless, as if she's speaking under hypnosis.

'Is that really the only route out of the village?' I ask her. 'Surely there's another way.'

She lets out a sharp, contemptuous laugh. 'Not unless you fancy swimming out to sea or scaling a sheer rock face,' she says, unhelpfully.

My teeth grind together; I can feel the pressure building in my jaw.

'We can't stay here forever, you know.'

'Of course not – and just as soon as the trains are back on track, we'll have you on your way.' Pamela's mouth makes a series of tiny, twitching, darting movements as if she's trying to stop herself saying something incriminating. 'Is there anything else I can get you? Ketchup? Toast? More coffee?'

Charles smiles at her. 'We're good for now, thanks, Pamela.'

'Super. Well, enjoy your breakfasts – and the minute communications are restored, I'll be sure to let you know.'

The moment she's out of earshot, Charles leans forward across the table. 'I wish you'd give Pamela a break,' he says mildly. 'The poor thing's doing her best.'

I shrug and stare down at my plate. All at once I seem to have lost my appetite.

Charles starts eating, shovelling food into his mouth in a rapid, anxious motion as if he's expecting it to be snatched away from him at any moment.

'God, this is good,' he says through a mouthful of baked beans. 'I'm really going to miss Pamela's breakfasts when we leave.'

I pick up my fork and prod the pile of grilled tomatoes on Charles's plate. 'I didn't think you liked these.'

He shakes his head. 'It's fresh tomatoes I don't like; these ones are delicious.'

'But your sister cooked tomatoes that time we stayed at her house and you refused to touch them. You said they made you gag.'

He looks at me indifferently. 'I don't remember that.'

'That doesn't mean it didn't happen.'

He starts dissecting a rasher of bacon. 'Eat up, darling, before it gets cold.'

I push my plate away. 'I'm not that hungry, actually. If it's all right with you, I think I'll skip breakfast and take my coffee into the sitting room.'

He doesn't even look up. 'No worries, I'll come and find you when I've finished this.'

'You haven't forgotten that we're going to check out some other guest houses today, have you?'

He pauses to take a gulp of coffee. 'Nope. I think it's a shame, though; the Jeffreys are clearly desperate for business and I know they're enjoying having us here.'

'Too bad,' I say flippantly. 'I just hope we can find another room, even if it means single beds.'

Charles regards me with undisguised horror. 'Seriously, Grace, single beds – on our *honeymoon*?'

I push my chair back from the table. 'At this stage, I'm open to any offer.'

Emerging into the hallway, I realise straight away that something has changed. The rotting chrysanthemums have gone (better late than never) and in their place is a lavish display of dried flowers. Mind you, it's not much of an improvement. As well as being far too big for the spindly console table, the arrangement is also displeasingly asymmetrical – something my inner neat freak feels compelled to rectify.

Pouting in disapproval, I place my coffee cup on the floor and set about reordering the brittle blooms. As I take a step back to appraise my adjustments, my gaze strays downwards, to the single drawer concealed beneath the tabletop. More out of boredom than anything else, I decide to take a look inside.

This is easier said than done. The drawer is so stiff that I practically have to wrestle it open and even then it jams halfway. I do my best to jiggle it free, but eventually I give up, worried that if I pull any harder the whole table will come toppling over.

At first glance, the drawer doesn't appear to contain much of interest: a child's colouring book, a clutch of leaflets for various local attractions, a few drawing pins and some well-fingered gobs of Blu-Tack, the usual household detritus. I'm on the verge of shutting it when something catches my eye. A slim red book peeking out from beneath a bus timetable. My curiosity piqued, I ease it carefully out of the drawer. When I see the words 'Guest Book' embossed in gold on the faux leather cover, I feel a twinge of excitement. This definitely requires further investigation.

No fire has been lit in the sitting room this morning, but I barely notice the chill in the air as I settle on the sofa under the window where the light is best. I may not have the luxury of Google to research the Jeffreys and their unconventional establishment, but this guest book is surely the next best thing.

The first entry dates all the way back to 2006 and it's effusive to say the least.

We enjoyed every second of our two-week break at this gorgeous guest house. The room was clean and comfortable, the sea views spectacular and the hospitality second to none. Our only complaint is that we can't stay at The Anchorage for longer!

The Abbotts

The irony of the final sentence is not lost on me. Here am I, desperate to escape this gloomy place and its spooky, shadowed rooms; here, the Abbott family is bemoaning the fact their stay has ended too soon. It doesn't make sense; it's almost as if they're writing about another place entirely. Bemused, I read on.

Michael and Pamela, thank you for looking after us so incredibly well. Everything about our stay was perfect and the flowers

in the room on our wedding anniversary were such a thoughtful
touch. We can't recommend your beautiful B&B highly enough.
With fondest regards,
Anne and David Henderson

Hmmm. How come the Hendersons got flowers, when Pamela barely had the energy to rustle up tea and biscuits for me?

As I work my way through the guest book, the entries continue in much the same vein. After a while, my eyes start to glaze over, but still I keep reading, convinced that if I look hard enough, this book will give up The Anchorage's secrets. And then, six or seven pages in, I spot something that makes me smile.

I love it here. Every day it's sunny and the breakfast is yummy.
Dad says if I'm good we can come again next year ☺
Charlie McKenna (Age 12)

A gust of emotion surges through me. My dear, sweet Charles; as endearingly optimistic then as he is now. I know that his family wasn't very well off when he was a kid, so a beach holiday on the Cornish coast must've seemed like a huge adventure to him.

As I trace the childish handwriting with my fingertips, my heart aches for the little boy I never knew. I've always envied couples that meet in childhood, who have the opportunity to watch each other's personality develop; to know the raw, unformed person they were in the beginning and the fully evolved person they eventually became. Unfortunately, Charles and I haven't had that privilege. He doesn't talk about his childhood a whole lot. Sometimes I get the feeling he's holding back on me; that there are aspects of his past he'd rather not talk about. But then again, don't we all do that? Present the best version of ourselves to the people we love and are seeking to impress?

Reluctantly, I tear myself away from little Charlie. After that, the clichés come thick and fast: 'a home from home'; 'a hidden gem'; 'Cornwall's best-kept secret'. Michael and Pamela were clearly doing something right. Back in the day, The Anchorage must have been making good money. There are a few small criticisms – one guest notes the absence of an electric fan in their room during a particularly hot summer; another references a fried egg that wasn't quite runny enough in the middle (seriously?), but there's nothing more concerning than that.

It's towards the middle of 2007 that the barbed comments start to creep in. These mainly concern lapses in housekeeping, as well as some frustratingly vague references to 'noisy neighbours'. One couple arrive only to find their booking unaccountably cancelled (and are only partly mollified by the offer of a larger room with a sea view at no extra cost). Worryingly, there are also a number of reports of food poisoning. The victims stop short of pinning the blame on Pamela's cooking – but if you read between the lines, the implication is clear.

As time goes on, the write-ups become increasingly sparse. Weeks go by without a single comment, and the few that do appear are brief and lacking in warmth. I wonder if the Jeffreys are suffering from a lack of bookings at this juncture – or if guests, struggling to find something nice to say about the place, decide it's best not to write anything at all.

It's not until the spring of 2009 that things start to pick up again, with the entries increasing in both quantity and enthusiasm. The momentum had clearly been lost however and, as I skim-read through the comments, it's clear that the Jeffreys never regained their early success. Something went badly wrong at The Anchorage – but what?

Then, in the summer of 2019, the guest book entries take another nosedive. There's an intriguing mention of a 'negative vibe' in one of the rooms followed, a few pages later, by a claim that personal items have been 'interfered with'. Other guests complain about being woken in the night by 'rowdy locals' and 'troublesome wildlife'.

A few months later, the entries come to an abrupt end. I don't understand why, not when a quarter of the guest book is empty, its blank pages waiting to be filled. Realising I've come to the end, I feel quite deflated. I don't know what I was expecting to find. An explicit account of some supernatural encounter, perhaps – or, at the very least, a no-holds-barred critique of the Jeffreys. But there's nothing like that, just hints and innuendo. It's a huge disappointment.

Then I notice something strange. Following the final entry, several pages have been torn out. I can see the jagged remnants of paper still attached to the spine. Who on earth would have done such a thing – and *why*?

I run my hand absent-mindedly over the blank page. But it's not blank. There's something there. The indentation of the words that were written on the preceding page, now missing, ripped out.

I turn on a nearby table lamp and hold the book up to the light. I see the faint impression of a few words, written in capitals in the centre of the page. I can make out the occasional letter, but nothing more. Fuck it.

I think for a moment and then a memory rises up, expanding, like something breaking the surface of water and rippling outwards. A school field trip in Year 6. Brass rubbing at a local cathedral. Bloody Eureka.

I lay the guest book on the sofa and return to the drawer, where I spend a few moments foraging for a suitable implement. Eventually I come across the stump of a red crayon. Not ideal by any means, but it will have to do.

Back in the sitting room, I waste no time in spreading the guest book across my lap and running the crayon lightly back and forth over the imprint of the words. As the message starts to come into relief, a victorious *Yessss!* issues from my lips. Then my smile fades.

The words look as if they've been written in haste, some of the letters barely formed. As I stare at them, they seem to jump off the page and float into the air, like black, buzzing insects, swirling, darting, following their own secret path.

Six words. Conveying an alarming message. With absolutely no room for misinterpretation.

DO NOT TRUST THEM. LEAVE IMMEDIATELY!

18

CHARLES

I spend longer in the dining room than I meant to. After I've polished off my full English, Michael brings me a toasted teacake with butter and jam. I didn't order it, but I figure it would be rude to send it back. Anyway, I'm starving, the way I always am when I'm suffering from a hangover.

Concerned that Grace's breakfast has been left untouched, Michael asks if she's feeling okay. He even offers to take some more coffee through to the sitting room for her. I decline politely, knowing she won't appreciate the interruption. He's very kind, they both are. It's just a shame Grace can't see it.

I'm sorry that it might be our last day at The Anchorage. In a funny sort of way, I feel I owe Michael and Pamela, the people who provided the backdrop for some of my happiest childhood memories. Despite Michael's hope that spring will bring a coach load of customers to his door, it's clear that the guest house is in dire straits; I just wish there was something I could do to help.

As I tuck into my teacake, Michael busies himself in the dining room, wiping down tables that are already spotless. I get the impression he'd like to chat, but I know Grace is keen to hit the road so I don't linger.

Having drained my coffee cup, I thank Michael for another excellent breakfast and make my way towards the sitting room. Just as I round the corner into the hall, Grace comes barrelling towards me.

'Whoa there, Mrs McKenna, where's the fire?' I say as she runs straight into my chest.

She looks up at me. Her lips are quivering slightly and her brown eyes are unnaturally bright. She's holding a book or album of some sort, gripping it tightly with both hands.

'I've found something,' she says, holding the book out to me.

'What is it?'

'A guest book.'

Hardly the discovery of the century, but Grace seems pretty excited about it. 'That's nice,' I tell her. 'We must remember to write in it before we go. Where was it?'

'In that drawer over there, buried under a pile of leaflets. Where they didn't think we'd find it.'

'Where *who* didn't think we'd find it?'

'The Jeffreys, of course!' Her voice swerves upwards, high and panicky. 'The woman in the cafe was right. We need to pack our stuff and get out of here.'

Before I can figure out what she means, she opens the guest book and starts turning the pages at speed.

'A previous guest wrote a warning. Except the Jeffreys didn't want us to see it, so they tore the page out. But the imprint was left behind on the next page and I used a brass-rubbing technique to make it legible.'

Grace is speaking so quickly her words are running into each other. She offers the book up to me. 'I don't care if we have to sleep on the street. I'm not spending another night in this place.'

I stare the page in bafflement; all I can see is a bunch of crayon scribbles, the kind a toddler would make. 'Sorry, Grace . . . what is it I'm supposed to be looking at?'

'That!' she shrieks. When I look closely, I can just make out a couple of sentences.

DO NOT TRUST THEM. LEAVE IMMEDIATELY!

'Other pages have been torn out too,' she goes on breathlessly. 'Four or five at least. I dread to think what *they* said.'

I look at her, not knowing how to respond. Her face is knotted into a shape I've never seen before, beyond worried or frustrated, bordering on fear.

'Don't you understand, Charles? I really think we might be in serious danger. I'm not making it up, we need to leave here – *now*!'

Just then I hear footsteps behind me. It's Michael. He's got a dishcloth in one hand and a tea towel over his shoulder. He looks concerned.

'I thought I heard raised voices,' he says. 'Is everything all right?'

Grace's eyes are filled with pleading. I don't know what she wants me to do. Say something ... or say nothing? I opt for the former.

'We're fine,' I say calmly. 'My wife was just browsing your guest book and she came across something that raised a bit of a red flag.'

'Oh yes?' Michael frowns when he sees the guest book that Grace is now clutching to her chest as if she's using it to ward off evil spirits. 'I haven't seen that old thing for ages. Where did you find it?'

'In that drawer,' Grace says, directing his attention to the console table. As Michael turns to look at it, she gives me a loaded glare. I realise now I was supposed to keep quiet about the guest book, but it's too late, I'm already committed.

I give a little grimace. 'Sorry, Michael, this is all rather awkward. Grace seems to think there's a hidden message in there and it's upset her a bit.'

'It wasn't hidden,' Grace adds frostily. 'A concerned guest wrote a warning for future guests and *someone*' – at this point, she fires a meaningful look in Michael's direction – 'decided to tear the page out to stop anyone else seeing it. Unfortunately for them, you can still see the imprint of that warning on the next page.'

Michael draws his hand over his face and in that moment he seems to age at least ten years. 'So what is this warning, exactly?'

'I think you'd better read it for yourself.' I pry the guest book from Grace's hands and turn to the page with the crayon scribblings. 'There you go; it's a little hard to see.'

Michael squints at the page, before spreading his hands apologetically. 'I'm sorry, I haven't got my reading glasses. Would you mind?'

I lick my lips; this really is hugely embarrassing.

'Okay, but these are their words, not mine.' I pause to clear my throat. 'It says: "Do not trust them. Leave immediately".'

I brace myself for Michael's reaction, but to my immense relief, he breaks into a taut smile.

'I can see why Grace was worried,' he says pleasantly. 'It is rather alarming at first glance, isn't it? But you'll be pleased to hear there's a perfectly sensible explanation.'

I heave a sigh. 'I knew there would be.' I give Grace a reassuring look.

'The author was one of our younger guests; a boy of eight or nine,' Michael continues. 'He was just larking around; he thought it would be amusing. His father caught him in the act and tore out the page to save us from any potential embarrassment, before reporting the incident to me.' He winks at Grace. 'Of course, nobody bargained on Miss Marple here.'

I put my arm around my wife's shoulders and draw her to me. 'You see, darling, there's nothing to worry about. It was just a kid, doing what kids do.' I give a little laugh. 'Actually, it sounds rather like the sort of thing I'd have done at that age.'

'We've had so much trouble with children over the years – destroying things, disturbing other guests – that we don't allow them to stay any more,' Michael divulges. 'Pamela and I feel bad about the blanket ban, but they're simply more trouble than they're worth.'

I feel Grace's body tense. 'Would a child of eight or nine use a long word like "immediately"?' she says coldly. 'Wouldn't they be far more likely to say, "Leave *now*"?'

My heart sinks. Why is she so suspicious, so disbelieving? Why can't she just accept Michael's explanation at face value?

Michael's eyes meet mine. I blink and purse my lips, trying to convey a silent apology.

Michael shrugs. 'I can't say; I'm not really familiar with the linguistic capabilities of young boys.'

'You don't have any children of your own then?'

I cringe inwardly, wishing Grace hadn't been quite so blunt.

Michael shakes his head. 'No, I don't.'

'What about the other pages that have been torn out?' Grace persists. 'What did they say?'

'I'm sorry, I can't quite recall,' Michael says, clearly flustered. 'I think the child may have done some obscene drawings.'

'Christ, what a little horror, eh?' I say with an eye roll. 'Anyway, I'm glad we've got to the bottom of it. We'll let you get back to work now, Michael, I'm sure you've got loads to do.'

'Hang on,' Grace protests, as he turns to go. 'Why are there no more entries after that one? There's plenty of space in the guest book.'

Please, Grace. Just let it drop.

Michael turns back. He really is being remarkably patient with her. 'We didn't think it looked very professional, having a load of pages torn out like that, so we took the guest book out of circulation.'

'Perfectly understandable,' I say. 'Right then, Grace, let's put our coats on and walk up to the station, shall we? You never know, they might have some good news for us.'

'In a minute,' she replies, glaring at me, before turning her attention back to Michael. 'Where do you keep your current guest book?'

'We don't bother with one any more. Everything's online these days, isn't it?' Michael starts walking away. He's clearly had enough – as indeed have I.

'You two be careful out there, won't you?' he says without turning round. 'The coastal fog can be treacherous.'

19

GRACE

I know I made Charles uncomfortable back there. I could feel the embarrassment coming off him in waves. That's something I've noticed since the accident – that I'm more attuned to other people's emotions. I wouldn't say I was thick-skinned before, but I was pretty unsentimental; you have to be that way when you work in HR and are required to make decisions about people's futures that aren't always popular.

I know Michael felt uncomfortable too; I did give him a bit of a roasting about those missing pages. Now that I've had a chance to think about it, I suppose his explanation is feasible. Perhaps I should give him the benefit of the doubt instead of tying myself up in knots about it.

The truth is, I wasn't myself when I woke up this morning. The extraordinary events of last night were lying heavy on my mind and I was light-headed from skipping breakfast. Added to that, my leg was in agony. The pain's been getting steadily worse since we arrived in Saltwater; I wonder if it's something to do with the weather.

I feel a bit better now that I've eaten a protein bar and swallowed a couple of my prescription painkillers. I don't like taking pills of any kind, but this morning I really needed them. It was either that or ask Charles to cut my leg off. And of course it's nice to be outdoors; I can't bear being cooped up in that house.

This fog is like no fog I've ever seen before. Soupy and

smothering, a dense white veil that seems to swallow every object in its path. As we leave the rail station and head back down the high street, I can hardly see the division between land and sea, sea and sky. Added to that is the fine, almost invisible rain that has soaked my clothes and hair within minutes.

It's almost as if the weather is mirroring my internal state. My mind is murky too, clouded with thoughts of haunted houses, killer landslides and mysterious hoteliers with ulterior motives. It would be easy to let myself believe I had the starring role in some real-life melodrama, but for the sake of my own mental health, I have to change my mindset completely, and focus only on the positives of my current situation.

We've already had a bit of good news regarding the trains. A member of rail staff has just informed us that the parts needed to repair the power cable are arriving this afternoon. The road is still blocked by the landslide, but the courier is going to park his vehicle beyond the roadblock and complete his journey on foot. This means the trains should be up and running by the weekend, leaving us with one whole week of our honeymoon to spend in St Ives. *Hurray!*

It would be helpful if we could let the hotel know our ETA, which will, of course, necessitate another tedious hunt for mobile reception. I'm keen to touch base with my parents as well. I don't usually go more than a couple of days without speaking to my mother.

It comes as no surprise when Charles, protective as ever, insists on going up to the war memorial alone. 'You're in enough pain with your leg as it is,' he says. 'I don't want you making things worse.'

Although I'd love to speak to my parents in person, Charles speaking to them is the next best thing. In any case, he's right – I've already done twice as much walking than the physio advised and from now on I need to take things easy.

'Say we're having a great time,' I say. 'And tell them that I absolutely love Saltwater, even if our hotel isn't quite as nice as the one we're supposed to be in.'

Charles gives me a look. 'You want me to lie?'

I smile. 'You don't mind, do you? I don't want Mum stressing. Oh, and if you manage to get through to the hotel, remind them that we paid for the full two weeks in advance, so they mustn't give our room to anyone else. Got it?'

He grins and plants a kiss on the tip of my nose. 'Got it.'

And then, in a wonderfully calm and encouraging way, in a way that reminds me just why I fell in love with him in the first place, my husband says: 'I know things haven't gone according to plan so far but trust me, Grace, this is all going to work out for the best.' Then he points to the antiques shop on the corner of the road and tells me to wait for him there.

I wander round the antiques shop for a while, but it smells horribly musty in there and it isn't long before I get bored examining badly stuffed squirrels, tarnished silverware and various other dead people's belongings. It's with a certain sense of relief that I leave the shop and step back out into the fog-bound street.

We walked past a shop selling postcards yesterday. I can't remember where it was, but it must be round here somewhere. Perhaps I could send one to my parents, the way people used to do in the days before social media.

If I'm going to leave our rendezvous point, I'd better let Charles know. It's only as I begin tapping out a text to him that I realise it's a waste of time. There's no mobile reception. *Duh*! This means I can't stray too far from the antiques shop, or he won't be able to find me.

Glancing across the street, I notice the village church. It's an attractive building with an ornate bell tower, almost Gothic in style, the top of which is now wreathed prettily in white candyfloss swirls. Maybe I could kill some time by wandering round the graveyard. So long as I keep the antiques shop in my sights, I'll be able to spot Charles when he gets back.

As I pass through the timber-framed lychgate, what strikes me first is how quiet and still the graveyard is. I can barely hear my own footfalls on the concrete path. I guess it must be the fog, deadening the sound.

I set off in a clockwise loop around the building. The grounds are a little overgrown in places, but generally well maintained. I walk slowly, taking in the ancient yew trees and the handsome stone mausoleum with its lichen-encrusted roof. Although I'm not particularly religious, I've always loved churchyards – the peacefulness, the sense of history, of continuity through time.

In the fog, this place seems almost magical. The headstones seem to reach into the coils of mist and merge with them, making me feel cocooned, removed from the real world.

Emerging from the rear of the church, I stop to admire a particularly striking memorial – a stone angel lying asleep atop a granite tomb, her hands folded neatly under her cheek the way a child would sleep.

My gaze drifts downwards, to the epitaph carved into the granite, and a cold hand wraps itself around my throat.

It wasn't a story. It really happened.

In ever-loving memory of Emma Rose Murrish,
dear wife and mother, and her children, Alice and Edward.
All taken by the cruel sea on 16th December 1876.

Also Captain John Frederick Murrish.
Died 4th June 1912. Aged 72 years.
We lived together in happiness.
Now we rest together in peace.

With a surge of dread, I realise that it was a day not unlike today when the SS *Albion* ran aground, resulting in the loss of so many souls. Fogbound. *Treacherous.*

As I stand there, absorbing the poignant tribute, I experience a peculiar sense of disconnection. The air seems to expand around me and although my gaze remains fixed on the tomb, the churchyard feels larger than it should, the lychgate receding in the middle distance.

I place a hand against my temple, praying it's not the start of a migraine. These chronic, post-traumatic headaches are another by-product of the accident. I haven't had one for several weeks now and I was hoping that they'd gone for good.

Unsettled, I take a step backwards. It's then that I see the bouquet of fresh flowers. They're lying on the ground at the head of the tomb, carefully arranged in a metal urn. Expensive flowers, not the cheap kind you get from the petrol station. Cala lilies, roses and baby's breath. They look fresh, as if they've only just been placed there. Emma Murrish's immediate descendants must be long dead, so who's been tending her grave?

Suddenly, I hear something. A brittle, snapping sound like a dry branch being broken underfoot. Startled, I look around. No one's there.

A slithering unease crawls into the pit of my stomach. It feels as if the dry, bony fingers of the past are reaching out to me. For some reason, I feel a connection with Emma. I'm not sure why, it isn't as if we have anything in common – except The Anchorage, of course.

I glance in the direction of the antiques shop, just to make sure Charles isn't there already. To my consternation, the high street has disappeared. All I can see is a blanket of fog swirling thickly between the yew trees, creeping through the cracks in the tombstones.

The thump of my heart fills my ribcage. The peace I felt just a few moments earlier has gone, evaporated in an instant.

Stop it, Grace, just stop it! I tell myself. *You're in a public place. Nothing can possibly happen to you here. The lychgate is just over there. All you have to do is walk though it and you'll be back on the high street.*

I start walking and then break into a clumsy jog, stumbling and almost falling to the ground as my foot catches on a yew tree's sprawling roots. As I hurry through the lychgate, not even pausing to latch the gate behind me, I startle a large, dark-coloured bird. It rises up and away over my head with loudly beating wings and a harsh, croaking cry that echoes all around the graveyard.

I'm out of breath and sweating slightly by the time I arrive back at the antiques shop. My fitness levels have dropped considerably since the accident and I'm unused to sudden bursts of activity. I push my rain-soaked hair out of my eyes and keep my gaze trained on the lychgate, but nobody else leaves or enters the graveyard.

By the time Charles returns, my pulse rate is back to normal. It feels like he's been gone forever and I'm hopeful that his trip to the war memorial has been a success. Then I see the look on his face.

'I tried for ages to get a signal,' he tells me. 'I must have looked ridiculous, wandering round and round the memorial, staring at my phone. I got talking to a couple of locals who were walking their dog and they told me that the nearest phone mast was damaged in the storm, so it was a waste of time me even trying.' He sighs. 'I'm sorry, darling, I feel as if I've let you down.'

Standing on tiptoes, I throw my arms around his neck and bury my face in the hollow beside his collarbone, breathing in the scent of his cologne, and enjoying the comforting solidity of him.

'Don't be silly,' I say, trying to keep the disappointment out of my voice. 'It was always going to be a long shot.'

'Did you see anything nice in the antiques shop?' he says into my ear. 'I'd like to buy you something before we go; a memento of our time in Saltwater.'

Discomfort slithers along my spine. This isn't a place I want to remember.

'Not really, I didn't stay there for long; I've been exploring the churchyard.' We draw apart and I look up at him. My husband is tall, almost a foot taller than me. If I stay in this position for too long, I'll get neckache. 'Guess whose grave I found?'

He smiles. 'Go on.'

'Emma Murrish's.'

He purses his lips. 'Emma *who*?'

'The wife of the sea captain who built The Anchorage. Her children are buried there with her.'

Recognition floods his face. 'Ah, right ... the woman in Rosario's told us that story about her.'

'It wasn't a story; they did die at sea. It says so on their tomb.'

He shakes his head sadly. 'That poor bloke; his wife and kids wiped out, just like that. I can't imagine what that must feel like.'

'I know ... heart-breaking, isn't it?' I draw away from him and glance back at the lychgate. 'For some reason I can't stop thinking about her ... Emma, I mean. In Victorian times, a female geologist must have been quite something. Not many women had careers back then.'

'Yes, she was certainly a trailblazer.'

'And she wasn't just super clever, you know, she was beautiful too.'

'How do you know that?'

'Because there's a portrait of her, hanging in the guest house.'

'Really, where? I haven't seen any portraits.'

'It's in one of the rooms on the first floor.'

Charles's mouth twists in surprise. 'You've been nosing around in the other rooms?'

'I wouldn't call it *nosing*,' I say, slightly indignant. 'I just had a look around on the first day, when you all went out in the car. I was curious to see how the other rooms compared to ours, that's all.'

'Well, don't mention it to Michael and Pamela,' he tells me. 'We don't want them thinking we're snoops.'

I snare my bottom lip in my teeth, feeling like a naughty schoolchild. 'I shouldn't think the Jeffreys care less, to be honest. If they didn't want people looking round, they would have locked the doors. In any case, they seem to *love* you. I doubt you could put a foot wrong in their eyes.'

'Fair enough,' Charles says, pushing a stray strand of hair off my cheek. He breaks into a grin. 'Just as long as there isn't anything else you haven't told me.'

A low thrumming starts up in my head, the persistent buzz of an uncomfortable memory. Sounds of movement in an empty house. A white kid glove on a bedroom floor. I blink hard, trying to banish it. I can't say anything to Charles; he wouldn't believe me. I'm not even sure I believe it myself.

I look off to the side. 'No, that's it,' I tell him. 'I've told you everything.'

20

I can't sleep. I haven't slept properly for weeks. No wonder I look like a ghost. My face is pale, my eyes are sunken, my skin is clammy.

Why are they doing it? What have I ever done to them? I'm not a bad person. I don't deserve this torture. How can I make them stop? Why won't they stop?

When it first started, I thought it was a joke, a game, maybe even an initiation ceremony of some sort. But it isn't funny any more. Not funny at all.

It's a horrible feeling, always looking over your shoulder, never knowing who to trust. No wonder my health is starting to suffer. All I want to do is live my life honestly, without fear of being judged. But that, it seems, is too much to ask.

He keeps telling me we need to be strong, that together we can weather the storm. I'm trying to keep my chin up, but as every day passes, I grow less and less convinced he's right.

What if it all falls apart? What are we supposed to do then? We'll be cast adrift, like shipwreck survivors, not knowing when rescue will come.

I wonder how far they're willing to go in pursuit of their ambition. They seem pretty ruthless. I don't think they'll stop until they get what they want. But if they don't stop soon, someone's going to get hurt. I'm sure of it.

21

GRACE

Charles's suggestion of coffee and cake at Rosario's is a tempting one, but my desire to leave The Anchorage is stronger. I manage to convince him that instead of procrastinating, we should be putting all our energies into finding another place to stay.

We had to throw away the sodden accommodation list that the rail staff provided, but we won't have any difficulty retracing our steps. Fortunately, Charles has an uncanny memory for places; he's like a human GPS. In fact, it was largely down to this ability of his that my life was saved that fateful day in Turkey.

In a re-run of our first night in Saltwater, we schlep from guest house to guest house. I start off with high hopes but, as one place after another turns us away, I realise that this isn't going to be as easy as I thought.

It quickly becomes apparent that just like us, the vast majority of our fellow evacuees are still stranded here. The few rooms that were empty before the landslide struck have already been filled with newcomers. Meanwhile, any guests who were poised to leave have been forced to extend their stay. The village is in lockdown: no way in; no way out.

As the final guest-house door closes in our faces, I have to admit that all our options are exhausted. We simply have no choice but to stick it out at The Anchorage. At least it's only two more nights, I tell myself. Then we'll be on the train to St

Ives and the honeymoon I planned so painstakingly can finally begin.

It's nearly lunchtime and Charles is concerned about the weather conditions. The wind has picked up and this, together with the fog and the unrelenting drizzle, means that being outdoors is pretty unpleasant. No doubt he's concerned about my leg as well. He hasn't said anything because he knows I hate to have my disability highlighted, but he can't fail to have noticed that my limp has become more pronounced with every hour that ticks by. The drugs are starting to wear off. I'm doing my best to pretend I'm not in pain, but it's becoming increasingly difficult.

Common sense dictates that we should head back to The Anchorage, but before we do I'm determined to buy a postcard to send to my parents. If I post it first class, it should get there tomorrow. I may not be able to talk to my mother, but the thought that she will soon be holding in her hands something that I have touched is a comforting one.

When we get to the gift shop, I find that it's much nicer than I thought. There's the usual tourist fare of fridge magnets and tea towels, but also some pretty throws and a colourful collection of ceramics. The well-dressed, middle-aged woman behind the till greets us warmly. 'Take your time looking round and if you need any help, just ask,' she says. 'I expect it's a relief to get out of that awful fog, isn't it?'

'You can say that again,' I reply, as I spin the carousel of postcards. 'You don't get weather like this where we're from.'

Charles picks up a glass paperweight and turns it over in his hand. 'I don't expect the weather's doing much for business, is it – not to mention the landslide?'

'We are pretty quiet, but that's fine. I've been running businesses in Saltwater for the best part of thirty years, so I'm used to the ups and downs.' The woman leans forward, resting her elbows on the counter. 'I'm Kirsten, by the way.'

'Nice to meet you, Kirsten. I'm Charles and this is Grace.'

'*Grace* ... that's a pretty name,' Kirsten says.

I smile. 'Thanks. I'm named after my mother's favourite aunt. She died two weeks before I was born.'

Charles puts down the paperweight and peers into a glass-fronted jewellery cabinet. 'Darling, come and look at this necklace, will you?'

'All our jewellery is handmade by a local designer,' Kirsten says, as I go over to join him. 'She draws her inspiration from the Cornish seascape.'

'Interesting,' Charles murmurs.

The necklace he's referring to is beautiful: a delicate silver ammonite, suspended on a slender chain. Instantly, my thoughts return to Emma Murrish. My eyes drift towards the price tag. It's not cheap.

'It's gorgeous,' I say.

'Then let me buy it for you.'

'No,' I say. 'It's far too expensive.'

Ignoring my protests, Charles asks Kirsten if she'd mind showing us the piece.

The necklace is even more lovely close up. I hold it to my throat and stare at my reflection in the glass, admiring the sheen on the ammonite as it catches the light.

'It compliments your skin tone perfectly,' Kirsten remarks.

'Is it sterling silver?' I ask.

She shakes her head. 'This entire collection is hand-crafted from Cornish shipwreck tin that was recovered from the seabed more than a hundred years ago.'

Charles looks faintly amused. '*Shipwreck* tin? That's a new one on me.'

'This particular ship sank off the coast of Cornwall at the end of the nineteenth century. Its cargo of tin was brought to the surface a couple of years ago using one of those underwater robots ... all perfectly legally, of course. The salvage operation even made the local news.'

A chill runs up my spine. 'You're talking about the *Albion*.' It's a statement, not a question.

Kirsten looks at me in surprise. 'Yes, that's right. You've heard of it then?'

I nod absently. A powerful sensation, almost like a premonition comes over me. It's as if I'm standing in the shallows, watching a rogue wave rising, then finding myself being dragged from the present and towed out into the past.

Meanwhile, Kirsten's sales pitch continues. 'The designer cleans off the barnacles and other encrustations and then melts the ingots down to make these stunning, one-off pieces. So, you see, you're not just buying a piece of jewellery, you're buying a piece of history.'

This is all too weird for words. First I stumble across Emma Murrish's grave and now I'm holding a piece of jewellery made from the cargo of the shipwreck that killed her – and not just any piece of jewellery, but a piece that symbolises her work as a geologist.

'What do you think, darling?' Charles asks, oblivious to my state of bewilderment.

A large part of me has no interest in taking home a memento of Saltwater, particularly one with such a macabre history. And yet part of me believes that this was meant to be.

I hand the necklace back to Kirsten. 'I love it.'

'In that case we'll take it,' Charles says decisively.

As she heads back to the till to ring it up, Charles grins at me. 'The SS *Albion*, eh? What a coincidence.'

'Isn't it just?' I say. Then, remembering my manners, I stand on tiptoes and kiss my husband's cheek. 'Thank you for my beautiful necklace.'

'It's my pleasure,' he says into my ear. 'Every time you wear it, I want you to remember our time together here.'

I don't reply. The truth is I can't wait to shake the sand of Saltwater from my shoes. But still, I can't help thinking that my experiences over the past few days will writhe and twist in my mind for a long time to come.

As we continue to browse, some more customers enter the shop, a trio of elderly women. Eavesdropping on their animated conversation, I quickly pick up that they're partway through a literary tour of the West Country.

Their conversation soon turns to the subject of the landslide. They talk about it as if it were some sort of special effect, laid on especially for them as part of the Cornish 'experience'. Unbelievably, they seem to find the prospect of being stranded in the village quite thrilling. Am I the only person who can't wait to get out of here? Just then, they spot a set of *Poldark*-themed table-mats and practically wet themselves with excitement. I take this as our cue to leave.

As well as the postcards – a pretty, harbourside scene for my parents, a sweeping shot of the beach for Charles's dad – I'm also treating myself to a box of clotted cream fudge and some handmade soap. Little luxuries that will make the remaining two days a bit more bearable.

'It's getting pretty gusty out there again,' Kirsten says, frowning as she looks out through the shop window. 'I hope the weather hasn't put too much of a dampener on your holiday.' She reaches under the counter for a paper carrier. 'Where are you staying anyway?'

Charles pats his jacket pockets, searching for his wallet. 'We're with the Jeffreys, up at The Anchorage.'

Instantly, Kirsten's relaxed demeanour changes. Her lips are still upturned, but there's something simmering in her dark eyes, something shrewd and knowing.

'Rather you than me,' she says with an odd cast in her voice.

'What do you mean?' I ask her.

She spreads her hands in apology. 'I'm sorry, I shouldn't have said anything.'

'It's fine,' I say. 'I'd love to know what the locals think of The Anchorage.'

She gives me that heartening smile people give you when the truth is something you don't want to hear and you have to be brave. 'I just meant that the house is a bit creepy. It's so isolated up there, all alone on the bluff.'

'Have you been inside then?'

'Just once, it was a few years ago now. The Jeffreys had an open day to try and drum up new business. It was for tourists, but I was interested to see what it was like inside. I was just being nosy, really.'

She gives a little shiver and draws her pink pashmina more tightly around her shoulders. 'I have to be honest and say that it really gave me the chills. It wasn't anything specific, just a feeling I had. I couldn't get out of there fast enough – and that's not all ...' She pushes the card reader across the counter so Charles can punch in his pin. 'You mustn't tell anyone I said this, okay?' Her voice has dropped to a near-whisper. 'But that place is ... how can I put this? *Unhealthy.*'

'I don't suppose you've got this in a medium, have you?'

My head swivels in the direction of the interruption. One of the elderly women is holding aloft a chunky cable-knit sweater.

Kirsten flashes her a smile. 'I think there's one in the stockroom. I'll take a look for you.'

She removes Charles's debit card from the machine and hands it to him, together with our carrier bag of purchases. 'Sorry, folks, you'll have to excuse me.'

I start to tell her that we'll wait, but Charles has already taken my hand and is pulling me towards the door. Anyone would think he didn't want me to hear what Kirsten had to say.

'You don't believe that bullshit she was spouting about the guest house, do you?' he says once we're out on the street.

'There must be something in it,' I reply. 'Kirsten's the second person who's warned us about The Anchorage … no smoke without fire and all that. What do you think she meant by "unhealthy"?'

He gives an exasperated sigh. 'No idea – but I'm sure it's just gossip. I've known Michael and Pamela for years and they're thoroughly decent people.'

I blow out a puff of air through pursed lips. 'I think "known" is a bit of an exaggeration. You spent a few weeks here on holiday and that's it. You don't seriously believe you got to see the real side of them, do you? You were their guest – and anyway, you were just a child at the time.'

'Oh, stop splitting hairs,' he retorts. 'We're leaving the day after tomorrow, so what does it matter?'

I don't want this to spiral into an argument, so I let it drop. I introduce the subject of lunch, proposing a quick sandwich at Rosario's where we'll have a chance to write our postcards. It might also be a good opportunity to pick up some more information about The Anchorage. Charles agrees, even though the weather conditions are worsening and I can tell he's anxious to get back.

As I eat my BLT, I replay Kirsten's words in my mind. 'Unhealthy' is an interesting choice of word, and was she implying that staying at The Anchorage would be detrimental to our physical – or our *psychological* – well-being?

I wish I could get to the bottom of this. It feels like I'm reaching down into a blocked drain and groping around with my bare hands trying to clear it. But there's nothing solid to get hold of, just a thick sludge. It coats my skin and burrows under my fingernails, its stink invading my nostrils, soaking up into the tiny blood vessels and poisoning my entire system.

Of course, what would really help is if I could talk all this through with Charles. But he's made his feelings on the subject abundantly clear. I know I shouldn't say this, but my husband can be frustratingly imperceptive at times. I love him, I trust him, I value his opinion, and yet his responses sometimes make me feel as though I'm talking to one of those computer programmes that mimic human behaviour. I watch him as he eats, the skin on the stubbled hinge of his jaw moving back and forth with the sounds of chewing. And it strikes me that there's still a lot about him I don't know.

Once lunch is out of the way, I borrow a pen from one of the waiting staff and we set about writing our postcards. Charles's message to his dad focuses on the weather and his re-acquaintance with the Jeffreys. Mine is resolutely upbeat, referencing the 'spectacular scenery' and the 'friendly locals'. Afterwards, I peel off a couple of stamps from the sheet I keep tucked in my purse and we brave the elements once more.

It's only when we get to the post office and see the handwritten sign taped to the pillar box, that we realise our utter stupidity. *Due to the landslide there will be no collections of mail until further notice.*

'You have got to be kidding!' I bawl as tears scuttle up like a ball in my throat. 'How could we not have thought this through? The road's blocked ... of course the postman can't get out.'

'Don't get upset, Grace,' Charles says, pulling me against his chest. 'It's not the end of the world. Just a couple more days and then I'm quite sure normal service will be resumed.'

'Will it?' I say in a thick voice. 'I'm beginning to think Saltwater is in some parallel dimension and we're going to be stuck here forever.'

Charles doesn't reply.

As we traipse back to The Anchorage, another storm seems to be waiting in the wings. The waves are pounding on the beach and the wind has returned with triple fury, howling around our ears like a pack of rabid dogs. At least the fog has dissipated. In its place is a strange, steely light that makes my eyes sting. It drains the colour from the landscape, turning everything black and white, so it feels as though the world is closing in.

22

GRACE

I'm shattered by the time we get back to the guest house. The searing pain in my leg has intensified, making it difficult to think of anything else. The minute we've taken off our coats, I go upstairs for my medication, leaving Charles to relax in the sitting room.

When I reach the top of the stairs, I know straight away that something's off. It's not just a feeling; the door to our room is half open and I know I closed it before we went out.

Inside our room, I'm unprepared for the sight that greets me. It looks as if a bomb has gone off. The wardrobe doors are wide open and the floor is littered with our clothes. A framed photograph of Charles and me that I had placed on the bedside table is now lying face down on the carpet, the glass shattered. It was taken at a friend's thirtieth birthday – an unposed shot of the two of us, slow dancing at the end of the evening. Charles is staring deep into my eyes, as if I am the only thing in that moment that matters to him. I wanted to be able to look at that image every day of our honeymoon and remind myself how lucky I am to have found a man like him.

Even more worryingly, my engagement ring, which I left lying on top of the chest of drawers, has vanished. I took it off this morning to apply hand cream and forgot to put it back on afterwards. I only realised when I got cold in the churchyard and went to put my gloves on.

The casement window is wide open, the curtains billowing wildly in the wind. As I go over to shut it, I wonder if an intruder could have entered this way. It doesn't seem remotely possible; we're too high up.

As I turn back to the room, I suddenly feel sick, saliva flowing into my mouth as if I'm about to gag. Not knowing what else to do, I go back out onto the landing, lean over the banister and shout Charles's name.

He's just as shocked as me when he sees the state of our room. 'Is anything missing?' he asks, surveying the mess.

My insides fold; I can hardly bring myself to meet his gaze. 'Just my engagement ring.'

His gaze switches to my left hand. 'Please tell me you're not serious.'

I stare at the floor, shamefaced. 'I was putting hand cream on; I only meant to take my ring off for a second. I obviously got distracted and forgot to put it back on.'

He sucks in his breath. 'Where did you leave it?'

'On the chest of drawers; I'm so sorry, Charles, I can't believe this has happened.'

His eyes are blazing with anger; I don't know if it's because of my own careless actions, or the intruder's. The ring has huge sentimental value; it's been in Charles's family for three generations and originally belonged to his grandmother. His dad inherited it and gave it to his own wife-to-be when they got engaged. As Charles's mum lay dying in hospital, she took the ring from her finger and gave it to him, with instructions that he should gift it to his own future wife. When Charles told me that story, I couldn't stop crying. Just thinking about it now brings tears to my eyes. What have I done?

It really is a beautiful ring. A square tourmaline, encircled by eight brilliant-cut diamonds. Eye-catching, but not showy. It isn't hugely valuable – a few thousand pounds at most – but it means the world to Charles, and because of that it means the world to me too. The thought that it's been stolen must be crucifying him right now. I watch him, amazed he's managing to stay as calm as he is.

He stalks over to the chest of drawers and begins looking all around it.

'What are you doing?' I ask.

'Maybe it isn't stolen, maybe it's just fallen on the floor.'

I think the chances of that are slim, but I go over to join him anyway. We spend the next few minutes on our hands and knees, desperately hunting for it. 'It's no good,' I say finally. 'Someone's taken it.'

Without saying another word, Charles rises to his feet and strides out of the room.

'Where are you going?' I call out after him.

'To find the Jeffreys,' he replies, in a tone I've never heard before. 'I want answers. Now.'

'Wait for me,' I tell him, grimacing through the pain as I limp after him.

A few minutes later, I'm standing with Charles outside a bland, single-storey building at the rear of the house. A light is on in one of the rooms, I can see it shining through the net curtains, but we have to ring the bell twice before anyone answers.

It's Pamela who comes to the door. She's wearing loose-fitting trousers and an oversized sweatshirt. Her eyes are bloodshot and she seems a bit out of it. I get the sense we've interrupted something – and yet, at the same time, she doesn't seem entirely surprised to see us.

'Hello Charlie, what can I do for you?' she says coolly.

Before Charles can answer, Michael appears in the doorway. He places his hands on his wife's shoulders in an oddly protective gesture.

'Is something wrong?' he asks.

'Someone's been in our room.' I can tell Charles is struggling to contain his emotion because there's a tremor in his voice. 'Our stuff's all over the floor and Grace's engagement ring has gone.'

'Oh, good Lord, no!' Michael cries. He seems genuinely shocked.

'Did you lock your door before you went out?' Pamela says, thrusting out her chin defensively.

'No, why would we when we're the only ones staying here?' Charles snaps.

Michael steps past Pamela and pulls the door to behind him. 'We'd better come and take a look.'

He glances at his wife and something invisible passes between them. It happens so quickly I almost miss it.

Michael steps over one of Charles's shirts that lies twisted in a question mark on the floor. Charles and I follow him in, but Pamela hovers on the threshold, like a forensics expert reluctant to contaminate the crime scene. Even though she's standing a metre away, I can hear her teeth grinding in her jaw, a sickening bone-on-bone crunch.

'Is this exactly how you found the room when you got back?' Michael asks, as he takes in the chaos.

'Yes,' I reply. 'We haven't touched a thing.'

'Was the front door locked when you came in?'

Charles nods. 'Yep, same way it always is.'

'Is there a back door?' I ask.

'Yes, Pamela and I use it to access the annexe, but we're the only ones with the key and it's always kept securely locked.'

Then I remember an important detail. 'I forgot to mention that the window was open when I came in. It was blowing a gale outside, so I shut it before I called for Charles.'

Michael looks at me as if I've just told him everything he needs to know. 'Ah,' he says, his facial muscles visibly relaxing. 'I think we might have our answer.'

'Nobody could have gained entry through that window,' Charles says. 'Not when we're two storeys up.'

'You're quite right – but what if the wind was the burglar?' Fired up by a new energy, Michael crosses the room in two large strides. 'Look at this,' he says, pointing to the metal bar securing the casement. 'See how loose it is. The stay doesn't fit snugly over the peg, the way it's supposed to. It needs replacing really, I've had it on my to-do list for ages.'

He places his finger under the stay and lifts it by a centimetre or two until it pops off the peg. 'Now, let's see how long it takes for the elements to do their worst.'

Within a matter of seconds, the wind has seized the unlatched casement and flung it wide, sending a blast of icy air into the room.

'This is only a single glazed window, so it's not completely air-tight,' Michael explains, as he grabs the casement and pulls the window shut. 'It's quite likely that a strong gust of wind rattled the stay, causing it to spring off the peg. You've seen what conditions are like out there; this must be a Force 8 or 9 … easily enough to wreak havoc in your room.'

Charles gives a scornful laugh. 'You're saying the wind sucked our clothes out of the wardrobe and dumped them all over the floor? I don't think so.'

'But Charles, none of our clothes were in the wardrobe,' I remind him. I point to the suitcase that's lying open on the luggage rack, just a couple of feet from the window. 'All our stuff was either in there or draped over the valet stand.' I turn to Michael. 'We only thought we'd be here for a couple of nights, so we haven't bothered unpacking.'

Charles's eyebrows contract. 'Let's suppose for a minute your theory *is* correct, Michael ... how do you explain Grace's missing engagement ring?'

His words send a trickle of panic down the back of my neck. If even Charles is starting to doubt the Jeffreys, then I really should be worried.

'Where was it?' Michael asks.

I go over to the chest of drawers. It's tucked in an alcove, as far away from the window as it's possible to be.

'Just here,' I say, patting the empty space beside a travel-sized tube of hand cream. 'I hardly think the wind would have carried off my ring and left my hand cream standing. In any case, Charles and I have looked everywhere; if it was still in the room, we would have found it.'

It's a real effort to remain civil. Is Michael being deliberately obtuse? Surely it's obvious there's been a break-in.

'Well, however they got in, I think we need to report this to the police,' Charles says in an authoritative tone.

I semaphore my support with a small dip of my head, pleasantly surprised to see my husband taking such a firm stance. He's usually so defensive on the subject of the Jeffreys and I half expected him to accept Michael's frankly ridiculous explanation at face value.

Michael sighs. 'As you wish – but I'm afraid you won't be able to do it right away. The phones are still down and there's no police station in the village.'

'For crying out loud!' I screech, unable to contain my frustration a second longer. 'This is an utter farce.'

'Calm down, Grace,' Charles says. 'We'll get to the bottom of this, I promise.'

I press my knuckles into my eyes until pinpoints of light dance before me. The pain in my leg is excruciating and I feel as if I could burst into tears at any moment. 'I really need my tablets,' I say, the words coming out as a whimper.

Charles give me a sympathetic look. 'Let me get them for you, darling. Where are they?'

'In the bathroom. On the side of the sink.'

'Back in two ticks.'

As soon as he leaves the room, I collapse onto the bed. For possibly the first time since we arrived, Pamela seems concerned about my well-being, although she's probably just a very good actress.

'I'm sorry you're not feeling well,' she says. 'Would you like something to drink? A nice cup of tea, perhaps, or some hot chocolate?'

I shake my head.

'We really are dreadfully sorry,' Michael says, raking his hands through his hair. 'Nothing like this has ever happened before.'

My eyes narrow to slits. 'I guess I'll just have to take your word for that.'

'Have you got travel insurance?' Pamela inquires. 'If the worst comes to the worst, you might be able to put in a claim for the ring.'

'That ring was a family heirloom; it's utterly irreplaceable.' My voice sounds choked: the words hard, angry clots. I'm sick of being polite, sick of pretending that everything's fine when nothing could be further from the truth. The Anchorage is toxic, its custodians uncooperative, and quite possibly thieves to boot.

'My ring's been stolen,' I hiss at them. 'Why can't you just accept that, instead of trying to pin the blame on the fucking weather?'

For a few seconds, nobody speaks. Then Charles's voice rings out from the other end of the corridor.

'Darling! Can you come here a minute?'

Groaning, I haul myself up from the bed and limp to the door.

'What's the matter, can't you find my tablets?' I shout back irritably.

When there's no reply, I start walking towards the bathroom. 'If they're not on the side of the sink, they'll be in the medicine cabinet.'

Charles appears at the bathroom door. He's grinning from ear to ear.

'Look what I've got,' he says as I approach. He uncurls his fist. Lying in the palm of his hand is my engagement ring.

I stare at it in disbelief.

'Where did you find it?'

'On the side of the sink, right next to your tablets.'

For a moment, everything goes quiet and very still inside my head. This doesn't add up.

'I ... I ... I don't understand,' I stutter. 'I left it in the room, on top of the chest of drawers.'

'You can't have done; you must be confused.' Charles's voice is gentle but chiding, as though he's talking to an adored but slightly dim-witted child.

'All's well that ends well, then?' comes a voice behind me.

I look around. Pamela is standing right behind me. That woman would make a brilliant assassin; how did she get within touching distance without me hearing her?

Then Michael's head bobs out from our room. 'You've found it?'

Charles holds the ring up triumphantly. 'It was in the bathroom all along.'

'Thank goodness for that. I take it there'll be no need for the police then?'

'Of course not.' Charles gives me a pointed look. 'I think we owe you two an apology, don't we, Grace?'

I feel the heat rising in my cheeks as shame live-wires through my body. It's such a cliché, but I really do wish the ground would open up and swallow me.

I try to say something, but it feels as if a fist is pushing into the base of my throat, starving me of oxygen.

'That's all right, it was an honest mistake, no harm done,' Michael says.

I can feel myself swaying, as my vision splits and wobbles. I grasp at the sticky, hot air, willing myself to stay upright, but the walls collapse in on themselves and the faded psychedelic pattern of the carpet rolls beneath my feet like waves. The next second, everything around me disintegrates to black.

23

GRACE

When I wake up, I don't know where I am at first. There's a buzzing in my ears, the force of my own blood pumping in my head. The room is dark and filled with shadows, but I know that I'm lying on a bed. There's something over me, a blanket; I can feel its roughness on the backs of my hands. As my eyes adjust to the gloom, I pick out a bulky shape in the corner of the room, a piece of furniture perhaps. All at once, the shape moves, causing me to yelp in surprise.

Instantly, a light comes on and I realise that the shape is Charles. He's sitting on a stool in front of what looks like a dressing table, his head haloed in the glow from an anglepoise lamp.

'Welcome back,' he says, springing to his feet.

I raise myself up onto my elbows, swallowing hard as bile rises in the back of my throat. 'What happened?' I say.

He comes over and sits down on the bed.

'You fainted, darling. You've been out for ...' He checks his wristwatch. 'Eight minutes and thirty-five seconds.'

It feels much longer than that. But I've noticed that time is different in Saltwater. It thickens and curdles, rolls and spins. It feels as if we've been here for three *months*, not three days.

As I lie there, memories come flooding back. A trashed room, a missing engagement ring, a harsh exchange of words with the Jeffreys. Ouch.

Charles brushes the hair off my forehead. His touch is gentle. Reassuring.

'How do you feel?'

I think about it for a moment. 'My leg hurts, but the rest of me's okay … I think.'

'It's lucky you didn't hit your head when you fell. I saw your knees buckle and I caught you just in time.'

He picks up the small amber bottle that's sitting on the bed-side table.

'You were just about to take your medication before you fainted. You'd better have it now.' He unscrews the cap of the bottle and shakes two of the small white pills into his palm. 'Pamela was kind enough to bring up a glass of water for you.'

I push the tablets between my lips and gulp down some water. I hate feeling so weak and helpless. I'm glad I'm not alone, that I've got Charles looking out for me, but even so I don't want to be dependent on him.

Since the accident, I've been susceptible to these blackouts. The triggers seem to be two-fold: intense pain and/or psychological stress, both resulting in a sudden drop in blood pressure, followed by a brief loss of consciousness.

My GP has advised me not to stand up for prolonged periods, to remain hydrated and maintain my blood-sugar levels. Common-sense precautionary measures I have largely neglected since we arrived in Saltwater. It's hard to be diligent when I have so many other things on my mind.

'I'm sorry, darling,' Charles says as he screws the lid back on the bottle. 'I should have spotted the warning signs earlier. I was too distracted by the thought we might have been burgled to appreciate how much pain you were in. From now on, I'm going to be keeping a much closer eye on you.'

I drink another mouthful of water, hoping the painkillers will take effect quickly. 'Do you still think we were burgled?'

'No, I don't,' he replies calmly. 'After all, nothing was taken, was it?'

'So you're convinced it was down to the storm and a dodgy window?'

'I think that's the most likely scenario, don't you? What else could it be?'

I don't respond. The truth is I don't know what I think any more. So much of what has happened since we arrived here doesn't conform to the usual laws of nature and physics. I cast my mind back to the first of these puzzling events ... the face of the little girl scratched out in the photograph. At the time, I dismissed it as the work of a disagreeable teenager, but now I'm not so sure. My mind is a swamp, deep and brackish, so many different theories, mingling and mixing.

I arch my back as my leg is gripped by another spasm. Hoping to divert my attention away from the pain, I look around the room. Nothing about it seems remotely familiar; it certainly wasn't one I visited during my earlier exploration.

'I insisted we move rooms, so this is where we'll be sleeping from now on,' Charles says, apparently reading my thoughts. 'I know our other room was bigger, but we don't want any more mishaps with that window.'

'Are we still on the second floor?'

'Yes – and we've got a lovely view of the sea, although we are a bit further away from the bathroom.'

I glance towards the tightly drawn curtains.

'I didn't want the light to hurt your eyes when you came round,' he explains. 'But now that you're awake ...'

He stands up and goes over to the window, yanking the curtains apart in one swift movement. The sound of the metal hooks sliding on the rail makes me wince.

'I'm so sorry about my engagement ring,' I say to his back. 'I was so sure I'd left it in the room. I obviously did put it back on after I'd used the hand cream – but then I must have taken it off again in the bathroom the next time I went to wash my hands.'

'There's really no need to apologise,' he says, coming back over to the bed. 'As Michael said, it was an honest mistake. I'm just glad we found it.'

'Where is it now?'

'Right here; close to my heart.' He reaches into the breast pocket of his shirt and pulls out the ring. 'There you go, Mrs McKenna,' he says, sliding it onto my finger. 'Back where it belongs.'

I look down at the ring. It feels cool and slightly alien on my hand.

'The Jeffreys must think I'm such a drama queen. First, I insist we've been burgled, then I get an attack of the vapours and collapse in your arms.'

'Oh, don't worry about them; I daresay they've seen worse during their time as hoteliers. They were really worried when they saw you were out cold. Michael even offered to drive to the doctor's surgery to get help. I tried to put their minds at rest by explaining that you had a history of this sort of thing and that you'd be right as rain in a few minutes.' He pats my hand. 'Speaking of which, I'd better pop over to the annexe and let them know you're back in the land of the living. Will you be all right on your own?'

'Of course,' I pick up the empty glass from the bedside table. 'Do you mind getting me some more water while you're downstairs?'

'No problem.' He bends over and kisses my forehead. 'I love you, Grace.'

'Love you too,' I whisper.

After he's gone, I prop myself up with some pillows and lie very still, waiting for the painkillers to kick in. Now that the curtains are open, the room feels overly bright, everything too vivid: the tick of the brass alarm clock at my elbow, the gurgling of the radiator, the angry roar of the wind outside.

This room is considerably smaller than our old room which, when combined with the steeply pitched ceiling, gives it a claustrophobic feel. I wonder why Pamela chose to move us here, when there are several, much nicer rooms on the first floor. I wouldn't have minded not having a sea view. In fact, I would prefer to be at the back of the house, where I wouldn't have to listen to the waves all night long.

Just then, I spot something that seems out of place. A pair of porcelain dolls in period costume, standing on a shelf above the door. I've never understood the appeal of china dolls; like a lot of people, I find them rather creepy. I'm guessing they belong to Pamela; it's just the sort of weird hobby I'd expect someone like her to have.

Feeling bored and not knowing how long it will be before Charles returns, I decide to have a closer look. I throw off the blanket and swing my legs to the side, taking care to stand up very slowly, so as not to trigger another sudden drop in blood pressure.

As I approach the dolls, it strikes me that this is a rather unique way to display a collectible item – *above a door*. I suppose the room's sloping ceiling does offer limited opportunities for shelving. Or perhaps they were placed there to put them out of the reach of curious children.

The dolls each stand around fifty centimetres tall. They're surprisingly lifelike with their pink cheeks and glittering eyes. They look pretty old; they might even be quite valuable. I wonder why Pamela has chosen to position them here, rather than in the sitting room, where there's a much higher footfall and more guests will be able to appreciate them.

Both specimens are, in their own way, rather striking. Unfortunately, I'm not quite tall enough to reach them. The doll on the left has long red hair that tumbles pre-Raphaelite-style down her back. She's dressed in a voluminous confection of cream-coloured satin, overlaid with lace. On her head is a gauzy veil, decorated with a coronet of artificial flowers. Her eyes are made of green glass and her rosebud lips are slightly parted to reveal tiny white teeth. Unfortunately, her beauty is spoiled by an unsightly crack that runs down one side of her face, from hair-line to chin.

Her companion, in stark contrast, is dressed entirely in black. A long, ruched dress with leg of mutton sleeves and a form-fitting bodice, trimmed with jet buttons. I can't see her hair because her head is covered with a wide-brimmed bonnet, also black, that's tied tightly under her chin. Her expression is dour and her navy eyes are hard and opaque, like an animal's.

The bride and the widow: a bizarre and rather macabre pairing.

As I stare at them, something sharp and deep goes through me, something I can't describe, a blade running up and under my ribs and making me gasp for breath. A moment later, it's gone.

I turn my back on the dolls and shuffle back over to the bed. Perhaps I did get up too quickly after all.

24

People can be so unkind. They broadcast their opinions to the world and his wife, never thinking about the damage they cause. And once the words are out there, they can't be taken back. They are there for all eternity.

I read something today that cut me to the quick. Savage words, words shot through with venom. Words that I can't even bring myself to repeat.

He says I should ignore them, that it's just people with nothing better to do with their time. That we need to look to the future and focus all our energies on getting ourselves out of this mess.

He's right. That's why I went to see someone I thought I could trust today. Someone who I hoped would be able to throw some light on this dreadful situation.

Sadly, I came away with a very different opinion. I tried to appeal to her good nature, to let her see how all this is affecting me. All I got were denials and platitudes. It actually made me feel quite sick.

She presents herself as an open book and yet everything she said seemed to have some kind of subtext shimmering just below the surface that I couldn't quite catch. Every word that came out of her mouth felt like grit under my eyelid.

I have a horrid feeling that she might be one of Them. And if that's the case, then we really are in trouble.

25

CHARLES

If I'd known I'd be spending huge chunks of my honeymoon on my tod, I might have thought twice about coming.

I'm just kidding; it is what it is. Grace can't help being unwell, poor thing. First there was the fainting episode and now she's got a headache. She refused to stay in bed and I don't blame her. Nobody likes feeling like an invalid, least of all Grace. I've left her lying on the sofa in the sitting room with her eye mask on to block out the light.

I did offer to stay indoors with her, but she told me she'd be fine on her own. She said I should do my own thing and not worry about her. My wife's good like that; she knows I go stir crazy if I'm cooped up inside for too long.

The wind has died down, but it's still chilly. I've got a woolly hat on and a tube scarf pulled up over my face. I've been strolling up and down the high street for the past half an hour, checking out the surf store and browsing for books in the charity shop. Now I'm starting to get hungry.

I don't particularly like eating on my own in cafes, so I buy a takeaway burger and head for one of the wrought-iron shelters on the esplanade.

Pretty soon, I'm joined by another person, who appears to be sheltering from the elements. He's roughly my own age, or possibly a bit younger. He's wearing earbuds and staring at his phone, so I'm not anticipating much in the way of conversation.

As I stand up to toss my empty burger wrapper in the bin, he pulls out his earbuds and asks if I've got a light. I don't, but we end up chatting anyway. It turns out he's a local plumber, enjoying some unscheduled time off work due to the landslide blocking his only means of exit.

He's pretty friendly and before long I find myself recounting the entire saga of our aborted trip to St Ives. He commiserates and says he feels bad moaning about a few days' lost work when I've had my entire honeymoon wrecked.

'Where's your wife now?' he says.

'Back at the guest house; she's got a headache.' I pause and lick my lips. 'We're staying up at The Anchorage. Do you know it?'

His reaction is predictable enough. First his eyebrows go up, then he shifts on the bench seat, clearly uncomfortable.

'I didn't know that place was still in business,' he says.

'It is, but hanging on by a thread by the look of things.'

He doesn't offer any further comment, so I give him a gentle nudge.

'All the other guest houses round here seem to be doing all right. Any idea why The Anchorage isn't faring so well?'

He strokes his jaw with the back of his hand, as if he's considering the best way to couch his reply.

'I don't want to freak you out,' he begins, slightly hesitantly.

'Don't worry about it. We're only there for a couple more nights anyway, just until the trains are up and running again.'

He snaps his tongue against the roof of his mouth. 'Well ... I think it's fair to say that a lot of weird shit has happened there – and it's not just me saying that, it's all over the internet.'

'Ah, Tripadvisor, every traveller's best friend,' I say dryly. 'What I wouldn't give right now for a minute's worth of Wi-Fi.' I motion to his mobile. 'I take it you've got no signal either.'

'Nope, I heard the mast got taken out in the storm – although, to be honest, the reception in the village is rubbish most of the time anyway.'

'Landline?'

He makes a slicing motion under his chin. 'Down as well. I've got no way of getting in touch with customers. It's a real pain in the arse.'

'What do the reviews say then?'

'Folk reckon they've been woken up in the middle of the night by strange noises. Banging, crying, moaning … you name it, they've heard it; one couple were so scared they checked out two days early. Things move as well. Some woman said she came back to her room and her stuff wasn't where she left it any more. She fronted up to the bloke who owns the place, but he denied all knowledge.'

'*Okaaay,*' I say thoughtfully. 'Anything else?'

'People get sick.'

'*Sick?*'

'Yeah, a whole bunch of guests came down with a mystery virus in the middle of their stay. They said they were so ill they were hallucinating. Some of them even had to go to hospital.'

'I expect it was just food poisoning, wasn't it?'

He shrugs. 'Doesn't sound like any sort of food poisoning I've ever had.'

'So what do you reckon's going on up there?'

He lets out a noise from somewhere between his nose and his throat. 'It's obvious, mate; it's haunted, isn't it?' He stands up and fumbles in his pockets for his earbuds. 'I'd better be getting back before my other half sends out a search party. I told her I was only coming out for cigarettes.'

'Right you are,' I say, wishing he didn't have to run off quite so soon. 'Nice chatting to you.'

'You too and listen, just a friendly piece of advice … don't leave your wife on her own in that place for too long.'

I remain in the shelter for a few minutes after he's gone, processing this new and rather startling information. I think he must have been joking when he said the guest house was haunted. I *hope* he was joking. Actually, it doesn't matter whether he was or he wasn't. There is no such thing as ghosts and no one will ever be able to convince me otherwise.

I cast my mind back, trying to remember if anything out of the ordinary happened during my previous stays at The Anchorage. On one infamous occasion, my sister claimed she saw a man in a raincoat watching her through the sitting-room window. But Ally was a shameless attention-seeker when she was younger and we all assumed she was making it up. The next time I see her I should ask her about it.

It's hard trying to reconcile all the bad things I've heard about The Anchorage with the place I knew as a kid. In fact, I was beginning to doubt my recollections, to wonder if perhaps I'd romanticised Saltwater and everything in it. But then Grace found the guest book and when I flipped through it, I saw that the reviews were *glowing*. There was even one I'd written myself as a boy – confirmation that my memories were accurate.

It's all very confounding. One thing is beyond doubt, however – I am *not* repeating a single word of the conversation I've just had to Grace; her nerves are frayed enough as it is. And she's obsessed with the idea that there's some sort of funny business going on at the guest house. The last thing I want to do is add fuel to the fire.

I suppose I should get back to check up on her, but I think I'll go the long way round. There's a place I need to see first.

*

There was always something magical about Saltwater's harbour when I was a kid. During holiday season it was a hive of activity, the shops and cafes packed to capacity, tourists jostling for position with fishermen unloading their catches. It's much quieter at this time of year, of course, but judging by the lobster pots piled up on the quay, this is still very much a working harbour.

I walk slowly, enjoying the rustic charm of the whitewashed fisherman's cottages and the wonderful sea views. The weather conditions may be challenging, but the magic's still there.

As I stop to admire the flotilla of fishing boats bobbing up and down on the swell, a memory stirs in my bones. A hot summer's day, a trip on a boat with a girl in a bikini, drinking bottles of Coke on deck, ice cold from the cooler. It's just a glimmer, like a light going on, then off again. I concentrate hard, trying to retrieve more details. Could the girl be my sister? Clearly not, because now I'm leaning forward, kissing her hard on the lips, feeling a surge of desire. The memory is so real, I can almost reach out and touch it. I can smell her suntan lotion, hear the seagulls overhead, feel the heat of the sun beating down on my closed eyelids.

Frowning, I dredge my memory, wanting more, but for now it seems that's all there is. It's funny how we remember some things and not others. It's almost as if our brain is programmed to retain the memories that benefit us in some way and bury the rest.

Thrusting my hands into my pockets, I turn my back to the offshore wind and continue walking, my eyes trained on the buildings that ring the horseshoe-shaped harbour. I'm looking for a restaurant, a seafood place called Fisherman's Hook that was very popular when I was a boy. The food was amazing, all locally sourced, and although it wasn't cheap, my father would treat us to a meal there at least once during our stay.

I feel a pinch of disappointment when I see it's not there any more. The distinctive whitewashed building with its striped awning is now home to a slightly pretentious-looking tearoom-cum-art gallery. If I wasn't so anxious to get back to Grace, I'd go in and have a coffee for old time's sake.

I used to be friends with the boy whose parents ran Fisherman's Hook. Jamie was a couple of years older than me, but it felt like we were kindred spirits. We'd spend hours together on the quayside, crabbing, swimming in the tidal pool, taking sneaky sips of beer from the dregs left behind by diners in the restaurant's outdoor seating area. My parents believed I was safe under the watchful eye of Jamie's parents, but the reality was they had their hands full with the restaurant and we were left unsupervised most of the time.

It's funny, but the longer I spend in Saltwater, the more I realise that a lot of what happened here when I was a child has shaped me into the man I am today. One particular incident, involving Jamie, as it happens, sticks out in my mind. It isn't something I think about very often, but when I do, it still has the power to shock me.

Having spent that first summer in each other's pockets, Jamie and I kept in touch even after I'd returned home to Wiltshire. With social media still in its infancy, we communicated mainly by text, although as I recall none of our exchanges were especially profound and revolved mainly around football. I had friends at school, of course, but none quite like Jamie, so when my parents announced that we would be returning to The Anchorage the following year, I was beyond excited.

That second summer in Saltwater, I was thirteen and a half and Jamie was fifteen. There was none of that awkward, getting-to-know-each-other-again stuff; we just picked right up where we left off.

Jamie's parents employed an eclectic brigade of staff at Fisherman's Hook. I'd got to know a few of them the previous year and they were a fun bunch, who always seemed pleased to have me around. This time, there was a new employee, a kitchen porter who'd come to Cornwall from Romania. He had a name that was difficult to pronounce, so Jamie and I took to calling him Mark, because that was the nearest thing to it in English.

We found ourselves running into Mark quite often – and not just in the restaurant either. We'd see him fishing on the jetty on his days off, or mooching along the beach, his brow deeply furrowed as if he were lost in thought. With his goatee beard and gravelly voice, Mark seemed much older than us – though in reality he was probably no more than seventeen or eighteen.

He wasn't the friendliest chap and always seemed rather surly, although I suspect some of this may have stemmed from his poor grasp of English. He didn't have any family in the UK and I felt quite sorry for him, especially when I caught him foraging for food in the huge industrial bin at the rear of the restaurant. I instinctively knew that Jamie's parents would take a dim view of this sort of behaviour, so I never mentioned it to them.

During that summer, my friendship with Jamie went from strength to strength. I virtually ignored my poor sister, preferring to spend all my free time with Jamie. Then one afternoon, about halfway through my holiday, as we skimmed stones from the end of the jetty, Jamie confessed he wouldn't be able to see me the following day due to an unexpected visit from a family friend. It seemed like a reasonable excuse and I thought nothing of it.

Instead, I spent the day hiking with my dad, while Mum and Ally visited a designer outlet village a few miles away. We came together in the early evening for a fish and chip supper, after which my parents gave me permission to play on the beach for a while.

At that time of day, the only other people around were dog walkers and I was pleased to have the beach almost to myself. I spent some time graffiti-ing the names of my favourite bands in the wet sand with a stick. Then I decided to explore the series of rocky inlets along the coastline that were only accessible when the tide was out.

The inlets were quite close together and separated by low-lying boulders, which were fairly easy to traverse, if a little slippery. I'd already explored the first of the inlets and I was preparing to move on to the next one when I heard the sound of laughter. It stopped me dead in my tracks; I hadn't figured on anyone else being here.

As I stood there, deliberating whether or not to turn back, the laughter stopped and was replaced by the sound of flesh smacking against flesh, swiftly followed by a guttural moan.

By this stage, I was grinning to myself, convinced I'd stumbled across a courting couple. Keen to catch a glimpse of the action, I dropped down out of sight and crept closer to the boulders that were the only thing between them and me. When I peered over the top, I saw a man kneeling on the sand with his back to me. His trousers were round his ankles and the sight of his hairy, thrusting buttocks made me snigger involuntarily.

My cover blown, the man leapt to his feet, staring around wildly for the source of the interruption. It was too late for me to hide and, as our eyes locked together, I realised it was the kitchen porter, Mark. I assumed I'd caught him with his girlfriend, one of the waitresses at the restaurant, perhaps – so imagine my surprise when the figure sprawled on the sand turned their head and I saw that it was Jamie.

In that moment, I was so shocked I couldn't speak. Jamie was supposed to be my friend; I thought we shared everything with each other. I was wrong. He'd lied to me. He'd been lying to me all this time.

Adrenalin squeezed my chest and my eyes were filled with explosions of colour. Had they been laughing at me? Had they spent the summer talking about me behind my back, keeping secrets from me? It felt as if something had snapped inside me, releasing a mist of sadness, humiliation and disappointment that wrapped itself around the muscles in my chest. These feelings were quickly replaced by something else. Something darker.

I glared at Mark, my fists flexing at my sides, hating every bone in his body. Jamie had betrayed me, but Mark, Mark was the reason why. As he stared back at me, his expression flickered first with uncertainty, and then with fear. The next moment, my rage was flaring like a lit match tossed into a pool of petrol.

In a sequence I was never able to reconstruct in my mind later, I was jumping over the boulders like a ninja and hurling myself at Mark, punching, kicking, spitting insults.

Although I was several years younger than him, I was tall for my age and well built. A forward in the school rugby team, I was used to physicality and knew my own strength. Mark, by contrast, was a skinny, malnourished-looking thing, who struggled to lift a crate of lobsters in the restaurant kitchen. The fact his trousers were still at half-mast didn't help him much either.

As I laid into Mark, Jamie watched from the sidelines, his eyes glazed over in horror. He seemed frozen, too taken aback to do anything. Or maybe he was scared that he was going to be next. Eventually, he sprang into action and dragged me off Mark, but not before I had landed a good many blows, leaving my opponent with a bloody nose and a fat lip.

'What the fuck's got into you, Charlie?' Jamie yelled, as he shielded his cowering lover with his own body.

I didn't reply. Instead, I turned my back on them and stomped back to the guest house, where I explained away my bruised and bleeding fists by telling my parents I'd taken a tumble on some wet rocks.

Up until that moment, I honestly didn't know I had it in me. I'd been in a few scuffles at school, but I'd never gone on the attack like that, especially without any sort of provocation. If Jamie hadn't intervened when he did, Mark's injuries would have been a lot worse. They could easily have reported me to the police for assault, but no doubt Jamie didn't want his parents to know what he'd been up to.

As I sat alone in the twin bedroom I shared with my sister, trying to process what had just happened, I knew that it was Jamie I really wanted to beat to a pulp. However that would have been too hard for me, emotionally speaking, so it was Mark who took the rap instead.

I wasn't angry because Jamie liked boys; I couldn't give a toss about that. I was angry because he had lied to me about the nature of his relationship with Mark, and about his commitments that day, so that they could sneak off together. I felt sidelined, like a sub left sitting on the bench for the entire match. I'd always prided myself on my people skills, but the experience dealt my confidence a severe blow, and left me doubting my ability to read people and situations. I thought Jamie and I were friends for life, blood brothers; I'd told him things I'd never told anyone else, things that make me cringe, thinking about them now. But he'd betrayed me and left me feeling like the worst kind of fool.

After I returned home, I tried to reach out to Jamie a couple of times by text and email. I didn't apologise in so many words, but I did say it would be nice if we could keep in touch. I missed him a lot, and his absence left me craving the kind of closeness we had shared over those two summers – the kind of closeness he was now reserving for Mark. I never got a reply.

That summer marked a turning point for me. My behaviour had frightened me; it was the first time I had truly lost control. I made a vow to myself that I would never lash out like that again.

What was the point when there were? easier, much more digni-
fied ways to achieve the same result?

I give the building one last, lingering look. I suppose a part of
me was hoping Jamie's family was still there. That I could just
breeze in and ask after him, as if that sordid event in our shared
past had never happened. Silly of me, really.

It's starting to get dark as I set off for The Anchorage. Dusk
falls much later here than it does inland. It's one of the things I
like about this place. As I walk briskly along the seafront, heading for the stone steps, I happen to glance up. There's a figure
in the distance, standing on top of the bluff, just beyond the
lifeboat station. I can tell it's a woman because of her long dark
hair that's blowing in the wind.

I must say it's very odd for someone to be standing in that
particular spot. She would have had to climb over the fence to
get that close to the edge. As I get nearer, I can make out a few
more details – not the woman's facial features, I'm too far away
for that, but I can see that she's wearing a long, pale blue gown.
It's very old-fashioned, almost like a fancy-dress costume.
There's something around her shoulders too, a dark-coloured
shawl.

As I watch her, the woman lifts a hand to her forehead, shield-
ing her eyes as she gazes out to sea. The whole thing looks very
staged and instantly puts me in mind of that film, *The French
Lieutenant's Woman*.

Then the penny drops: the woman's an actress. Loads of costume dramas have been filmed in Cornwall, not to mention that
long-running TV show about a country GP that my mum was
addicted to.

Yes, that's it; they're filming up there on the bluff. Mystery
solved. I breathe a sigh of relief. For one awful moment there I
thought she might be contemplating suicide.

I wouldn't mind seeing a film crew at work; I'm quite interested in photography myself. Disappointingly, when I reach the top of the steps, there's no sign of the woman *or* the production crew. With the light fading fast, they've clearly called it a day. Never mind, it'll be a good story to tell Grace. She'll be sorry she missed out; she loves the movies, she might even know the actress's name.

26

GRACE

I stare at my reflection in the dressing table mirror. I look terrible. My skin tone is uneven and there are purplish blooms beneath my eyes, testament to my lack of sleep. I've done the best I can with my thick, ill-disciplined hair, but I'd kill for a professional blow-dry. Our hotel in St Ives has a spa with a beauty room. The first thing I'm going to do when we get there is book an appointment.

At least my leg isn't hurting any more. I've resigned myself to taking a pre-emptive dose of medication twice a day, instead of waiting until I'm in so much pain I can hardly breathe.

I'm so bored right now, deeply, maddeningly bored. I feel as though I've achieved absolutely nothing since I got up nearly nine hours ago, a state of being I am wholly unused to.

The day began, as usual, with breakfast in the dining room. Yet again, we were the only guests. I was worried things might be a little tense with the Jeffreys after the drama of yesterday, but we saw Michael only fleetingly and Pamela not at all. Michael said he hoped our new room was satisfactory and Charles replied that he'd slept the sleep of the dead. I've always thought that was an unfortunate turn of phrase.

After breakfast, we played games in the sitting room for several hours – first backgammon, then cribbage. Later, Charles popped into the village to pick up some lunch. I'd like to have gone with him, but it's better if I keep the weight off my leg.

Instead, I sat on the windowsill, observing a couple of lads kicking a football around on top of the bluff. I always feel strangely removed whenever I'm at The Anchorage. It's as if life is happening to other people and I am watching it from a distance.

When Charles returned, we ate our sandwiches and read our books for a while. Then Charles asked if I'd mind if he went for a run. I didn't particularly want to be left on my own again, but there's no reason we should both be prisoners here.

I went up to our room after he'd gone and did my exercises. Afterwards, I decided to have a nap. But as soon as I lay down on the bed, I felt wide awake, so I got up again.

I wish Charles would come back; it's lonely here without him. It feels as if he's been gone for ages, but when I check my watch I realise it's less than an hour. I go to the window and rub away the condensation on the glass with the heel of my hand to make a peephole. There's a good view of the sea from here. It's calm, for once, the water shining like mercury as it laps the shore in slow, rhythmic waves. I'd love to walk along the beach, to clear my mind and lift my spirits, but with my leg the way it is, I don't want to push my luck. Maybe tomorrow.

I turn away from the window and survey our cramped quarters. My husband has left a pile of clothes draped over the end of the bedstead, so I start folding everything up, ready to put back in our suitcase. I know my unwillingness to unpack amuses Charles. I haven't told him this, but I have a terrible feeling that if we do, we'll never leave this place.

As I pick up a T-shirt, I get the unpleasant sensation that I am being watched. My skin prickles and the fine hairs on the back of my neck stand up. I turn my head slowly towards the door. There's no one there, only the pair of porcelain dolls, maintaining their eerie vigil. Around us, the silence spins and spins like a silk cocoon.

*

It's half an hour later before Charles bursts into the room. He's pink-cheeked and soaked in sweat.

'Good run?' I ask him.

He fiddles with the activity tracker on his wrist. 'Just shy of 10k; not bad. I went up to the landslide site to see how things were progressing.'

'And?'

'They're hard at it with the heavy-lifting equipment. Half the road's cleared already; another twenty-four hours should do it, I reckon.'

'Fantastic, I'm sure everyone will be happy to see that road open again.'

Charles rests his heel on the end of the bedstead and leans forward, stretching his quads. 'I called in to the railway station on my way back. They've put up a poster, confirming that the trains will be running as normal from eight o'clock on Friday morning.'

'Even better,' I say, thrilled at the prospect of our imminent escape.

'Oh, and I've booked a table for dinner tonight.'

'Great, where are we going?'

'The Sundowner, it's a Spanish restaurant. I spotted it yesterday when I went for a wander around the harbour. It looked really nice, so I stopped by just now to make a reservation. Seven o'clock okay?'

'Perfect,' I say, smiling. An evening out is exactly what I need.

Charles peels off his running jersey and drops it on the floor. 'I'm going to take a shower; I won't be long.' He pulls me towards him and kisses me hard on the mouth. 'Unless you'd care to join me, Mrs McKenna.'

I don't need asking twice.

The Sundowner doesn't disappoint. The walls are painted a soothing shade of terracotta and the soft lighting from the

Moorish-style lanterns creates an intimate atmosphere. Despite the scratchy veil of fatigue irritating my eyes, I'm feeling relaxed and looking forward to a romantic evening with my husband.

I've dressed up for the occasion in a figure-hugging wrap dress that falls to mid-thigh. It's one of my husband's favourites; he likes me to show off my figure when we go out. I haven't been able to wear heels since the accident and standing next to Charles in my ballet flats, I feel tiny and fragile. I'm wearing the necklace too, the one that Charles bought me. The ammonite nestles at the base of my throat where my collarbones meet. I like the way it feels against my skin, cool and strangely reassuring.

After greeting us at the door, a friendly waiter scoops up a couple of menus and offers to take us to our table. The restaurant is busy, but I spot them straight away. Sitting at a table in the corner of the room, overlooked by a giant frieze of a posturing bullfighter.

I have to bite my lip to stop myself swearing. It really is unbelievable. We've escaped our prison for a few short hours and who do we have the bad luck to run into? Only our jailers, that's who.

It seems I'm not the only one who's made an effort this evening; I almost didn't recognise Pamela with her hair up. She and Michael are deep in conversation, their heads bowed together. I don't think they've seen us. Yet.

Instinctively, I move closer to our waiter, using him as a human shield. With any luck, we'll be seated on the other side of the restaurant and any interaction with the Jeffreys can be avoided. I wonder if Charles has spotted them. If he has, we'll almost certainly have to go over and chat briefly, but hopefully it won't come to that.

Our waiter hangs a right, leading us towards the opposite side of the room. I think for one delicious moment we're home free, but almost immediately my hopes are dashed.

'Charlie ... Grace!' Michael's baritone booms across the restaurant.

I stop, my fingernails carving sickles into the palms of my hands. Michael is waving madly at us, as if he hadn't just seen us a few short hours ago at breakfast. Charles waves back and tells the waiter we want to say a quick hello to our 'friends'.

'Fancy seeing you two here,' Pamela says as we approach the table, our waiter following close behind. She's wearing a pink ruffled dress and oversized gold earrings that snatch greedily at the light when she turns her head. Michael has pulled out all the stops too, in a tweedy suit and open-necked shirt. It looks like he's even trimmed his beard.

'Yes, what a pleasant surprise.' Charles jerks his thumb towards the bottle of sparkling wine in the ice bucket at the side of the table. 'Special occasion, is it?'

Pamela beams. 'Our wedding anniversary. Thirty years.'

'Wow, congratulations, that's definitely something worth celebrating – isn't it, Grace?'

'Absolutely,' I say perkily. 'Anyway, it's nice to see you both and enjoy your evening.'

'Why don't you join us?' Michael says. 'We haven't even ordered yet.'

'Oh no, we couldn't possibly impose,' I say, maintaining a rictus smile.

'You wouldn't be imposing at all – and look, there's plenty of room.' He gestures to the two empty seats at the table. Anyone would think they were expecting us.

I give Charles my best emergency eyebrows, but he's not looking. 'Well, if you're sure ...' he says.

Immediately, our waiter begins transferring cutlery from a nearby table onto the empty place settings opposite the Jeffreys. The decision, it seems, has been made.

'I love your dress, Grace,' Pamela remarks, as we take our seats at the table. 'Only someone with a fantastic figure like yours could carry it off.'

The compliment sounds contrived, almost as if she's reading from an autocue.

'You look nice too,' I tell her. 'Your hair suits you like that.'

She smiles and pats her hair self-consciously, seemingly unaware that her up-do is beginning to collapse on one side.

Michael gives me a concerned look. 'Are you feeling better now, Grace? You gave us quite a scare when you collapsed like that.'

'Much better, thank you.' I take a breath, fortifying myself. I need to get this out of the way now; otherwise this dinner is going to be super awkward. 'I don't think I've apologised properly for my behaviour yesterday; in fact, I know I haven't.'

Pamela reaches across the table and pats the back of my hand. Her fingers feel like ice and I flinch instinctively. 'Don't be silly, you couldn't help fainting.'

'I'm not talking about the fainting,' I say, discreetly drawing my hand away. 'It's what I said about my ring being stolen. I just want you to know that I wasn't accusing you of anything. I was upset and I wasn't feeling well; I was venting, that's all. But anyway, I'm sorry.' I force the words out.

Michael wipes my words away with a brisk wave of his hand. 'All water under the bridge now. How about we have a lovely evening and forget about yesterday?' He reaches for the wine bottle. 'Will you join us in a glass of cava?'

I nod gratefully; alcohol will help take the edge off my ruined evening. I hate occasions like this. Conversing with people in that fake way that guarantees you'll know less about them at the end of the evening than you did at the beginning.

It's patently obvious that Charles and I have got zero in common with the Jeffreys. Try as I might, I just can't figure them out. They've clearly made a royal fuck-up of their business; I don't know why they don't just sell up and move on. I can't wait to get back to civilisation and read all the Tripadvisor reviews. Maybe then I'll get the real story. But first, I need to get through tonight. It shouldn't be too difficult. I have to make small talk with interview candidates all the time at work. It's just a question of smiling and asking lots of questions.

'So how did you two meet?' is my opening gambit. A nice easy one, to break the ice. It should keep the conversation going until our starters arrive.

Sadly, I'm wrong. Pamela's answer consists of three words: 'Sixth-form college.' Then she swiftly changes the subject, by pointing to the bullfighter on the wall and asking me if I've ever visited Spain.

As the evening wears on, it's a tactic both she and Michael employ repeatedly. Every time I ask them a personal question, they manage to deflect it.

'Oh God, ninety-nine per cent of the time it's very humdrum; you really don't want to hear about it,' Pamela says when I enquire about the challenges of running a guest house. And when I ask Michael how difficult it was to fit in when they moved here from London, he offers an enigmatic smile and says: 'Fitting in is always difficult at first, but you just have to persevere.'

By any standards, these are fairly innocuous questions, so what are the Jeffreys afraid of? That they might let slip some precious trade secret? Or could it be something more sinister?

After a while, I get fed up with being stonewalled and stop asking questions. This opens the door for the Jeffreys to introduce a series of increasingly banal conversation starters: property prices, the weather, the upcoming local elections. We jump from one subject to another with dizzying speed, like diners at an all-you-can-eat buffet who can't bear to leave any dish untasted.

By the time the main course arrives, I have lapsed into almost total silence. The Jeffreys emit a noxious energy that sucks the life from me. Charles, meanwhile, seems oblivious to the fact our hosts have talked and talked while divulging almost nothing about themselves. Instead, he appears utterly rapt, lapping up the conversation like someone receiving a visit in prison after a long period of solitary confinement.

As we consider the dessert menu, I take advantage of the brief lull in the conversation to blurt out a question.

'Do you two know much about Emma Murrish?'

Pamela straightens her spine, the movement betraying a concern that I suspect she would rather not have revealed. She looks at Michael and something ponderous and painful passes between them.

Michael sets down his menu. 'You've heard about the Murrish family then?'

He thinks I don't know what he's doing, posing an open-ended question like that, but I do. He's fishing, trying to find out what I already know, before he commits himself to revealing anything else.

I'm still framing my response when Charles beats me to it. 'One of the locals filled us in. We got chatting in Rosario's and we happened to mention where we were staying.'

Pamela leans forward. I feel a change in her. A flex of muscles tightening under the skin. 'What did she tell you?'

'Just that a merchant seaman called Captain Murrish built The Anchorage and that his wife and kids drowned at sea in a horrible accident.' Charles twists his lips in distaste. 'It's a pretty grim tale.'

Michael sighs. 'Grim but true, unfortunately.'

'I believe Emma was a geologist,' I say, my fingers straying to the pendant at my neck.

Pamela nods. 'That's right, a real pioneer in her time. There's a portrait of her in one of the guest rooms. We inherited it when we bought the house.'

Under the table, I feel a gentle pressure against my foot. It's Charles, warning me not to admit I'm already aware of the portrait's existence. He needn't worry; I've no intention of saying anything.

I quirk my eyebrows. 'You mean the previous owners left it behind?'

'That's right. They felt it would be bad luck if the painting was ever removed from The Anchorage.'

'It was a condition of the sale that the portrait remained on permanent display in the house,' Michael adds. 'Quite an unusual request, but hardly a deal-breaker.'

Charles frowns. 'Pretty hard to enforce though, surely.'

'I suppose so, but we don't want to jinx the place so we were happy to comply.'

'Are you superstitious then?' I say.

Michael shifts in his seat. 'Not especially.'

'The fact is, it's such a lovely painting and we like showing it off,' Pamela says quickly. 'It's received a number of compliments from guests over the years. And it's a part of the history of The Anchorage.'

'It sounds very intriguing,' Charles says.

'And just as intriguing is the fact that several of the locals have suggested The Anchorage is haunted,' I say quickly, keen to continue this line of enquiry. 'I must say I've heard a few unsettling things in the house myself – and I'm sure I'm not imagining them.'

'What things?' Charles says sharply.

'A child crying, the first night we were here. I told you at breakfast, if you remember.'

Michael laughs awkwardly. 'It's an old building with Victorian plumbing and windows that badly need replacing. It makes all kinds of queer noises, especially when the wind's up.'

'So how do you explain the singing I heard outside the bathroom window two nights ago?'

'*Singing?*' Pamela says in a high, glassy voice.

'Yes, an old sea shanty; it was quite chilling.'

Now it's Charles's turn to laugh. 'Come *on*, Grace, don't be so dramatic. It was probably just a load of pissed people coming back from the pub.'

'It was a *child's* voice,' I say stiffly.

He leans over and kisses my ear. 'Don't worry, darling, if any ghouls try to carry you off in the middle of the night, just wake me up and I'll wave my crucifix at them.' He glances at Michael and Pamela, grinning, clearly hoping to diffuse the palpable tension in the atmosphere.

Right now, I could quite happily punch my husband. Instead I turn to Pamela and fix her with a stare, willing her to volunteer an opinion. She says nothing, but I can see how tense she is, vibrating like a violin string, every bit of her pulled taut.

I pick up my glass and take a slug of wine. After the cava we moved on to a rather good white Rioja and I've lost track of how much I've drunk.

Before I have a chance to probe the Jeffreys any further, Michael starts telling us about his plan to build a self-contained holiday let in The Anchorage's sizeable garden. He gets very excited when he learns that Charles works in the construction industry and starts asking him all sorts of incredibly dull questions about building regulations and underfloor heating.

As he drones on, I cast furtive glances at Pamela. There's a sparkle in her eyes tonight, a bloom on her cheeks. Maybe it's just clever makeup, but she looks years younger. Despite this, there's a rigidity beneath her features, it's almost as if she's wearing a mask. I wouldn't bat an eyelid if, after dessert, she peeled off her face to reveal the reptilian horror beneath and immediately embarked on a bloodthirsty colonisation of Saltwater. Christ, I really *am* drunk.

I'm so bored of this conversation. My throat has developed a hollow ache from holding back my yawns. Discreetly, I gaze around the room, observing my fellow diners. At least three-quarters of the tables are occupied, not bad for a Wednesday night. Mind you, with the coastal road still shut, I guess The Sundowner has a captive audience.

My gaze slides over the walls, taking in the vibrant artworks, before drifting to the floor, which is made up of dozens of brightly painted tiles. Canary yellow, fuchsia pink, cobalt blue, a dazzling clash of colours and patterns.

Just then, I see something in my peripheral vision. Something dark and fist-sized, moving very quickly across the tiled floor. Startled, I push my chair back. The impatient grind of its legs on the tiles makes everyone at the table look up.

'What is it, Grace?' Charles asks.

I stare at the floor. It is flat and unmoving, the way floors are supposed to be. I've had too much to drink and I'm seeing things that aren't there. I need to get out of here before I make a fool of myself – or fall asleep, whichever one comes first.

I turn to our hosts. 'It's been a lovely evening, but would you mind if Charles and I skipped dessert and called it a night? I haven't been sleeping very well and I'm absolutely shattered.'

Instantly, Michael is falling over himself to be solicitous, apologising for keeping us out so late, waving his hand in the air for the bill. Pamela, meanwhile, says nothing. She reminds me of one of those porcelain dolls. Cold and emotionless.

*

It's just gone eleven when we leave the restaurant. I'm glad the Jeffreys decided to stay for dessert. I don't think I could have tolerated another second in their company.

On top of the bluff, The Anchorage lies in wait, a monster crouching in the darkness. The street lamp outside the house is still out and we forgot to leave the light on in the hall. When we get to the front door, Charles has to use the torch on his phone to light the keyhole. Inside, I take off my coat and ask Charles for the room key. I head upstairs, while he lingers in the hall, emptying his jacket pockets.

As soon as I step into the room, I feel it. A tension in the air. A long, supple ligature winding around my chest, squeezing the air out of my lungs. I flick on the light switch and go over to the dressing table, perching on the chintz stool as I take off my jewellery. Then, in the reflection from the mirror I see something lying on top of the bedclothes. Something that wasn't there when we left.

Jumping to my feet, I turn around, my eyes widening as I try to make sense of what I'm seeing. Then I scream, a long piercing shriek that reverberates against my eardrums.

27

GRACE

'Hang on, Grace, I'm coming!'

As Charles thunders up the stairs, something shifts in the air, the resistance I'd felt earlier fading to a ripple, then it's gone. A moment later, Charles appears in the doorway of our room.

'What is it?' he says, grabbing hold of both my arms. 'What's wrong?'

I put a hand to my throat; I'm finding it hard to breathe. Tendons, blood vessels, vital organs. Everything inside me is shrinking. 'Over there,' I manage to squeeze out. 'On the bed.'

His face contorts in horror when he sees it. 'Jesus Christ!' he blurts out. 'What *is* it?'

I point to the shelf above the door where one porcelain doll, the black widow, stands alone. The bride is lying on our bed. Her body is intact, but her head has gone, smashed to smithereens. Shards of her pale skull litter the duvet cover, some of it with strands of auburn hair still attached. Her veil has been torn to shreds and the coronet of flowers is sitting on her chest, like a funeral wreath.

Charles claps a hand to his forehead and exhales, a long and measured breath. The words that come out of his mouth are not what I was expecting:

'Look Grace, I get it, I really do. You hate it here, you wish we were in St Ives – and so do I. But right now, there's nothing that either one of us can do about it.' He flings an arm towards the decapitated doll. 'I'm not sure what you were hoping to achieve by this – except, perhaps, to make me feel even worse about bringing you here than I already do.'

I draw my hand up against my stomach, suddenly feeling nauseous. Is he serious? The look on his face tells me he is. A wave of indignation, mixed with cold fury, rises up inside me. 'You don't think *I* did this?'

He looks at me reproachfully. 'Come on, Grace, I wasn't born yesterday. Who else could it be? The room was locked; we're the only ones with a key.'

'That's not true,' I respond fiercely.

'You're not seriously suggesting Michael and Pamela had anything to do with this, are you?' Charles says, nostrils flaring. 'We've been with them the entire evening; they can't be in two places at once. In any case, what possible motivation would they have for terrorising their guests with a sick stunt like this?'

He's really angry; I can hear it in his voice.

'I don't know who did it. All I know is that it wasn't me.'

My head is spinning – with alcohol, with confusion, with disappointment that my own husband thinks I'm capable of such a perverse act.

'Bad things have been happening since the day we arrived and I don't know how much more of it I can take,' I say, gulping as I try to hold back the tears. 'I keep trying to tell you about it, but you won't listen.'

He laughs, a brittle, humourless sound. 'Ah, now I know what all this is about. It's your way of getting back at me for not taking your concerns seriously enough. That's it, isn't it?'

If my heart had not been breaking, I might have laughed aloud.

When I don't reply straight away, he takes it as a *yes*. 'Oh Grace,' he says, his tone softening as he extends a hand towards me. 'I don't know what's got into you lately. You haven't been yourself since the day we got here; you never used to be this uptight.'

I duck my head away from his hand, which is still hovering near my face as though looking for somewhere to put itself. 'Believe what you like,' I say wearily.

Far-fetched as it sounds, I'm convinced this is personal. It hasn't escaped my notice that, just like me, the headless corpse on the bed is a newlywed. The realisation sets off something inside me, a violent tremor of fear. Around me the walls of the room seem to rear up like sentries, leaning inwards and blocking out the light and space in my head. This house doesn't want us here, but Charles can't see it. He thinks I did this myself – acted like a spoilt kid, destroyed my favourite toy to teach the grown-up a lesson. It's not a nice feeling, knowing my husband doesn't believe me.

I have to get away. I need a few moments to myself.

'I'm going to brush my teeth,' I tell my husband as I walk towards the door. 'Don't wait up.'

I sit on the side of the bath for a while, trying to absorb the implications of this evening. Charles does have a point; the Jeffreys can't have staged the doll. But if it wasn't them, then who? A human being – or something else? Something without form or conscience?

A twinge of pain in my leg makes me gasp. If I take any more of my medication, I run the risk of exceeding the maximum daily dosage. These are powerful drugs, my GP warned me, and potentially addictive. I need to be careful. I open the medicine cabinet and remove the bottle of tablets, holding it up in front of my face so I can read the small print on the label. My suspicions are confirmed; I'm already up to my limit. There's something else on the label; something I hadn't noticed before. A warning: *Do not drink alcohol.* Shit. Oh well, too late now.

I'm too tired and too drunk to think clearly. A fog is descending over my brain and my thoughts are gently squashed up against each other like cotton wool. All I want to do is lie down. I'll consider my options in the morning. But the truth is, I don't really have any. I'm stuck. Trapped like a rat in a maze. I don't feel safe here any more. Worst of all, I don't know who to trust.

28

I think I need to see the doctor again. My insomnia is getting worse and I seem to have a permanent headache. I spend half the night awake, my thoughts churning, my heart racing. Meanwhile, he lies next to me, sleeping like a baby.

I often think I'm at my loneliest when we're in bed together. Last night, I thought about killing him, about putting the pillow over his head so I don't have to be reminded of what it's like to be at peace. See what these things, these hideous creatures, have reduced me to?

Daytimes aren't much better. I can't seem to concentrate and I keep getting my words muddled. Even basic tasks like getting dressed or making the bed seem like huge achievements.

I can feel myself becoming more feral as each day passes. I'm like a wild animal. Pulling at my hair. Howling. Snapping at anyone who tries to talk to me. I can't seem to stop myself. I'm scared that one day I'll take it a step further and lash out at someone.

Or maybe I'll do something to myself. That would solve a lot of problems – not just mine, but everyone else's too. Will he miss me when I'm gone? I doubt it.

29

CHARLES

'We need to talk.' That's the first thing Grace says to me when she wakes up.

'Look, if this is about last night, I'm sorry,' I tell her. 'I shouldn't have spoken to you the way I did. I know you've been under a lot of stress these past few days, but tomorrow we'll be out of here and then we can put all this nonsense behind us.'

She looks at me, stony-faced. 'It isn't nonsense, Charles, it's real. And just so there's absolutely no room for doubt, I'll say it again: I did *not* destroy that doll.'

This is one of those occasions where I'm going to have to bite my tongue. Anything to keep the peace. 'Understood,' I say.

She throws back the duvet and gets out of bed. I wait for my good morning kiss, but Grace clearly isn't in the mood for intimacy.

'And anyway, it isn't about last night.'

'Oh? So what is it about?'

'Let's have breakfast first and then we can talk.'

Maybe I'm getting ahead of myself, but this sounds serious. Grace and I rarely disagree about anything, but now the dynamic between us is shifting, I can feel it. I need to get things back on track – and fast.

I was stupid to behave the way I did last night; with hindsight, I probably sounded quite patronising. I have to keep reminding myself that Grace is scarred – not just physically, but psychologically. She needs careful handling; I should have been more sympathetic.

In my defence, I'd had a few drinks and I suppose I was a bit fed up of walking on eggshells, the way I have been ever since we arrived in Saltwater. Even so, that's no excuse. She's my wife and she needs to know I'm on her side. Even if that means pretending I believe her when she says she didn't destroy that doll.

Grace can protest as much as she likes, but all the evidence points to her. She was upstairs for several minutes before I heard her scream. Long enough to stage the whole thing. I know it was only a doll, but it was a pretty shocking sight; the old Grace would never have even *thought* to do something as warped as that, especially not to someone else's property.

I cleared everything away while she was in the bathroom. Stuck all the pieces in a plastic carrier bag. The doll's beyond repair, but I can't just throw it away as it might be worth something, but if that's the case then the Jeffreys really ought to keep it under lock and key. I still haven't worked out what I'm going to tell them. I don't want to embarrass Grace; I'll probably say it was an accident – that I slammed the door too hard and the doll fell off the shelf. Naturally, I'll have to offer them some sort of financial reimbursement.

I thought that once she was sober, Grace would admit what she'd done. But I'm starting to realise she's having difficulty separating fact from fantasy. I think she really believes she didn't do it – and that's a very disturbing thought.

I'm not a psychologist, I don't know what's going on inside her head, but she's clearly more fragile than I thought. Once we get home, I'm going to speak to her parents. Share my concerns. They can afford the best; they'll be able to get Grace the help she needs.

*

Downstairs in the dining room, we make polite conversation, like a couple of strangers. I don't bring up the subject of the doll. Grace already looks as if she's ready to bite my head off, I don't want to antagonise her any further.

When Pamela comes to take our breakfast order, I thank her for a pleasant evening. She smiles and says they both had a good time, especially Michael who's still in bed, sleeping off his hangover. Grace doesn't say anything, just stares moodily out of the window.

I know my wife hasn't warmed to the Jeffreys. It was probably a mistake to accept their dinner invitation. She made an effort in the beginning, but I could see her tuning out as the night wore on. Maybe that's why she trashed the doll – to get back at them. I sincerely hope not; that would be unforgivable.

I wonder what Grace wants to talk about. As she eats her bacon and eggs, she isn't giving anything away. Her silence makes me nervous and by the time we finish breakfast, my stomach is in knots.

We go to the sitting room and take up position in two armchairs, side by side. Grace sits very straight-backed, stiff and formal, as if she's a headmistress, about to announce my suspension.

I wait for her to speak, but she says nothing. The silence between us grows, chewing at the air.

'Come on, Grace,' I say with a nervous laugh. 'The suspense is killing me.'

She levels a serious gaze at me. 'I want to talk about what happened in Turkey.'

My initial feeling is one of relief. For a minute I thought she was going to say she wanted a divorce.

'The thing is, you and I have never discussed the accident in any detail,' she says. 'The precise sequence of events, I mean.'

Am I imagining it, or is there a hint of censure in her voice?

'You never asked me about it,' I say quickly. 'And I didn't want to bring it up because I thought you'd find it too painful. Was I wrong about that?'

'No, you weren't wrong,' she says carefully. 'I wasn't ready before; the whole thing was still too raw.'

I give her a searching look. 'Are you sure you're ready now? One's honeymoon is hardly the best time to revisit a traumatic experience. Wouldn't it be better to wait until we're back home?'

She looks down at her hands, folded neatly in her lap. 'I've put it off for long enough, Charles. I need to know exactly what happened. It's the only way I'll be able to move on.'

'Of course, I understand completely.' I'm at pains to keep my tone light, neutral. 'So what did you want to know?'

She lifts her head and looks me in the eye. 'Everything,' she says.

That's what I was afraid of.

30

GRACE

This conversation is long overdue. I know it isn't going to be easy, but I can't put it off any longer. In the beginning, I was happy not to dwell on the minutiae of my accident. I didn't need to know every little detail, I told myself. What purpose would it serve except to cause me more pain and anguish? I had emerged from the experience alive, if not quite unscathed. Surely *that* was the only thing that mattered?

But things have changed. I've had a lot of downtime in the last few days. It's given me the space to think, to appreciate the potential benefits of getting everything out in the open.

There's something else too. It feels as if my continuing ignorance of the facts is creating a barrier between Charles and me. The accident is there all the time, sitting between us like the last piece of cake at a party. It's seeping in more and more when we're together, an indefinable ache that colours every look and touch. We seem to be growing more distant as each day passes; I'm hoping that getting everything out into the open will help us reconnect. It might not work, but it's got to be worth a try.

But before I talk to Charles, I need to get the story straight in my own head. So here it is: this is what happened, as well as I can remember it.

It was Charles's idea to walk the Lycian Way. One of the world's great long-distance hiking trails, it's a 540-kilometre route through the mountainous hinterland of southern Turkey. We weren't planning to tackle the whole thing, just an 80-kilometre section that takes in some of the highlights, including the Roman ruins at Patara and the legendary Turquoise Coast. We were both fit, both experienced hikers. We were more than up to the challenge. Or so I thought.

For a while, we tossed around the idea of joining an organised group, but in the end we decided to take the self-guided option. The tour company would provide maps and route instructions and arrange for our luggage to be transported from pension to pension. It would give us more freedom, more time on our own.

The trip came at a critical time in our relationship. In the run-up, things hadn't been going too well between Charles and me. I'd been very busy at work, putting in long hours as I helped set up a new internship programme. As a result, we hadn't seen as much of each other as we usually did. It felt as if we were drifting apart. As we set off for the airport, I remember thinking that by the end of the holiday I would know whether or not our future lay together.

The trip started promisingly. The weather at the end of September was perfect for hiking – dry, but not too hot – and the Turkish hospitality second to none. On the third day of our trip, we found ourselves negotiating a vertiginous and impossibly beautiful stretch of coastline. It was a lovely day, with an expanse of blue sky rinsed clean and bright by an early morning shower. Neither one of us had any foreboding of the horror that was about to unfold.

On impulse, I decided to take a selfie at the edge of the cliff, something to make my Instagram friends jealous. With scarcely a second thought, I stood with my back to the sea and held up my phone, grinning for the camera. And that's the last thing I remember.

I don't know how long I was unconscious for – probably no more than a few minutes. When I came round, I was lying on my back, with my left leg at a very peculiar angle. Above me, I could see Charles running back and forth along the cliff top, trying to find a way down to the slender strip of beach where I had landed. Unfortunately, that cliff face would have presented a challenge to even a skilled mountaineer, never mind a weekend hiker like Charles.

'Don't try to move, Grace,' he bellowed, having established that I was conscious. The unpalatable truth was that I *couldn't* move, even if I'd wanted to.

I wasn't in too much pain at that point, thanks to the vast quantities of adrenalin surging through my veins, but I knew I was in a bad way. As well as my broken leg, I was struggling to breathe. I didn't know it at the time, but a broken rib (one of several) had pierced my right lung, causing it to collapse. Meanwhile, it hadn't escaped my attention that the tide was coming in. Pretty soon, the beach where I lay, utterly defenceless, would be under water.

I am by nature practical and no-nonsense – the sort of person who, by definition, ought to be good in a crisis. But as I observed Charles's futile attempts to reach me, I was ambushed by a feeling of blind panic. 'It's no good, you'll never make it,' I called breathlessly to him. 'You have to get help.' He gave me a thumbs-up and disappeared from view.

I had studied the map before we set out that morning and I was painfully aware that we were some distance from the nearest settlement. Charles had a mobile phone, but we were in a very rural area and I wasn't sure he'd be able to get a signal. I must have dropped my own phone when I fell. Certainly, there was no sign of it as I looked around from my prone position. Once the alarm had been raised, I had no idea how long it would take the Turkish emergency services to turn out. And even when they did, how on earth would they reach me? It was a horrifying and brutally surreal situation to find myself in.

As the minutes leaked away and no rescue came, the fear really took hold. I'd never known anything like it could exist: all-consuming, ravenous, a whirling black vortex that made me feel I was being eaten alive, bones gnawed, marrow sucked.

Mercifully, I slipped into unconsciousness at some point. I don't know how long I was out. The next part's a bit woolly; all I have is fragments of memory. They're framed in my mind like slides on a projector, nothing in between them, but an empty screen and the harsh click of one rotating away as the next one dropped into place. And then, to my immense relief, there was a man wearing an orange boiler suit and an abseiling harness, kneeling next to me on the sand as he gently strapped a surgical brace around my neck.

As I was airlifted to hospital, one of the paramedics told me that Charles, unable to get a signal on his mobile phone, had run nearly twelve kilometres to raise the alarm. Somebody less fit, less determined, would never have made it in time. I owe everything to him, because by the time the men in orange boiler suits got to me, the waves were already lapping at my ankles.

I was grateful that our travel insurance covered the cost of my emergency medical care in Turkey, as well as my repatriation back to the UK, where I continued my recovery. Although I had numerous injuries, none of them was life-threatening. The backpack I was wearing had cushioned my fall, almost certainly saving me from a serious spinal injury.

All things considered, I'm doing pretty well, but there's still a long way to go. I really thought this break with Charles would be just what the doctor ordered: restful, therapeutic, *grounding*. But it's turning out to be quite the opposite. I feel like the needle on a compass, endlessly spinning, unable to find my way home.

31

CHARLES

I always knew this day would come. I thought I was prepared for it, but now that it's here, I'm not so sure. My right leg is juddering. Betraying my anxiety. Giving the game away. I put my hand on my knee and squeeze it hard.

'Let's start at the beginning?' she says.

'Good idea,' I reply.

She looks at me with the intensity of a cat watching an injured bird. 'Did you see the exact moment I fell?'

Jesus, talk about cutting to the chase. 'Not as such. I was tying my bootlace at the time.'

'So just before it happened, you don't remember thinking I was standing too close to the edge?'

'Like I said, I wasn't even looking at you. If I'd thought for one second you were in any danger, I would have told you to come away.'

She nods thoughtfully, taking this in. 'So when did you know something was wrong?'

'When you screamed ... actually, it was more of a yelp than a scream. I heard you yelp, I looked up from my boot and you weren't there any more.'

'Just like that?'

'Just like that. I don't know if you tripped on some loose shale and lost your footing, or if your bodyweight caused the ground underneath you to give way. I guess we'll never know.'

'No, I don't suppose we will.'

She pauses, her hands twisting in her lap.

'Is this too difficult for you? We can stop any time.'

'No, I'm fine ... just thinking, that's all.'

I nod and wait for her to continue, reluctant to volunteer any information unless she specifically requests it.

She clenches her fists, as if galvanising herself.

'When you saw me lying at the foot of the cliff, did you think my injuries were serious?'

'I didn't know for sure, but nobody gets up and walks away after falling thirty feet. Frankly, it was a miracle you were conscious.'

'Thirty feet? Was it really that far?'

'I reckon so. I was utterly distraught; all I could think of was how I was going to get to you.'

Her forehead creases. 'But if you suspected I had serious injuries, wouldn't it have been better to summon help straight away?'

I pinch the end of my nose. This is starting to feel like a police interview. 'I had the medical kit in my rucksack; I thought I might be able to give you first aid.'

'Even though you could see the tide was coming in?'

'But I didn't see it, not right away. My entire focus was on trying to find a way down the cliff. I knew you'd be terrified; I just wanted to give you some reassurance.'

'But you couldn't find a way ... *could* you?'

'No, I couldn't. That's when I told you I would go for help.'

'No, you've got that bit wrong,' she says sharply. 'It was me who told you to get help.'

I think for a moment. She's right. 'My mistake ... *you* told me to get help, but when I checked my phone, the battery was dead.'

'Dead? I've always assumed you couldn't get a signal.'

'No, it was dead, I'd forgotten to charge it the night before.' I'm such an idiot. Who goes for a hike in a foreign country without checking their phone?

She glares at me, her disapproval obvious. 'So then what happened?'

'I started running.'

'Towards the nearest village?'

'Of course, where else would I be running to?'

She smiles, but it fails to reach her eyes. 'Sorry if these sound like stupid questions, I just want to get it clear in my mind.'

I sigh heavily. 'I want you to know that leaving you alone like that was one of the hardest things I've ever had to do. It broke my heart seeing you lying there, so helpless; so *vulnerable*.'

I close my eyes for a second, replaying the scene. I remember exactly how I felt – as if I'd stuffed a kitten in a sack and dropped it in the canal. I could hear it mewing, but there was nothing I could do to save it.

'How long did you think I had until the tide covered the beach?' she asks, interrupting my reverie.

'An hour and a half … two hours at most. The only thing I knew for sure was that I didn't have a second to waste.'

'So you ran to the village. What's that … 12k?'

'Something like that.'

'And what did you do when you got there? Tell me *exactly*.'

The muscles in my abdomen tighten. This is it. Decision time. The urge to lie is overwhelming, but I can't. I mustn't. No matter how bad the truth makes me look.

'I didn't make it to the village,' I say hoarsely.

Grace does an actual double take. 'What? But that's what you told me … you ran to the village and called for help.'

'Actually, it was one of the paramedics who told you that. I'm not sure how his wires got crossed; I guess there was a lot of confusion that day.'

She stares at me, not understanding. 'But if you didn't run to the village, how did you manage to call the emergency services?'

'I didn't.'

I hear her breath come hissing out of her, as if she's been struck hard, in the chest. 'So who did?'

'The captain of a yacht, out at sea. It seems that somebody on deck saw you fall from the cliff and the captain radioed the coastguard. That's the only reason the emergency services got there as quickly as they did.'

Grace's face registers such a tumbled mix of emotions that I can't read a single one.

'How do you know all this?' she asks.

'The day after the accident, the yacht passenger who raised the alarm called the hospital to find out how you were doing. During the conversation he explained what had happened and the nurse who took the call passed the information on to me. I wish I could have thanked him, but he didn't leave his details.'

'And you didn't see fit to tell me this until now, five months later?' Grace says, anger flaring in her voice. 'I can't believe what I'm hearing. You *knew* I thought it was you who saved my life and yet you did nothing to set the record straight.'

I'm struggling to find the words; they've been sucked away into a subterranean cave of shame. 'I could see how traumatised you were. I thought it would only make things worse if I told you the truth and you realised what a desperately close call it was.'

She eyes me suspiciously. 'What do you mean?'

I sigh again. 'Are you sure you want to do this, Grace?'

'Quite sure,' she says firmly.

'Well, okay then. The fact is that if it wasn't for that eagle-eyed passenger, you probably wouldn't have made it.'

She blinks hard. 'But if the captain hadn't radioed the coastguard, you'd have called it in when you got to the village – right?'

I shake my head. 'I would never have got there in time. I might have stood half a chance if I'd been wearing my running shoes and I was familiar with the route. But in my hiking boots and having to stop every ten minutes to check the map … not a chance. I was still 5k from the village when the rescue chopper flew over my head.'

Grace stares at her lap, plucking at a loose thread on her skirt, then smoothing it down, as if she needs time to let this awful truth sink into her bones.

'But why keep up the pretence in front of all our friends and family?' She glances up and fires a venomous look at me. 'Actually, you know what, you don't need to answer that because it's obvious. You enjoyed being hailed as the great hero, didn't you? *My* hero? I bet you loved that party my friends threw for you, while I was in hospital. And what about the bottle of Château Margaux my father gave you from his cellar? He was saving that to wet his first grandchild's head. Did you know that?'

'No, I didn't,' I say quietly, my humiliation complete. 'I'm sorry, Grace, I should have told you sooner but I didn't know how. It didn't help that before we'd even flown back to England you were posting on social media, presenting the paramedic's account as fact.'

'So it's my fault, is it?'

'I'm not saying that. It's just that the more people kept thanking me, the more difficult it became to put them straight. I became trapped in a lie that wasn't even of my own making.'

Grace's reply is shot through with steel: 'Well, at least now, we both know where we stand.'

Her words are bruising, but it's only what I deserve. I just hope she can find it in her heart to forgive me, and realise why I couldn't say anything earlier. 'I did everything in my power to save you that day, I really did.'

She leans forward so our noses are almost touching. 'You know what really hurts, Charles? It's not the fact you didn't manage to get help; it's the fact you lied – if only by omission. We're married now and husbands and wives shouldn't have secrets.'

I don't answer. How can I? It would mean peeling away all the layers until we got to the one dark place I don't ever want to shine a light on.

32

Till death us do part. That's what they make you say when you get married. I sometimes think that line should be optional.

It feels as if we're growing further and further apart every day. The fabric of our relationship unravelling, knitting back together in an entirely different way, the edges no longer seamless.

We don't argue as such, but a quiet antagonism underpins all our interactions; I find it quite exhausting.

He likes to fix things. But he can't fix this. Can't fix me. More and more I find myself fantasising about what it would be like to leave him. But I don't know if I've got the strength. I worry too about what he would do without me. He relies on me for so much. As I do on him.

I close my eyes and try to imagine life on my own. A vice settles around my heart as the implications rush at me and I squeeze my eyes tighter because it's all I can do. But it's not enough. Nothing is enough.

I used to think love was like a dog. Faithful, loyal, sturdy. The sort of beast who would always chase the stick after it was thrown and come back happier than ever. I know now that love isn't like that. It's a fragile thing that can vanish so easily, destroyed by a few careless actions or thoughtless words.

Love isn't a dog; it's a spider monkey, a tiny jittery primate with eyes that are permanently peeled open in fear.

33

GRACE

I'm alone in the sitting room. Charles has gone out for a walk. I told him I needed space to process what he'd just told me. Before he left, he kissed me and said again that he was sorry.

I wonder why he decided to tell the truth at last. Did he suspect it would eventually wriggle free – and if so, was it a case of damage limitation, a feeling that it was better off coming from him? Finding out what happened in Turkey was supposed to bring me closure, but instead it's thrown up more questions than it's answered.

Charles's revelation has left me reeling. It feels as if some pivot has shifted between us, a relentless mechanism that threatens to derail our marriage before it's even begun. I was already feeling insecure, incarcerated in this mysterious house, cut off from the outside world, and now I feel more alone than ever.

I'd always regarded Charles as both capable and caring, but the accident elevated him to another level entirely. After Turkey, he became my protector, my saviour, my knight in shining armour. I felt that nothing bad could happen to me while we were together – or that if it did, he would magically make it better.

This naive notion that I was dating some sort of superhero is unquestionably a large part of the reason I agreed to marry him. Would I still have said yes if I'd known that I owed my life not to him, but to a sharp-eyed stranger? I can't answer that question right now. Not yet, not while I'm still trying to figure out why it took so long for him to own up.

I cast my mind back six months or so. Was I truly in love with Charles before the accident? I know the answer almost before I finish asking the question. *Absolutely*. I can pinpoint the exact moment.

It was a couple of months after we met. Our first weekend away together. A camping trip. Not the sort of camping I was used to, on a proper site with a convenience store and a shower block. This was *wild* camping – which was, according to Charles, the only kind of camping worth doing.

He said he knew the perfect spot, and he wasn't wrong. A fairy-tale glen beside a lake, with wooded fells in every direction; utter peace and privacy. We pitched our tent, went for a long walk, stopped at an ancient coaching inn for sausages and mash, eaten in the beer garden as the sun went down.

Later, in our tent, Charles made love to me. Not frantically or selfishly, but slowly, tenderly. Afterwards, I lay with my head in the hollow of his arm, listening to him breathe, feeling him wake just enough to find my hand and hold it. It was then that I realised I had been starving for him, craving him for as long as I could remember.

But this isn't the time to get sentimental; I need to keep my wits about me. I close my eyes. Keep them tight shut, until I generate the strength to swallow the memories back down.

In the next moment, it occurs to me, with a hot rush of horror, that perhaps this was Charles's plan all along: to withhold the specifics of my rescue until his ring was safely on my finger. Could he really be that cold and calculating? I'd like to think not, and yet I can't shake the persistent mosquito-whine of suspicion that sings in my ear.

My father certainly had his doubts. In the run-up to the wedding, he proposed a pre-nup. He and my mother were wealthy people, he explained, as if I didn't know that already, and I was their sole heir. In the event of a divorce, a pre-nup would protect me from any nefarious claim on their estate.

It makes me ashamed now, remembering how I brushed the suggestion aside with scarcely a second thought. Could it be that Charles had an ulterior motive in asking me to marry him? I swiftly reorder my thoughts, pushing that appalling notion to the back of my mind.

I'm restless now and sick of sitting here alone. Outside the wind is hammering at the windows. Yesterday, we enjoyed a brief respite from the weather, but I can sense a drop in barometric pressure. My joints are aching and the air feels curiously charged. It's chilly too – the second day in a row that the fire hasn't been lit. There's coal and sheets of newspaper and kindling, but I wouldn't have a clue how to go about laying a fire. With any luck, Pamela is still around, cleaning up after breakfast. I'll see if I can find her. If she's already beetled off to the annexe, I shall have to go upstairs and put on a jumper.

When I get to the dining room, there's no sign of life. Our breakfast dishes have been cleared away, the tablecloth dusted of crumbs. I'm not sure where the kitchen is. I could try and find it, but something tells me Pamela would not appreciate the intrusion. I go back out into the hall and call her name very loudly, two or three times, but get no response.

My feet begin to climb the stairs. One, two ... the third one creaks and my whole body tenses. After finding the doll on our bed last night, I'm even jumpier than usual. As I reach the first-floor landing, I half expect a fist to slam into me, pushing me back down, but there is nothing there, just a sense of unease sticking to me like a second skin.

Instead of continuing to the top floor as I had intended, I decide on impulse to take a detour. As I walk down the corridor to the smallest room, an unsettling thought occurs to me: am I walking towards something I should be running away from? I shrug the feeling off; my desire to see the portrait is too powerful.

As before, the door is unlocked. I push it open and step across the threshold, my ears alert to the slightest sound. I don't know what I am anticipating ... wafts of laughter, perhaps. Tattoos of running feet. But all I hear is the creaking bones of the old house.

The colours of the portrait seem more vivid today, the figure of Emma more lifelike. She looks down at me with her storm-coloured eyes, almost as if she's trying to reach inside of me. I'm glad the previous owner insisted the painting remain here. Emma belongs at The Anchorage; she is the mistress of this house, the first and only.

I find myself wondering if her marriage to John Murrish was a happy one. Everything I've heard so far suggests it was. Would the discovery that her husband had deceived her have led Emma to reassess their relationship? Perhaps, but I suspect her options would have been limited. A Victorian wife – even one with a successful career – would risk penury and social exclusion if she ever got divorced. But the time I live in is very different to hers.

Tearing my eyes away from the portrait, I go to the small window on the other side of the room. It's a pleasant enough vista, looking out across the harbour and the wide-open sea. The sky is darkening; Charles ought to be thinking about making his way back soon. Unless I'm very much mistaken, another storm is brewing.

I put the back of my hand to my forehead. The events of the last few days are flooding my brain, filling the fissures, welling up in the hollows. Everything is connected, I'm sure of it.

I'm positive the Jeffreys know more about these events than they're letting on. They can't have lived here as long as they have and not be aware of this building's idiosyncrasies. Other guests may even have experienced the same things I have.

I wish I could take an axe and split the house open, letting its secrets ooze out, as dark and unappetising as they might be. So this can be over, forever. For everyone. But time is running out; Charles and I are leaving in the morning.

Suddenly, a shrill sound pierces the silence. It's so strange, and yet so familiar, my heart leaps in my chest. The insistent ring of a phone – a *landline*, unless I'm very much mistaken.

In an instant, I'm moving towards the door. I can't remember ever seeing a telephone in the house, but the sound seems to be coming from the ground floor. I hurry down the stairs as fast as I can, but my gait is jerky and awkward. As I reach the entrance hall, my foot catches the newel post and I stumble, just catching myself in time before I crash to the floor. The ringing sounds so near, I must be right on top of it, but I can't see a phone anywhere. I do a frantic three-sixty, eyes desperately searching. And then the ringing stops.

I swear out loud. I *need* to find that phone. Where the hell is it? My gaze settles on the row of coat pegs behind the front door. There are several items of outerwear hanging there besides ours. With no other guests here, I can only surmise that they belong to Michael and Pamela. Is it possible that a cordless handset is stashed, forgotten, in one of the pockets?

I go over to the pegs and start feeling inside the coats, but all I find are some balled-up tissues and half a packet of chewing gum. I walk back towards the stairs, my teeth pressing hard into the flesh of my lip.

All at once, I spot something hiding in plain sight. A small doorknob set into one of the wooden panels under the stairs. I pull on it and a door opens, automatically activating an interior light. With a shock of surprise I see a mini-office laid out in front of me. A desk with a laptop and printer and in front of it, a wheeled stool. And there, sitting atop a small filing cabinet is a corded, push-button phone.

In a heartbeat, I snatch up the receiver and press it to my ear. The dial tone is suddenly one of the most beautiful sounds I have ever heard in my entire life.

Quickly, I punch in my mother's mobile number. I know she'll be at her dental practice right now; I just pray she picks up.

'Hello.' It's only one word, but the voice is so soft, so kind that my throat constricts.

I sink onto the stool, clutching the receiver with both hands. 'Mum, it's me.'

'Grace!' she cries. 'How lovely to hear from you. How are things in St Ives?'

'We're not in St Ives,' I say, frowning. 'Didn't you get Charles's text?'

'What text?' she replies. 'We haven't heard a thing from either of you since you left Salisbury.'

I experience a small tearing sensation, deep inside me. Charles lied about that too.

'If you're not in St Ives, where are you?' my mother asks. I can hear the worry in her voice.

'About fifty miles away, in a place called Saltwater; we've been stuck here since Monday. A tree came down on the railway line and our train had to be evacuated. I thought you might have seen it on the news.'

'Gosh no, your father and I heard that Cornwall had been hit hard by the storm, but we didn't know anything about a train evacuation. You're both all right though, aren't you?'

'We're fine. We're staying in a B&B – I think *quirky*'s the best way to describe it. It was the only place in the village that had any vacancies. There's no mobile reception here and the landline's been down for days. We did think about hiring a car, but a landslide has blocked the only road out of the village.' I speak quickly, urgently, the words falling over themselves like dominoes in a line.

'Oh Grace, how awful for you,' my mother says with a sympathetic sigh. 'Your father and I were surprised we hadn't heard from you, but we assumed you were just too busy having lovely romantic adventures. What's the weather like there now?'

'Not great, I think another storm might be heading our way.'

'So when do you think you'll be able to get to St Ives?'

'Tomorrow morning, once they've finished the repairs on the railway line.'

'Oh well, at least you'll be able to salvage *something* of your honeymoon.'

A tear rolls down my cheek and plops onto the desk. 'I miss you, Mum.'

'I miss you too, my love, but try not to get too upset. You and Charles are together, that's the main thing.'

Hearing my mother say his name makes my breath catch in my throat. 'Listen, Mum, there's something I really need to talk to you about. A few things, actually.'

I hesitate, wondering if I should discuss the newly discovered details about my accident in a phone call. I think I'd rather tell my mother in person when we get back. But the other issue that's weighing heavily on my mind can't be put off.

'This is going to sound pretty crazy, but just bear with me, okay?' I lick my lips, trying to find the words to explain the unexplainable. 'Some weird things have been happening at our guest house. I wouldn't mind getting your take on it.'

'Sorry, Grace, can you hang on for a sec?' I hear the sound of her hand covering the phone, followed by muffled voices. When she returns, her voice has taken on a harried tone. 'I'm afraid I have to go. My next patient's just arrived. Do you have the number of the place where you're staying? It didn't come up on my phone. I'll give you a call this evening and we can have a proper chat then, if that works for you.'

'That would be wonderful,' I tell her. 'It's called called The Anchorage. I don't know the number; you'll have to google it. Oh, wait a minute, here we go.' I pick up a compliment slip that's lying in the in-tray and start reading off the phone number at the top. I'm halfway through when I get the sensation that I'm speaking into a void. An anxious drumbeat starts in my chest.

'Are you there?' I say. My mother doesn't answer.

'Mum? Can you hear me?'

Silence.

I jiggle the switch where the handset rests, trying to restore the connection. It's no good. The line is dead.

34

GRACE

How can a phone be working one minute and not the next? Hoping it's simply a loose connection, I follow the electrical cord to the socket in the wall. It looks all right and seems to be securely plugged in.

Exasperated beyond words, I turn my attention to the laptop that's sitting on the desk. It's a clunky thing, practically a museum piece. As I flip the lid and hit a key at random the screen springs to life, but when I click on the web browser, all I get is an error message telling me that *this device is not connected to the internet.*

The thought that I might not be able to speak to my mother tonight after all is unbearable. I put my face into my cupped palms and breathe in, then out again, trying to calm myself down.

My nerves steadied, I turn my focus back to the computer. The desktop is cluttered with folders: *Tax Returns, Bookings, Invoices, Insurance.* It all sounds spectacularly tedious. Just as I'm about to close the lid, something catches my eye. I lean forward, glowering at the screen. I can hardly believe what I'm seeing, but it's right there in front of me. A folder with my name on it: *Grace.*

Heart pounding, I double click the folder. It springs open to reveal dozens of files – word documents, PDFs, Jpegs, each one with a padlock symbol attached. When I try to open one, a password prompt appears. I click on a few more, but every one is encrypted. I close the folder and scan the desktop, looking for any other folders with names, but there aren't any. Just mine. I accept that there might be a perfectly reasonable explanation, but right now I'm struggling to think what it could be. I have the overwhelming sensation that this isn't mere coincidence; it's something more sinister.

My lungs tingle as an invisible band tightens around my chest. Why have the Jeffreys got a folder with my name on it – and *what* is it? There must be forty or fifty files there. I've got the usual social media presence of a person my age and my CV appears on a couple of professional networking sites, but that's about it. Apart from being hugely disturbing, the Jeffreys' dossier almost certainly breaches data protection regulations – a subject that, given the nature of my job, I am well versed in.

This is beginning to feel more and more like a bad movie. Real life isn't supposed to be like this. People don't get trapped by storms in haunted houses run by fiendish hoteliers for days on end. How on earth did I end up in this situation? Haven't I had enough bad luck recently? Or maybe it wasn't luck; maybe it was deliberate. Maybe I was brought here for a reason. Maybe *Charles* brought me here for a reason.

I check the time on the laptop. It's been more than two hours since he left. When I said I needed some time by myself, I didn't imagine he'd be gone this long.

Taking care to leave the office exactly as I found it, I walk to the other end of the hall and open the front door. Outside, a row of parked cars is obscuring my view of the road ahead. Putting the door on the latch so I don't get locked out, I go to the gate. As I step into the road, the wind catches my hair, lashing it across my eyes and mouth.

There are no dog walkers or football players on the green today. In fact, looking around, I can't see a single soul. I wonder where Charles is. With the coastal road impassable, he can't have gone very far. Above my head, there's a low rumble of thunder. The sky is black, I'm sure the heavens are about to open and I know Charles hasn't taken an umbrella.

Behind me I hear the persistent clang of metal against metal, the sound of something banging in the wind. I glance over my shoulder, wondering if I've forgotten to secure the front gate. Then I realise it's the *side* gate that's slipped its latch, the one that leads to the back garden and the annexe. I daresay I'll be able to hear the banging inside the house, so I'd better go and shut it.

As I walk over to the gate, I catch a flash of something orange – the laces on a pair of sturdy hiking boots. The boots are sitting on the rubber mat outside the front door of the annexe. They're Charles's, I'd recognise them anywhere; mine are the same make. We bought them together as an early Christmas present to ourselves. What the fuck is Charles doing in the annexe?

I go through the gate, sliding the bolt home behind me. Up ahead, the annexe is ablaze with light. Inside, every lamp, every bulb seems to be on, burning against the encroaching darkness. There are net curtains at all the windows, but the illuminated interior makes it easy to see inside, and not so easy for those *inside* to see out.

I move towards the building, flattening my back against the gable end like a cat burglar. Maintaining this position, I edge around the corner, up to the first window. I lean forward slightly, twisting my neck so I can look inside. It's the kitchen. I can see some dated wall units and a sink piled high with dirty dishes.

I inch forward, past the front door, to a second, much larger window. My breath hitches. There they are, Michael, Pamela and Charles, grouped cosily together in front of a gas fire. Charles has taken his coat off and he's sitting on the sofa, next to Pamela. Michael is opposite them in an easy chair. Bathed in the light of a standard lamp, shadows pooled in the hollows of his cheeks, he looks like a cadaver.

There are three mugs on the coffee table and a half-empty plate of biscuits, suggesting that this isn't a brief visit for the purposes of some casual request or enquiry. Charles and I spent the whole of yesterday evening with the Jeffreys; what possible reason could he have for wanting to spend more time with them now?

Just then, Pamela reaches for something lying next to her on the sofa. As she lifts it onto her lap, I see that it's a foolscap wallet. I watch as she opens it, removes a sheaf of papers and hands them to Charles. He studies the uppermost document in silence for a long moment, seemingly lost in thought. When he starts to talk, Michael and Pamela stare at him solemnly, as if they're hanging on his every word.

I have a sudden flush of icy-cold certainty that spreads from my chest along my arms, to the tips of my fingers. These aren't three people who have just renewed a casual acquaintance after many years, there's a much deeper connection here. An *intimacy*. Given what I've just discovered on the Jeffreys' laptop, it's a deeply disturbing thought. My hands begin to shake. I bunch them into fists and tuck them into my armpits.

Shocked and bewildered, I take a step back, colliding with a metal watering can that's been abandoned on the patio. It topples over, making a loud noise as it strikes the paving stones. Instantly, Pamela's head swivels towards the window. She reminds me of a wild animal, eyes glinting, ears pricked. Quickly, before she has a chance to bare her teeth, I turn and run towards the gate.

It's half an hour or more before I hear the sound of the front door opening. It's followed by the rustle of a coat being removed, and then the soft thud of stockinged feet making their way along the hall.

I don't call out a greeting. Instead, I wait for Charles to find me in the sitting room. I'm staring at the pages of my book, but the words are a blur, my thoughts a million miles away.

'Hey,' he says, regarding me warily as he slips into the arm-chair beside me.

I look up from my book. He's so handsome in his faded pink shirt, his hair all tousled from the wind, even if he has only walked the short distance from the annexe.

'Hey yourself,' I reply, straining to sound as if nothing's wrong.

He tries to clear his throat but it unravels into a dry, tentative cough. 'I just want to say again that I'm sorry. I didn't mean to hurt you, Grace, that's the last thing I would ever want to do.'

My brain is full of static. I know what I want to tell him, but given what I've just witnessed, I must think very carefully before I say – or do – anything. I'm stuck in this house with this man ... this man who all of a sudden seems like a stranger. I think it's probably wiser to tell him what he wants to hear.

'Apology accepted.' My voice is calm, deliberate, even though my pulse is racing.

'Great,' he says, visibly relaxing. 'I'm glad everything's out in the open now.'

'I really hope it is, because it isn't a nice feeling, knowing that you held out on me like that.'

He fixes me with his bottomless eyes. 'I've told you everything, Grace, I swear. I know I should have clarified things sooner, but I was only trying to protect you.'

His remarks feel true – I hear the clean, clear sound of them as they chime in my heart – and yet ...

I close my book and wedge it in the space between my thigh and the side of the armchair. 'You were gone for ages. Where did you get to?'

He leans back in his chair and offers the careless yawn of a bored silverback gorilla with all the time in the world to forage.

'Down to the harbour, along the seafront, all the way up to the landslide and then back via the high street.'

I tilt my head, studying his expression, looking for a subtle tell. 'You must have been walking very slowly to string that out for two hours.'

His cheeks flush and I think he's about to confess. Until he doesn't.

'I stopped at Rosario's for a coffee and a read of the paper.'

'Busy in there, was it?'

'Not particularly.'

I don't say anything for a few moments, waiting for him to tell me the truth. Instead, he gets down on his knees in front of the hearth.

'It's freezing in here, how about I get this fire going?'

I watch in silence as he begins screwing sheets of newspaper into balls and laying them on the grate. Next, he pulls the basket of kindling towards him and begins stacking it in a grid formation on top of the newspaper. A final layer of coal is added before he takes the box of matches and sets light to the newspaper. The flames take hold quickly, licking the kindling like a hungry beast. I had no idea my husband was such a competent fire starter. Just one of many things I didn't know about him.

He leans back, resting on his haunches, and brushes his hands together to get rid of the coal dust. 'So what did you get up to while I was out?' he asks.

'I spoke to my mother,' I say in a casual tone, as if this wasn't a major achievement.

His eyebrows shoot up. 'You managed to get a signal on your mobile?'

I shake my head. 'I used the landline.'

'How did you know the line was up again?'

'I heard a phone ring and I tracked it down to the office.'

Charles makes a puzzled face. 'What office?'

'In the understairs cupboard.'

'Wow, well done you for finding it.'

He takes another lump of coal from the scuttle and adds it to the fire. 'Did you phone our hotel in St Ives to let them know we'll be arriving tomorrow?'

'I didn't get a chance to. The phone suddenly went dead while I was talking to Mum. Almost like someone had cut the line.'

'Perhaps the engineers are still running tests; that might explain why the service is intermittent.'

I pluck an imaginary speck of lint from my sleeve. 'I didn't realise you were a telecoms expert.'

'I'm not; it's just a guess.' He runs his finger back and forth across his lips. He's starting to look a little uncomfortable. 'So how is your mother anyway?'

'She was surprised to hear we were in Saltwater; she didn't know we hadn't made it to St Ives. Why did you tell me you'd sent her a text when you hadn't?'

'But I did text her,' Charles says, sounding quite indignant.

I hold out my hand. 'Can I see your phone, please?' I hate the imperious tone in my voice, but I can't help it. I need to see the evidence with my own eyes.

For a moment he looks at me as if I am a puzzle piece and I am not fitting nicely in my designated slot. Then he gives a little shake of his head and tears open the pocket of his cargo pants. He pulls out his phone, unlocks it and hands it to me without saying a word.

I go straight to his text messages. I'm almost disappointed when I see he was telling the truth. He did send a text to my mother, the day after we got here.

'Satisfied?' Charles says in a quiet voice.

'Yes and no.' I show him the screen, drawing his attention to the red exclamation mark beside the message. 'You sent the text, but it was never delivered.'

His mouth gapes open, he seems genuinely surprised. 'But I had a signal, I know I did.'

'It must have dropped out before the text went through.'

'Shit, Grace, I'm so sorry, I didn't even think to check,' he says, taking the phone from me and putting it back in his pocket. 'Has your mother been worried sick about us all this time?'

I blink slowly. 'Not really. She didn't see anything about the train evacuation on the news; she just assumed we were safely holed up in St Ives.'

I stare into the fire as the beginnings of a headache creep slowly across my forehead. I am burning to confront Charles, to demand the truth about his relationship with the Jeffreys and find out what he knows about the folder on their laptop. But some instinct in me knows that to verbalise my feelings would be a mistake.

After all, there are three of them and only one of me.

35

I don't feel safe here any more. It feels as if I am being watched. It's the same way you can tell a burglar's in the house, even when your eyes are closed.

Just now, I was relaxing in the sitting room when I thought I saw something out of the corner of my eye. It was barely half a second – the smooth gliding of a shadow, something half-seen and snatched away. It could have been a trick of the light, but I don't think so.

I got up and went over to the door. The hall was empty, but the arrangement of dried flowers on the console table was trembling slightly, the aftershock of someone pushing past it.

I have a creeping, vague sense that something terrible is about to happen – or maybe it's already happened and I just don't know it. I can feel it moving through me like a cold and salty wave made of every unnameable feeling.

I sit in the armchair, gathering these thoughts and trying to squash them down, but they keep springing up like jack-in-the-boxes, taunting me with their gruesome smiles.

36

GRACE

Twelve hours. Twelve hours and I'll be on the train to St Ives. Time slows and stretches in Saltwater, but it still goes forward. Tomorrow I shall be free of this house and its whispering walls. Dawn can't come soon enough.

It's dark now and the sitting-room curtains are drawn. I can hear the rain slapping in rugged gusts against the windows and the guest-house sign squeaking as it swings in the wind.

The storm arrived early in the evening, just as Charles was returning with food from the Chinese takeaway on the high street. We listened to a local news programme on the radio while we ate. The occurrence of two violent storms in such quick succession is unprecedented, the weather presenter said, as he advised listeners to stay indoors. The talk of potential travel disruption made me feel sick. If the trains don't run tomorrow, I don't know what I'm going to do.

We've got an early start in the morning, so after our meal we packed our suitcase and left it ready by the front door. There are still several hours of the evening yawning ahead and I'm not sure how we're going to fill them.

The atmosphere between Charles and me is more tense than it's ever been. Despite our conversation today, there is so much that is still unresolved. We've barely had any physical contact all evening. My husband is usually very tactile, always touching me, holding my hand, stroking my hair, kissing me. I like that he does that; it makes me feel wanted, desired, protected. But our only contact this evening came when he accidentally brushed my hand as he passed me the prawn crackers. We were perfectly civil to one another, but although we appeared to be communicating, there was no spark of connection. It's as if some invisible wall lies between us, which neither of us is able to penetrate.

We've given up talking for now. I wish there was a TV here, so we could watch a wildlife documentary, or even one of the soaps ... anything to lighten the mood. Instead, we're stationed in a pair of armchairs, reading our books in silence. I keep sneaking furtive looks at my husband. He seems so ill at ease. He's staring down at his book, but he hasn't turned the page for nearly ten minutes. I can see a muscle ticking in his jaw. That usually only happens when he's stressed – which is hardly ever. When I ask him what's wrong, he says he's worried the storm might torpedo our departure plans. But he's spent the last five days acting as if he couldn't care less whether or not we get to St Ives. What's changed, I wonder?

His anxiety is most concerning. Has he sensed some threat, some foreshadowing that all is not as it seems? I'd like to probe him on the subject, but I can tell he isn't in the mood.

Around ten-thirty, Charles announces he's ready for bed. I'm not nearly tired enough to sleep and so, after a cursory good-night kiss, he goes upstairs alone.

Another hour crawls by and my mind is still free and restless. But I can't sit here all night. It's getting cold. The fire is dwindling in the grate, nothing left of it but glowing embers.

Upstairs, Charles has left the landing light on for me. He's fast asleep and doesn't stir as I change into my pyjamas. His face looks so peaceful, so untroubled by any sense of guilt or shame, stress or anxiety. It makes me wonder if I am right to be suspicious of him; if it wouldn't just be easier to give him the benefit of the doubt and draw a line under everything's that happened. The past can't be changed; all we can do now is look to the future.

As I head to the bathroom to brush my teeth, I'm conscious of a flare of pain in my leg. I'm reluctant to take my medication; I don't think as clearly when it's in my system. But without it, I won't be able to sleep. I strike a compromise, taking one – instead of the recommended two – tablets and wash it down with a mouthful of tap water.

Even by Saltwater standards, it's been a strange and upsetting day. Should I have brought up the accident at all? All it's done is increase my anxiety levels. I can feel the knots clustering in my stomach and the fear tight around my throat like a cord.

As I stare at my reflection in the medicine cabinet mirror, I try to give myself a wry, 'isn't life interesting!' look but it's not enough to lift my spirits.

Back in our rapidly cooling room, I put on a pair of socks and slip in beside Charles. The sheets on my side of the bed are freezing. I'd love to curl around my husband's body, steal his warmth, feel the beat of his heart. But instead I lie on my back, stiff as a board, listening to the wind.

I'm not sure what time it is when I awake from a particularly unpleasant dream, the finer details of which are already fading from memory. Beside me, Charles is sleeping peacefully, his intermittent snores barely audible above the artillery fire of rain on the roof tiles.

Hoping I'll be able to get back to sleep before the alarm goes, I keep my eyes shut and roll onto my side. As I adjust the pillow under my head, my hand brushes against something sharp. My eyes snap open.

What the hell *was* that?

My fingertip is smarting like I've just been stung. I reach out a hand, feeling for the lamp on the bedside table. When I press the switch on the base, nothing happens. I press it again. Still no light. Don't tell me ... another power cut? Wouldn't that just be the icing on the cake?

Sighing, I lean over the side of the bed and grope around on the floor for my phone, remembering with a spike of alarm that the battery was down to ten per cent the last time I looked. Thankfully, there's still sufficient charge to operate the torch. Directing the beam onto my right hand, I see a tiny bead of blood on the tip of my middle finger. Frowning, I wipe it away and lift up my pillow.

Nothing prepares me for what I find. A wave of revulsion rises in me like a tide.

I am staring at an eyeball. And it's staring right back at me.

I want to scream, but my larynx is frozen.

I blink several times, as if to prove I'm not dreaming. Then I see that the eyeball is attached to something: a long white shard. I prod it gently. Porcelain.

I let out a long, slow breath. It isn't real; it's only a glass eye, from the bride doll. The porcelain shard is sharply pointed at one end, like an arrow, sharp enough to prick my finger. But how did it find its way under my pillow? It wasn't there this morning; I distinctly remember plumping the pillows when I made the bed. I would have noticed it.

A throb of vertigo hits me in the solar plexus; it's powerful enough to make me recoil.

The eye. Is it a sign? A warning of some sort? What does it mean? Above my head, there's a growl of thunder. The storm is getting worse.

It was Charles, not me, who tidied away the doll's broken body. I didn't ask him what he did with the pieces, because I didn't care. But I care now. I direct the torch beam towards his side of the bed.

Then I get another surprise: Charles isn't there.

With a mounting sense of panic, I shine the torch under my pillow again. It's then that I see something I didn't notice before. Five or six pieces of ruled paper, roughly torn; each one approximately three centimetres square. They're scattered around the eye like confetti, each one covered in dense, angry handwriting. As the beam of light sweeps over them, three words, written in jagged capitals on three separate scraps, jump out at me. GRACE. MUST. DIE.

I press my hand to my mouth. A seam of fear has opened up inside me. This isn't a game, or a dream, or a figment of my imagination; this is really happening.

As I stare at the hateful words, something chimes in my brain like a radar. I know this handwriting; I've seen it before.

A moment later, I am frantically scrolling through the pictures on my phone. It doesn't take me long to find what I'm looking for: the list of car hire firms that Pamela wrote down for us; I took a photo of it so we wouldn't lose it.

I pick up one of the scraps of paper and hold it against Pamela's list: the elaborate curl of the 'G', the sharply pointed apex of the 'A', the slight downwards slant of the text: there's absolutely no room for doubt; the handwriting is identical.

I turn off the torch, clasping my phone to my chest as questions crowd in on me. Nothing makes sense. Why would Pamela do something like this? What does she mean by it? What have I ever done to her? Does she want to hurt me? Am I in imminent danger of being murdered in my bed? And where is Charles? I never heard him get up. He rarely stirs in the night, he's such a deep sleeper. Suddenly, the safety of St Ives seems a very long way away.

My breathing has quickened. The air in the room feels heavy and thick. I can barely see a thing, but I sense something in the atmosphere – a malevolence, a great diffuse evil silently undulating all around me in the darkness. A series of images runs rapidly through my mind like a video on fast forward: the defaced photo, the otherworldly voices, the warning in the guest book. It's all on the verge of coming together. Right here, right now.

Suddenly, my whole body tenses. I thought I heard something. There it goes again. It's not the wind or the rain or the thunder. It's not even coming from outside. It's coming from *inside*, from the corridor on the other side of our bedroom door.

My heart starts hiccupping violently in my chest. I don't understand. How can this be happening? This was supposed to be my honeymoon, but it is fast turning into a nightmare.

I crane my neck towards the door. Footsteps. Definitely footsteps. But ever so light, like a child's. I move further up the bed, clinging to the headboard. The footsteps stop and for a few moments there is silence. Then I hear another sound, one I've heard before. A child's sobbing, high-pitched and frightened, just like the first night. It bounces off the walls and vibrates inside my head. I feel the blood draining out of me, to be replaced by an icy nausea.

After twenty seconds or so, the ghastly aria fades. Now I hear voices. More than one. Broken whispers. Angry hisses, the words indistinct. A current of dread cuts a valley from my throat to my intestines.

I am alone. In the dark. Filled with a lurching, sick-to-the-stomach sense of helplessness. My throat is dry, I barely have any saliva in my mouth. I lick my lips and bring my hand to my chest, trying to press my heart back to its normal rhythm. The nervous tension in me is ready to explode.

With trembling fingers, I turn the torch back on and shine it round the room. I don't know what I'm expecting to see – a handy portal, opening into another world, perhaps. But it only confirms what I already know: there is no means of escape.

I wish I knew where Charles was. If he'd just popped to the bathroom, he would have returned by now. I'm tempted to lie back down, pull the duvet over my head and hope that whatever it is out there that wants to hurt me goes away. But I am stronger than that. I have faced demons before – when I lay at the foot of that cliff in Turkey, watching the tide come in. On that occasion, I was utterly powerless; I had to rely on others to save me. But this is different. This time, I'm not going to sit here and accept my fate.

Slowly, silently, I get up from the bed and start moving towards the door, my torch lighting the way. The single pain-killer I took before I went to bed has worn off now and there is a serrated pain unfurling along the full length of my leg. Only the bedroom door stands between them and me: a five-foot space, swimming with uncertainty.

I take two steps forward. The voices are still there, but they're growing quieter; perhaps they're trying to lull me into a false sense of security. I don't care what their tactics are; I'm going to face them head on. I make it to the door. I reach for the handle. And then, at the precise moment the door swings open, the battery on my phone dies – and I am plunged into darkness.

I hover in the doorway, teetering on the edge of something I don't understand. The voices seem to be all around me: up, down, left, right. I don't know which way to turn.

Suddenly, there's a flash of lightning. It penetrates the sky-light, illuminating the narrow corridor. It's just enough time for me to make out the silhouette of a person raising a large object, a curved blade, above their head.

Before my brain has time to make sense of this, the corridor is pitch black once more.

Seconds later, a heavy thud shakes the floorboards beneath my feet. Then, from the shadows, comes a great, gusty sigh. I feel it on my face, cool and sour. A voice starts speaking, foreign words I've never heard before, like some sort of incantation.

Air leaves my lungs in shallow puffs. There is something solid in my chest, an obstruction past which I can't breathe. Every nerve in my body shrieks, telling me to run, but my feet are welded to the floor.

And then, from behind me, I hear the sound of feet pounding up the stairs.

'Darling?' a voice says.

I don't reply.

'Darling?' the voice says again. 'Is that you?'

I take a deep breath – and with it a leap of faith. 'Yes.'

The next moment, my husband's solid form is beside me. 'Come on,' he says, grabbing my hand.

'What's happening?' I ask him, my thoughts rapidly unspooling.

Before he can answer, another voice comes drifting through the air. It's different to the one I heard before. It's soft and light, but each word shivers with certainty.

'*Charlie.*' The elongated vowels hang in the air. '*Why?*'

Unseen hands squeeze my lungs. I am shrinking, dwindling. Fear floods through me, filling me from my toes to my scalp and threatening to pull me under.

'We need to go, Grace – now!' Charles says.

The urgency in his voice is unmistakeable and yet still I hesitate. Something is holding me back – keeping me here. Can I trust him?

The next moment, Charles is pulling me towards the stairs.

37

CHARLES

I'm lying, bare-chested, on the sand in a sheltered cove that only the locals know. A soft, salty breeze is coming in off the sea. Above my head, a plane trails a frothy white tail across a clear blue sky. The remains of a picnic are laid out beside me: ham sandwiches, crisps and chocolate biscuits that are rapidly melting in the heat. There's a girl with me; a pretty girl in shorts and a pale-yellow T-shirt. I reach for her, pressing my face into her neck, feeling her warm skin. In that moment, I remember thinking: this is what it feels like to be home. Here. This beach, this skin, this smell, this girl. But almost as soon as I've grasped it, the memory slips away like a wave from the shore.

A flash of lightning brings me back to the present. The rain is bucketing down and the wind's so strong the telegraph wires are swaying. It's dark. The power failure must be village-wide because every street lamp is out.

Down below, at the foot of the bluff, the waves are smashing against the sea wall. But despite this, faced with either the house or the storm, I'll take my chances with the storm any day.

As we burst through the front gate, Grace's voice reminds me that I'm not here alone. 'What do we do now?' she wails.

I think for a moment. The bandstand is close by, but after what just happened, I'd prefer to put more distance between The Anchorage and us.

'There's a bus shelter a hundred metres or so away,' I tell her. 'We'll be safe in there.'

As we set off down the road – Grace hobbling, me carrying our suitcase and backpack that I grabbed from the hall – I try to process what just happened. It's not easy; the situation unfolded so quickly. Everything's a blur.

Once we're safely inside the shelter, we swap our pyjamas for warm clothes and shoes from our suitcase. Grace has barely said a word since we left, but I can see from her body language she's shaken.

'Are you okay?' I ask her, as I ball up our wet things and stuff them in a corner of the suitcase.

'I am now we're out of *that* place,' she says, rubbing her upper arms through her waterproof jacket.

'Are you cold? Do you want one of my jumpers to put on underneath that?'

'No, it's all right. I'm just in shock. I don't know what happened.'

'Me neither.' I reach for her shoulders, pulling her towards me. 'Don't worry, Grace, nothing's going to hurt you now.'

She looks up at me, for a moment I see her cinnamon-coloured eyes soften. The world seems to slip sideways and I have to hold her tight to keep from falling.

'What do you think that was?' she says in a quiet voice.

'I don't know,' I say, my words sounding strangled.

'I'm sure it said your name.'

'I heard it say *something*, but I don't think it was my name.' I'm glad she can't see my face; it makes it easier to lie.

I glance at my wrist. But then I remember my watch is still in the room, together with some loose change and the clothes I was planning to wear today. As luck would have it, all our other valuables were safely stowed in the backpack, ready for our departure. Bending down, I unzip the front pocket of the backpack and reach inside for my phone.

'It's four-oh-seven,' I say, and pause, considering our options. We really don't have any. 'The train station won't be open for another couple of hours. Shall we just sit tight in here? At least we're out of the rain.'

Grace sighs as she sits down on the narrow bench seat. 'What choice do we have?'

Just then, the street lamp outside the bus shelter flares into life. I stick my head out into the rain and watch as, one by one, pinpricks of light appear all over the village.

We haven't been there for very long when I notice a car approaching, the first one we've seen. It's a newish estate, its windscreen wipers beating furiously against the driving rain. It drives past slowly before drawing to a halt a little way down the road. Suddenly, it reverses and stops again, directly opposite the bus shelter this time. The window opens and I go over, thinking that maybe the driver needs directions. But when I bend down to peer inside the car, I realise it's the woman from the shop where we bought Grace's necklace.

'I thought you two looked familiar,' she says, shouting to be heard above the din of the rain. 'What on earth are you doing out here? If you're waiting for a bus, they don't start running till nine, you know.'

I wipe the raindrops out of my eyes. 'Unfortunately, we had to check out of our B&B a little earlier than planned. We're just sheltering here until the train station opens.'

'But that won't be for ages,' she says, looking at me aghast. 'You can't possibly stay out here till then.'

'Don't worry about us, we'll be fine,' I say, as if this is the sort of thing Grace and I do all the time. 'Where are you off to?'

'The shop,' she says, grimacing. 'I don't usually start work so early, but I'm expecting a delivery of ceramics first thing. I need to clear some space in the stockroom before it arrives. Why don't you two come with me? You're going to catch your deaths otherwise.'

I look around for Grace, but she's already reaching for the door handle. 'Thanks, Kirsten,' she says as she slides into the back seat. 'You're a life-saver.'

38

I have an ache that runs through me like a steel blade. It slices down from the crown of my head to my stomach. I can feel my insides leaking from the gash.

I want them to DIE. Slowly and painfully. I want them to beg for mercy while I gouge their eyeballs and tear out their spleens. Only then, like me, will they know the true meaning of the word suffering.

Everyone thinks it was an accident, but I don't believe that. It was Them; it MUST be. I don't have any evidence, of course; just a mother's instinct.

They think they will get away with this, but they won't. One day my words will find the light and make their secrets known.

I went out into the garden earlier. I knelt on the lawn and snatched up handfuls of soil from a flowerbed, rubbing it into my face and mouth. I wanted the earth to soak into my skin and replace me, cell by cell, and if I couldn't be replaced, I wanted to disappear.

Of course, none of these things happened. All I could do was whisper your name over and over again to myself, like a catechism. GRACE, GRACE, GRACE ...

39

GRACE

It's only been six months, but already Saltwater feels like another lifetime. We never did make it to St Ives. We thought about it long and hard, but the weather forecast was grim and rather than trying to make the best of a bad situation, we decided to cut our losses and come home. The hotel would only give us a part refund, but that's fine, the money's not important.

Although we've spent hours and hours talking about it, Charles and I are still no nearer to understanding what went down at The Anchorage. I've told him everything I experienced there, each tangled thread, and he's sorry he ever doubted me. I'm sorry too. Sorry that I had doubts about *him* and even suspected he might be in league with the Jeffreys.

I was in a very peculiar frame of mind the whole time we were in Saltwater. The Anchorage, with all its little turning wheels and moving pieces, played with me, bent me out of shape until I hardly recognised myself any more. Although it's not an experience I would ever wish to repeat, I think it's brought Charles and I closer together.

Needless to say, our friends and family were incredulous when we recounted the tale. I directed any doubters to Tripadvisor, because it's all there in the reviews. Frankly, it's a wonder The Anchorage hasn't been investigated by the authorities – but perhaps, in these politically correct times, paranormal activity is not a sufficient excuse to shut a business down. Ghosts have rights too, I guess.

As for Charles's confession regarding my accident, I am slowly coming to terms with his misrepresentation of the facts. I'm still pretty pissed off about it, but I'm not about to throw my marriage away on the basis of one mistake. At least this way, if *I* ever fuck up – and quite frankly it's only a matter of time – my husband will be duty-bound to return the favour and forgive me back.

The therapy has helped a lot too. It was meant to improve my anxiety issues, which it has done – I'm definitely sleeping better these days – but during the sessions, my relationship has also come under scrutiny.

My therapist helped me understand that my expectations of marriage were too high from the outset. I thought that finding someone I actually *wanted* to marry was the hard part and that after that it would be all plain sailing. I realise now that I need to be more flexible and adjust my expectations to reflect reality; otherwise, I run the risk of being continually disappointed. I have to keep reminding myself that married life is supposed to be us against the world – *not* each other. And that's how I want it to be: Charles and me, back to back in the water, fighting off sharks for the rest of our lives.

I appreciate that Charles is putting a lot of effort into our marriage too. He offered, rather gallantly, to tell our friends and family what really happened in Turkey. After giving it some thought, I said I was happy for things to stay as they were. I don't want my nearest and dearest to think badly of my husband – and I know my parents, in particular, would take a very dim view of his failure to come clean sooner. He knows what he did was wrong and he's apologised for it a hundred times. I really don't see the point in making him grovel any more.

One thing I was very keen to do after we got home was thank the people who played such a vital role in my rescue.

After a few phone calls, I managed to track down the cruise line whose yacht was in the right place at the right time that day. They in turn put me in touch with the captain who radioed the coastguard. I sent him an email, expressing my undying gratitude and saying that without him I would probably be dead.

A couple of days later, I received a self-effacing reply from the captain in which he insisted that he had only been doing his job. Regrettably, the cruise line hasn't been able to identify the individual who saw me fall. There were two hundred and forty-two passengers on board that day and the chances of ever finding my saviour are slim to non-existent – but I live in hope.

Continuing on a positive note, I've seen a significant improvement in my health. The flexibility in my leg is so much better than it was and I rarely need to take painkillers these days; one more appointment with the physio and I'll be done. Meanwhile, things are going very well at work and I'm starting to regain some of the confidence I lost as a result of the accident. I've just produced a standardised social-media policy for our employees, which was very well received by the CEO. On the back of that, my line manager indicated that there might be scope for a promotion later this year. So all in all, I'm feeling pretty good about the future.

The weather this summer has been glorious and now that it's the weekend, I'm looking forward to a lazy day, soaking up the sun on the south-facing balcony of our apartment. Charles has gone to play tennis with some friends, but he'll be back at lunchtime. If the weather holds, we're planning a barbecue, just the two of us.

No sooner have I settled in the sun-lounger with a cold drink, when my phone chirps, signalling the arrival of a text. It's from Olivia, my cousin.

Check out this podcast, her message says. *You'll find Episode 8 riveting – I guarantee it!*

Olivia is a bit of a podcast aficionado. She listens to them every day on her lengthy commute to work. She knows I'm not much of a fan; I can't think why she's passed on the recommendation. Still, I'm sufficiently intrigued to click on the link she's provided.

It takes me to a true crime series called *When Death Comes Calling.* I swipe up, scrolling through the list of episodes until I reach number eight. As I scan the programme synopsis, a bitter rush of bile slides up my throat.

Episode 8: Hotel of Horrors
When detectives probe a suspicious fire in a Cornish fishing village, they expose the shocking secrets of a haunted guest house and a twisted tale of revenge that left two people dead.

In an instant, I'm on my feet and running into the lounge for the earbuds that I left lying on the coffee table. As I slide the jack into my phone and tap play, I notice that my hand is shaking.

At first glance, it was an open-and-shut case: a lightning strike that set a seaside guest house on fire, tragically claiming the lives of its two owners. But as detectives searched for the truth, they uncovered a real-life murder story that was stranger than any work of fiction.

Michael and Pamela Jeffrey were the owners of The Anchorage guest house in Saltwater, a picturesque fishing village on the south coast of Cornwall. The couple had moved there from London in 2006. Like so many others before them, they were seeking an escape from the rat race, the chance to swap the smog of the city for clean sea air, and the promise of a more relaxed way of life.

I tap Pause as I struggle to digest what I've just heard. The lugubrious narrator has barely begun, but what I've learned so far has knocked me sideways. Michael and Pamela are dead. Not just dead, but quite possibly murdered.

I pace around the lounge, casting my mind back over the past six months and trying to work out when this horrific incident might have happened. A story this big would surely have made the national news. Why didn't Charles and I know anything about it? I take a deep breath, bracing myself for what's to come.

Prior to their relocation, both the Jeffreys had worked in the financial services industry. Thanks to hard work and some wise investments, they had built up a sizeable nest egg – enough to buy an imposing, three-storey home in Saltwater and convert it into a nine-room bed and breakfast.

For more than a decade, they worked tirelessly to make the business a success, even when times were tough – but earlier this year, their dreams were violently shattered. As dawn broke on Friday, February the twenty-first, one of the Jeffreys' neighbours looked out of his bedroom window, and saw to his horror that The Anchorage was alight.

Fire crews were rapidly dispatched, but sadly they arrived too late. Michael and Pamela Jeffrey were discovered, entwined in each other's arms, on the third floor of the Victorian property. Both were pronounced dead at the scene.

Frowning, I tap Rewind, certain I've misheard. I haven't. February the twenty-first: the same day Charles and I fled the guest house, never to return.

Something is twisting my windpipe, robbing me of air. I don't understand. The Anchorage was perfectly fine when we left it – and yet, just a couple of hours later, two people were dead. What were Michael and Pamela doing in the main house anyway, when they should have been safely tucked up in the annexe? It's just one of many questions whirling in the tornado of my mind.

The narration jumps to a summary of the post-mortem findings, delivered in an inappropriately upbeat tone by a local newspaper reporter who covered the story. Wishing to be spared the grisly details, I fast forward through this part before picking up the story.

> *The blaze occurred during a thunderstorm, the second severe weather event to hit the West Country in the space of a few days. Initial reports suggested it might have been caused by a lightning strike. But, as fire investigators painstakingly combed through the badly damaged building, they made a chilling discovery.*

At this point, the podcast cuts to an interview with one of the investigators who worked on the case. He describes how burn patterns indicated that the 'point of origin' was a linen cupboard on the ground floor, just off the kitchen. A lump rises in my throat when he reveals the fire was started deliberately.

Once the fire took hold, the expert explains sombrely, anyone trapped on the top floor of the building would not have stood a chance.

When I hear that, there's a stinging across the bridge of my nose, the unmistakeable sign of approaching tears. I hardly knew the Jeffreys, I never liked them or trusted them, but I can't bear to think of the suffering they went through that night. Part of me doesn't want to hear the rest, because I know I'll be in bits by the end of it. But I need to know who did this to them. With a leaden feeling in my gut, I continue listening.

> *The question now facing detectives was who killed the Jeffreys – and just as importantly, why? On the face of it, this unassuming*

couple in their mid-fifties had no enemies. Police even consid-
ered the possibility that the fire may be the result of a robbery
gone wrong. But, with no sign of forced entry, this was quickly
ruled out.

It was only after months of exhaustive legwork that a possible
motive for the killings emerged – and what detectives unearthed
tore away the village's veil of cosy respectability, exposing a dog-
eat-dog world where only the most ruthless survive.

As the narration segues into a dramatic orchestral arrangement, I find myself in a state of shocked disbelief. Are they really talking about sleepy little Saltwater? This can't be the same place where Charles and I spent those five miserable days in February. And yet, I *know* it is.

With its pretty harbour and golden sands, Saltwater is a pop-
ular destination for visitors from all over the world – its appeal
boosted in recent years by a number of high-profile TV dramas
that have been filmed along the same stretch of coastline.

For a village with a population of less than a thousand,
Saltwater boasts a surprisingly large number of guest houses.
In such a crowded marketplace, one would expect prices to be
fiercely competitive. And yet strangely, until the Jeffreys opened
the doors of The Anchorage, there wasn't a single budget option
in sight.

I'm starting to get impatient. I wish the narrator would skip the background stuff and cut to the chase. At a loss to see what all this has to do with the Jeffreys, I fast-forward a couple of minutes.

… what Detective Inspector Nick Gibson had discovered was
that almost every hotelier in the village was part of a price-fixing

cartel. It should be pointed out that the consequences of break-
ing UK competition law are severe. Business owners can be
fined as much as ten per cent of their turnover and banned
from operating for up to fifteen years. In the most serious cases,
individuals can even go to prison.

For many years, the cartel's illegal activities ensured that
prices for bed and breakfast accommodation in Saltwater re-
mained artificially high, especially during the peak summer
months.

But then, in the spring of 2006, the Jeffreys tore up the
rulebook. Seemingly unaware of the cartel's existence, they set
about undercutting their competitors, initially with a great deal
of success.

Furious to see the new arrivals enjoying an influx of visitors,
the members of the cartel were intent on revenge. With a wom-
an called Kirsten Masters as their ringleader, they orchestrated
a vicious and sustained campaign, designed to drive the Jeffreys
out of business.

At this, my whole body stiffens. *Kirsten.* Quite an unusual name.
But even with a population of less than a thousand, it is possible
there might be two Kirstens living in Saltwater. *Isn't it?*

They sent anonymous threatening letters to the Jeffreys, made
fake bookings and even, on one occasion, posted live cockroaches
through a cat flap in The Anchorage's back door, hoping to
cause an infestation.

In a bid to scupper the guests' chances of a good night's sleep,
they also created various noise nuisances. These included play-
ing loud music through a tannoy and riding a noisy motorbike
up and down outside the property.

A member of the cartel, who came forward only after police
offered him immunity from prosecution on price-fixing charges,

revealed that as time went on, Kirsten Masters' behaviour be-
came increasingly concerning.

On one occasion, she intercepted The Anchorage's vege-
table delivery, replacing a box of chestnut mushrooms with
a poisonous variety that she had picked herself. After the
mushrooms were unwittingly served as part of a cooked
breakfast, six guests became ill, two of whom required hos-
pital treatment.

Several months later, she slashed an elderly guest's car tyres.
Unaware of the damage, the guest drove off and promptly lost
control of his vehicle, crashing into a wall not far from the prop-
erty. Fortunately, he didn't sustain any serious injuries, but the
writing was on the wall for anyone who cared to look: Kirsten
Masters was dangerous.

This is almost too much to take in. I've never heard anything
like it. Such hatred; such deception. How must the Jeffreys have
felt, being victimised in this way? I'm amazed they had the
strength to keep on going. So much of their strange behaviour
is starting to make sense. Pamela's awkwardness, her coldness
towards me. The way Michael always seemed to be carrying the
weight of the world on his shoulders.

In the face of such attacks, The Anchorage's popularity began
to wane, its hitherto excellent reputation tarnished by a string
of critical online reviews.

It's clear from conversations they had with family members
at the time that Michael and Pamela Jeffrey suspected they
were being deliberately targeted. However, without sufficient
proof – or any indication of who was behind the attacks – they
were reluctant to go to the police.

Speaking exclusively to When Death Comes Calling, Mi-
chael's brother, David Jeffrey, suggested that the couple were

also keen not to sour relations with the community by pointing the finger of blame.

The sabotage campaign only came to an end in 2009, with the sudden death of the Jeffreys' fourteen-year-old daughter Grace, who tragically drowned at sea. At this juncture, it's believed cartel members unanimously decided to halt their activities, believing the couple had already suffered enough.

My finger hits the Pause button so violently that my phone drops to the floor, jerking out my earbuds in the process.

Grace.

The Jeffreys had a *daughter*. With the same name as me. How can that be when Michael told me they didn't have any children? I suppose, though, if she was dead, he was telling the truth.

How horrendous it must be to lose your child. I can't help being reminded of The Anchorage's original owner, John Murrish, who found himself in the same heart-breaking position. Three young people, all onetime occupants of the same house, all drowned; a macabre coincidence.

Struggling to keep a lid on the swelling tide of emotion inside me, I tap Play.

The Jeffreys worked hard to rebuild their business, while trying to come to terms with the loss of their only child. They launched a new website and staged an open day in a bid to attract new customers, as well as restore goodwill among the community.

Meanwhile, in the wake of an acrimonious divorce, Kirsten Masters had opened a second business, The Pink Ribbon gift shop, in Saltwater's high street. By 2018, however, she was struggling financially and was forced to lay off a number of staff at her six-bedroom luxury guest house.

Kirsten. The Pink Ribbon. It is the same person after all.

The following year, Masters' guest house was repossessed, an event that seems to have reignited her animosity towards the Jeffreys, who had somehow managed to keep The Anchorage afloat. She became obsessed with the couple and made up her mind not just to ruin their business, but also their entire lives.

In a course of action that almost defies belief, Kirsten Masters set out to convince the Jeffreys' guests that The Anchorage was haunted. During police interviews, she admitted that she had staged supernatural happenings on numerous occasions, in an attempt to scare guests away and encourage them to post negative reviews.

Her bizarre acts included playing sinister audio recordings, defacing photographs, destroying guests' personal property and writing alarming comments in the guest book. On several occasions, she even placed macabre items – such as dead birds and threatening notes – in guests' rooms. Many of these incidents occurred at night, when the owners had retired to their living accommodation, housed in a separate annexe at the rear of the main building.

Critical to the success of her plan was the set of master keys she had stolen during The Anchorage's open day, meaning she was now able to enter and leave both the guest house, and the annexe, at will.

The notion of a spoof haunting will no doubt be perceived as laughable by some, but it was certainly a traumatic experience for those who experienced it first-hand. Some of the guests targeted by Masters were so disturbed by what they experienced that they fled in the middle of the night, often leaving belongings behind in their haste to get away.

By this stage, my head is spinning. All those things that happened to me in the house, all the perplexing events I took as evidence of some psychic force. It was make-believe, pure pantomime, nothing more than smoke and mirrors.

I have a feeling of abrupt drainage, as if a plug has been pulled on the pool of some inner world. I realise with a painful fibrillation of the heart how much I wanted it to be real. It certainly felt real in the moment. But now I know it wasn't. I was duped. Cheated. And the fact that I was not the only one is scant comfort.

But, as she entered the property in the early hours of February the twenty-first, Masters' behaviour took a deadly turn. Her initial intention was to terrorise two guests, thought to have been staying in a third-floor room. Due to a power outage affecting the entire village, the property lay in almost total darkness.

At some point, Michael Jeffrey left the annexe and entered the main house via the back door. His reasons for doing so are unclear, but an inspection hatch in the kitchen, which concealed the main fuse box, had been left open. This led police to suspect the hotelier had been attempting to restore power to the property. It's thought he heard a suspicious noise and, armed only with a torch, went upstairs to investigate.

Startled by Michael Jeffrey's appearance on the third-floor landing, Kirsten Masters lashed out with the nearest object to hand – a decorative metal sculpture of a heron, its steel beak carving a fifteen-centimetre gash in the defenceless hotelier's head.

As her victim lay bleeding and unconscious on the floor, Masters made her way back downstairs – but she wasn't finished yet. In an act that was described in court by the prosecuting barrister as 'depraved and utterly senseless', she set fire to the ground-floor linen cupboard before making her escape.

It's impossible to know what happened next, but it's likely that when Michael Jeffrey failed to return, his wife went to look for him. Alarmed to find the linen cupboard on fire, Pamela Jeffrey apparently ran upstairs in an attempt to save her husband's life. But, as the flames took hold, the couple found themselves trapped.

A shudder moves through me and I gulp, as tears push themselves out of my eyes, choking my throat.

Following an anonymous tip-off to police, Kirsten Masters was quickly arrested. Officers searching her home found the metal heron concealed inside a chest freezer. DNA analysis revealed it had been used to assault Michael Jeffrey.

Masters was also in possession of a diary, belonging to Pamela Jeffrey, which she had stolen from the annexe several months earlier. In a series of intimate entries, Pamela expressed her mounting anxieties about the villagers' behaviour and the strain that their relentless bullying was placing on her marriage.

Chillingly, the diary suggests Pamela had a premonition that the villagers' harassment campaign would end in tragedy. In one of her entries she even alluded to the Ten Plagues of Egypt from the Bible – specifically 'the death of my firstborn'. Little did she know that, within the space of a few years, her entire family would be dead.

The last diary entry came the day after Grace Jeffrey's body was recovered from the sea off Saltwater, several hours after she had left her home for reasons unknown. In it, Pamela revealed her conviction that the cartel may have had a hand in the death of her daughter – although police insisted she had not brought her concerns to them at the time. Several subsequent pages of the diary had been torn out, although it was never established who was responsible for this.

After the diary entries were aired at the trial, the Jeffreys' relatives called on police to look again at the circumstances surrounding Grace's drowning. Fearing a public backlash, Devon and Cornwall Police agreed to review the case file. However, they later declared themselves satisfied that the teenager's death was nothing more than a tragic accident.

At her trial, Kirsten Masters insisted she had not been responsible for the fire, pleading guilty only to charges of theft, breaking and entering and inflicting grievous bodily harm. Jurors were not convinced, however, and it took them less than eight hours to find her guilty on two counts of murder.

As he sentenced her to life in prison, with a minimum term of twenty-eight years, the judge described the businesswoman as 'a wicked individual with no moral compass'. Family members in the public gallery stood up and applauded as she was led from the dock, with one shouting: 'I hope you burn in hell.'

With Kirsten Masters locked up for the foreseeable future, only one mystery remains – the identity of the two guests believed to have been staying at The Anchorage in the days leading up to the tragedy. Fire investigators found no trace of their bodies – or their belongings – indicating that they had vacated the property before the fire started.

Believing these individuals might be able to provide vital information, police tried in vain to trace them. They studied the charred remains of The Anchorage's guest book in a desperate search for clues and even launched a campaign in the media, appealing for the mystery witnesses to come forward. But all their efforts came to nothing.

If those guests are listening to this podcast now, they should be congratulating themselves on a very lucky escape.

Sadly, The Anchorage – a landmark in Saltwater for nearly a hundred and fifty years – sustained serious damage in the fire and is scheduled for demolition later this year. Soon there will be nothing left of it, but the memory of what is surely one of the darkest chapters in the village's history.

As the closing credits begin, I collapse onto the sofa, feeling slightly dizzy, as if I've turned my head too fast. The last few pieces are falling into place. The 'Grace' folder on the Jeffreys' laptop: my assumption had been wrong, it was nothing to do with me, and those files almost certainly contained precious mementoes of their daughter's brief life. The words under my pillow in Pamela's handwriting: clearly ripped from her journal and callously repurposed ... just one more attempt by Kirsten to mess with my mind.

Remembering those five days in February, I have a grudging admiration for the energy and imagination my persecutor put into her undertakings. All those tiny little details that made it seem so real. I wonder how many people in the village knew – or at least suspected – what she was up to, but did nothing. And now two innocent people have paid with their lives. The narrator was right. Charles and I *were* lucky. A few more minutes and we would have been dead too.

40

GRACE

How could I have been so gullible? I thought she was our guardian angel. Riding to the rescue in her silver Volvo. Offering us refuge from the storm. Giving us hot cups of tea and towels to dry our wet hair. How kind, how *community-spirited*, I thought.

If I'd known then that Kirsten Masters was a psychopath, I would never have got into her car.

I can't believe how normal she seemed when she picked us up, fresh from her attack. She was calm, quite charming, in fact – but then psychopaths have that ability, don't they?

Did she really have an early morning delivery at the shop, I wonder? Or did she come looking for us, worried that before we absconded from the guest house, Charles and I might have seen something that could incriminate her?

Of course, I did see something – the precise moment she assaulted Michael with the sculpture – but at the time I didn't understand its significance, too brainwashed by what had gone before. Too scared for my life. If I'd realised for one second what was really going on in the corridor outside our room, I would have done whatever it took to protect Michael. But I left him there to die. At the thought, the realisation, of the part I played in this, something snarls up in my throat, hard-edged and acrid.

Looking back, the shop owner was fishing for information when she quizzed us about what had driven us from the guest house that night. Charles tried to play it down, but I was more forthcoming. After all, I reasoned naively, hadn't Kirsten tried to warn us about The Anchorage the day Charles bought the necklace? I informed her, without a hint of self-consciousness, that the guest house was haunted and that Pamela Jeffrey was a warped and unfathomable individual who seemed to have it in for me.

She must have felt so smug, so self-righteous when she heard that, but she masked it well. 'You two did the right thing,' she reassured us. 'Who knows what might have happened if you hadn't left when you did.' With the benefit of hindsight, her words have taken on a disturbing new meaning.

Having apparently satisfied herself that we posed no threat, she left us alone in the shop, dismissing Charles's offer to help her in the stockroom, in anticipation of her impending delivery. 'You two stay here and relax,' she said. 'And when you're ready to make a move, I'll give you a lift to the station.'

It wasn't until we were safely on the train that Charles and I had a chance to properly discuss the night's dramatic events. In the wake of his admissions about Turkey, it felt as if my feelings for him had changed. But I was grateful he had rescued me from the guest house and, in that moment, he was all I had.

He told me he'd been unable to sleep, and had gone outside to observe the storm at close quarters, just the way he used to when he was a boy. After slipping on boots and a waterproof jacket over his pyjamas, he went to the bandstand on top of the bluff. He was out there for nearly an hour he reckoned, watching the lightning, listening to the roar of the waves. It was strangely peaceful, he said, even with all that going on around him. It must have been during this absence that first Kirsten – and then Michael – entered the guest house.

I suppose there's a chance things might have worked out differently if Charles had stayed in bed, but there's no point dwelling on that now.

Returning to The Anchorage, he saw that the light in the hall had gone out and realised there'd been a power cut. As he removed his coat and boots in the pitch darkness, he heard a loud thud overhead, as if a heavy object had fallen over. Worried I might have fainted again, he came to find me, his concern growing when he heard voices that he didn't recognise. There was something else too: a presence that he described as a cool hand caressing the back of his neck; I got the shivers when he told me that. He said it was one of a handful of times in his life he'd felt genuinely scared. When he spotted my shadowy outline in the doorway of our room, his immediate impulse was to get me out of there – otherwise, he feared something very bad was going to happen.

When I heard that, I was pleased. *Vindicated.* At last, Charles had accepted what I had known all along: that there were unnatural forces at large in the guest house. And if a diehard sceptic like him was convinced The Anchorage was haunted, then it *must* be true, I told myself.

I shared my own experiences with him – the doll's eye, and the threatening message under my pillow, as well as the figure I'd seen in the corridor, with the blade raised above its head. He was shocked – but not as shocked as when I told him about the folder bearing my name that I'd found on the Jeffreys' computer. I remember his jaw hitting the floor in complete disbelief.

'But that's insane,' he said. 'The Jeffreys didn't even know you existed until we arrived on their doorstep.'

All I could do was shrug. 'I don't understand it either,' I told him. Little did I know that the truth about those encrypted files was deceptively simple.

I knew I had to ask about his visit to the Jeffreys' annexe. Nothing would make sense until he told me the truth. He was surprised I knew about it, but despite being caught unawares he had a ready explanation. It seemed he'd bumped into Pamela in the high street, after I'd banished him from the guest house. She asked him to take a look at some drawings they'd had done for the holiday let they wanted to build in the back garden – eager, it seems, for his professional opinion.

It was a plausible enough scenario – but why, I asked Charles, had he failed to tell me sooner. His response? He didn't think I'd approve of him spending time with them, especially as he was already in the doghouse. He turned the question back on me: 'If you knew I'd been to the annexe, why didn't you ask me about it?' I didn't have an answer.

We continued talking for the whole train journey, until at last we had no more to say, like a storm that blows itself out. And when we were done, Charles placed a hand beneath my chin and raised my face until our eyes met.

'I want you to know that you are the most important thing in my life and you have been ever since the day I met you,' he said. 'I know I can be thoughtless at times, but please believe me when I say that I love you and I will do anything in my power to protect you and keep you safe.'

It felt good to hear him say those words and, even though a splinter of doubt remained in my mind, I leaned forward and kissed him on the mouth. Perhaps I should have given him a harder time, but I didn't. He's my husband and if I don't trust him, then what do we have left?

The podcast's revelations have put a whole new light on our time in Saltwater, and I know I need to speak to Charles. But at the same time, I dread telling him that the Jeffreys are dead. He was fond of them both and I know he'll be devastated.

At first, he struggles to take the news in, as well as the unedifying truth about Kirsten. In the end, I sit him down and play the entire podcast from beginning to end. Only then can he appreciate the full enormity of what happened. Like me, he now understands that there were no ghosts living at The Anchorage, only two desperate people whose lives had been destroyed not once, but twice.

'Losing a child must have had such a profound effect on Michael and Pamela,' I say, as I tuck my feet up on the sofa and lean into Charles. 'I wish you'd told me about Grace. If I knew what they'd been through, I wouldn't have been so hard on them.'

'I had no idea,' he says.

'That their daughter had died?'

'That she even existed.'

I turn my head, staring at him in surprise. 'But you would have been around about the same age as Grace. You must have met her when you were a boy.'

Ridges appear in his forehead. 'No, if we'd met, I'm sure I would have remembered it. It's quite possible she never came in to the main house and stayed in the annexe the whole time. Or perhaps she was sent away to relatives, or some sort of summer camp during the holiday season. Michael and Pamela were always rushed off their feet; it makes sense that they wouldn't want the added stress of looking after a kid.'

I rest my head on his shoulder. 'It makes me feel funny, knowing she was called Grace too – almost as if we're connected in some psychic way.'

Charles gives an odd, rueful little laugh. 'Yeah, weird, huh?'

'Do you think that was her in the photo?'

He yawns loudly. 'What photo?'

'The one in the wall montage, just outside our bathroom. There was a picture of a couple with a little girl. She had her face scratched out; I thought some kid must have done it for a laugh, but I guess it was Kirsten.'

'I guess so.'

We sit in silence for a few moments. I chew my thumbnail, thinking hard. 'Should we contact the police?'

I feel his shoulders twitch, a quick gesture of exasperation.

'Why would we do that?' he says.

'To let them know we're the two guests they were pulling out all the stops to find. I'm sure they'd appreciate us getting in touch.'

'I really don't think that's necessary,' he says brusquely. 'They managed to crack the case without us, didn't they? Kirsten's in prison now. She can't hurt anyone else.'

'I suppose so ...'

He gently extracts his shoulder from under my head and stands up. His face is smooth and unconcerned. 'Right then, I'll get the barbecue going, shall I?'

He disappears through the patio doors and I'm left alone with my flyaway thoughts.

41

CHARLES

From the moment I fell in love with Grace, I've been waiting for the truth to be cracked open and all the hundreds of tiny lies I've told to come wriggling out, like maggots feeding on a rotting corpse.

I was convinced our unplanned holiday in Saltwater would be the undoing of me, stirring the silt of my past and choking my future. But amazingly, my secret remains intact.

I returned to The Anchorage with the best of intentions. I thought it was the right thing to do – but perhaps, with the benefit of hindsight, I was being too optimistic. I'm truly sorry the situation worked out the way it did and it would be very easy for anyone not in possession of the full facts to point the finger at *me*. After all, I had the opportunity, if not the motive.

I would like to state for the record that I did not kill Pamela and Michael Jeffrey.

But I did kill their daughter.

Whenever I try to visualise Grace Jeffrey, I find that I can't quite pin her down. I can see the blue of her eyes, the fullness of her lips, the galaxy of freckles on the bridge of her nose, but the image is vague and shifting, as if I'm watching her underwater.

The first year my family came to Saltwater, I barely noticed her. Although she was only ten months younger than me, she was small for her age and seemed quite immature. We were never formally introduced, but somehow I knew her name and I knew that she was the Jeffreys' daughter.

I'd see her at breakfast, setting out the miniature pots of jam or helping Pamela collect the dirty plates after a table had been vacated. I think we probably smiled at each once or twice, but I don't recall us actually speaking.

The following year when we visited, Grace had the chicken pox. For obvious reasons, she wasn't allowed to mix with the paying guests and I only saw her once during our two-week stay. My sister and I spotted her through the window of our first-floor room, playing with her kitten in The Anchorage's back garden. She looked awful, her face and arms covered in livid blisters. I remember laughing when Ally referred to her as 'the leper'. Thinking about that now makes me cringe.

It was my third and final summer in Saltwater that Grace and I got to know each other properly. I hardly recognised her at first. She'd just turned fourteen and she'd grown at least a foot since the last time I'd seen her. Her limbs were long and tanned and her dirty dirty-blonde hair hung in loose, surfer-girl waves around her pointed face. She wasn't classically beautiful, but she was striking in her own way and she had a floating, sashaying style of walking that I found utterly mesmerising.

Now that Grace was older, she had been entrusted with wait-ressing duties and that first morning, we made lingering eye contact across the dining room. On the second morning, I staged a napkin-dropping incident. We both bent down to pick it up at the same time, exactly as I had planned. As my hand brushed against hers, every nerve in my body seemed to throb with electricity.

Mid-morning on day three, I saw her through the sitting-room window, emerging from the side gate that led to the annexe. It was a beautiful sunny day and she was wearing frayed denim shorts and a vest top, a pair of white-framed sunglasses perched on top of her head. The towel peeking from the top of her striped shoulder bag suggested she was heading to the beach.

I told my mother I was going out for a stroll and set off after Grace, following at a discreet distance as she made her way across the bluff and down the stone steps to the beach. It was such an instinctive thing that I didn't know I was making a conscious decision, let alone what I was setting in motion.

With a mounting sense of excitement, I watched as she spread her towel on the sand, then removed her vest top and shorts to reveal a hot pink bikini.

I'd had some experience with the opposite sex, but Grace seemed so different to the pasty-skinned girls at school, so exotic and untouchable. It was at least half an hour before I eventually plucked up the courage to approach her. After falling out with Jamie the previous year, I'd been wondering how I was going to amuse myself – and now, it seemed, I had my answer.

'Hey,' I said, smiling down at her. 'It's Grace, isn't it?'

She looked up from the magazine she was reading and smiled a slow, lazy, radiant smile that made me go weak at the knees.

We spent almost the entire day together on the beach. I don't remember what we talked about – the usual teenage stuff, I expect – school, music, our favourite box sets. I felt a quiver of unease when Grace let slip that she and Jamie were acquaintances, but after some gentle probing, it turned out he hadn't even mentioned me. I was relieved – but at the same time, rather hurt.

Grace was smart and spiky and funny and I liked her a lot. By the time I offered to go to the kiosk and buy some chips and a drink for our lunch, I was smitten.

We agreed to meet at the beach the next day – and the next, and the day after that. Thankfully, I had reached an age where my parents were happy to let me off the leash. I didn't want to rush things with Grace, but I was acutely aware that our time together was limited. As I leaned forward to kiss her at the end of our second day together, I wasn't entirely sure how she'd react. I needn't have worried. She kissed me right back, her mouth soft and hungry, her hand on the back of my neck, drawing me closer. Never would I have imagined that less than a fortnight later, she would be dead.

Right from the start, Grace impressed on me the need to keep our romance under wraps. Her parents thought she was too young to be dating and Grace was worried she'd be grounded if they found out about us.

Consequently, we were very careful to make sure we were never seen together and I told no one about our relationship, not even Ally. I can't deny that all the sneaking around added an extra air of excitement to our activities and when I wasn't with Grace, I walked around in a daze, unable to believe my good fortune.

While I was desperately fond of her – as she clearly was of me – I was riddled with the typical teenage insecurities. As the date of my family's departure drew ever nearer, I somehow convinced myself that once I returned home, Grace's interest in me would quickly wane. With the twisted reasoning that passed for logic in my undeveloped brain, I decided that the only way to save myself from the pain of being dumped was to dump her first. I think a large part of me hoped that when I broke the news, Grace would beg me to reconsider and pledge to keep our relationship alive by any means necessary, thus providing me with a much-needed ego boost. But, as I was about to learn in the most painful way imaginable, real life rarely conforms to our fantasies.

I recount the next part of this saga now only reluctantly and without hope of forgiveness, because nothing should be omitted.

Though I have braced myself time and time again to go back over it, it still cuts me like a knife.

The last day of my holiday was squally and generally quite unpleasant. My family was scheduled to set off from Saltwater at noon and I had arranged to meet Grace in the bus shelter at the end of the road an hour or so beforehand. We hadn't really talked about what would happen when I returned home, but I don't think Grace was anticipating the grenade I was about to toss in her direction.

I wish that morning the clouds had arranged themselves in the sky, spelling out a warning in big marshmallowy letters that I couldn't fail to heed. But they didn't, and so our fates were sealed.

As I approached the bus shelter, my feelings were a curious mix of the heady excitement of being the one holding all the power, combined with the more sober consciousness that I was about to deliberately hurt someone who I cared about very much.

The minute the words were out of my mouth, I wondered if I'd made the right decision. Grace gazed dumbly at me for a few seconds, as if she didn't trust herself to speak. The light went out of her eyes and her shoulders sagged.

'We can still stay in touch,' I told her breezily. 'But I'm too young to be tied down, I want to be free to see other people.' I felt so grown up, saying those words. So important.

She nodded once, then closed her eyes, as if the sight of me was more than she could bear. I took a step forward, intending to give her a farewell hug, but she recoiled, pushing me away with both hands.

'Don't touch me!' she shrieked, as she fled from the shelter, heading back in the direction of The Anchorage.

I called out after her, begging her to stop so we could talk about it, but the wind caught my words, carrying them off in the opposite direction. I followed her as she ran not back to the house, as I had anticipated, but straight across the bluff, towards the stone steps.

'Please come back,' I shouted. 'I don't want to hurt you; I just want a chance to explain.'

By the time I got to the edge of the bluff, Grace was already halfway down. It had been raining on and off all morning and seeing how wet the steps were, I made the decision not to follow her, worried that if I continued my pursuit, she might lose her concentration and slip.

From where I stood, I had a bird's-eye view of the coastline below. The tide was in, so the beach had all but disappeared and due to the shitty weather, the promenade was deserted. The waves were pretty big, too gnarly even for the surfers to be out, and they were slamming against the sea wall, sending plumes of spray shooting into the air.

I thought that once she reached the bottom of the bluff, Grace would turn right, towards the high street. I didn't expect to see her climb on top of the sea wall and make off in the opposite direction. I had no idea where she was headed; the only thing that lay over there was the lifeboat station.

I checked my watch: eleven-thirty. I was aware I ought to be getting back so I could help my father load up the car with our luggage. I turned over my shoulder to see if there was any sign of him outside The Anchorage, but there wasn't.

I took my eyes off Grace for a matter of seconds, but when I turned back she wasn't there any more. Surprised, I scanned the length of the sea wall, left and right, but there was no sign of her. I assumed she'd had a change of heart and had now turned back, heading towards the high street. It was impossible to know for sure however, as the walkway that led into the village hugged the bottom of the cliff and wasn't visible from my vantage point. I lingered for another minute or so and then, deciding there was nothing to be gained from standing out there in the cold, I made my way back to the guest house.

It was several weeks before I found out what had happened to Grace. Up until then, I hadn't attempted to contact her. I was embarrassed and I thought she'd still be angry with me. But then one evening, alone in my bedroom, I decided on impulse to check her Facebook.

When I saw the initial post, from one of her friends, declaring 'I'll miss you so much and I hope you're happy, wherever you are', I thought the Jeffreys must have moved away from Saltwater. But as I scrolled down and read the dozens of other messages and tributes, their nauseating implication was clear. Still hoping it was some sort of sick joke, I dashed to the bathroom, where I emptied the contents of my stomach into the toilet bowl.

A short time later, I was back at my laptop and frantically googling Grace's name. My heart fractured when I found out it was true: Grace was dead, her body recovered from the open sea just hours after I had last seen her. No one knew how she came to be in the water, but with a post-mortem ruling out any suggestion of foul play, her death was ruled a tragic accident.

It didn't take too much effort on my part to piece together the likely sequence of events. I'd seen how big the waves were and the way they were breaking over the sea wall; I should have called out a warning to her.

With a rush of revulsion that almost sent me running back to the bathroom, I realised that the responsibility for Grace Jeffrey's demise lay squarely with me; that my own clumsy actions had, quite literally, driven her to her death.

I never shared my secret with anyone. Instead, I swallowed it down, where it sat like a lump of clay in my stomach. For the longest time, I kept hoping I'd wake up in the morning and find that time had folded and I'd missed a few weeks or months, that I'd be given a choice of alternative endings and be able to select the one that would save Grace.

A kind of emotional hypothermia set in. I became sullen and withdrawn; my schoolwork suffered and I lost my appetite. I spent hours locked in my bedroom, playing computer games, watching porn, smoking weed, anything to take my mind off the agony of being me. I dated one girl after another, a never-ending carousel of meaningless relationships. But there wasn't enough pornography, or drugs, or girls in all the world to stop the truth revolving in my mind. There could never, never be any peace or silence while the voice in my head repeated on a loop: it's *your* fault; *you* killed her.

As time went on, the ache lessened somewhat, but I never felt true happiness or contentment. It was like having a tapeworm writhing in my gut, a lithe and greedy parasite, gobbling any goodness I might hope to own.

But then I met the other Grace and everything changed, literally overnight. The first time she told me she loved me, it was as if the putrid slick of filth that had clung to me for years had been rinsed away and I emerged all clean and sweet-smelling and new.

It was, of course, the bitterest of ironies that the two women who had such a huge impact on my life should share the same name. In the beginning, I dismissed it as mere coincidence, but then one day I found myself at the top of another cliff in another country, while another woman who meant the world to me fought for her life. Seriously ... what are the chances?

As I stared down at my wife-to-be, her beautiful body twisted and broken, I had a terrifying flashback and in an instant, I was right back there in Saltwater. I had failed Grace Jeffrey miserably on that occasion but here, at last, was a chance to redeem myself. At least that was the theory.

Yet again, I fucked it up bigtime. The whole thing was a cat-alogue of errors: I didn't call for help immediately, my phone battery was flat, I couldn't run fast enough. Thank God someone else rose to the occasion that day – and for that, I will be eternally grateful.

Afterwards, I was so terrified I'd lose Grace if she knew how I'd fallen short that I took advantage of the paramedic's confu-sion and let her believe it was me who'd saved her life. Then, just to seal the deal, I asked her to marry me. Having exchanged our vows, I thought I would finally be able to move forward – but when our train got stuck in Saltwater, the past elbowed its way back in, shoving everything else aside and standing there with its chest puffed out, demanding my attention.

Perhaps it was a mistake to take Grace to The Anchorage, but there was nowhere else to go – and anyway, I was anxious to see Michael and Pamela, to reassure myself that they too had been able to move on with their lives. Of course they hadn't; their daughter's death had changed them in ways I could never have imagined. Their business had clearly suffered too. I assumed this was simply down to neglect – but now I know that other factors were at play.

I enjoyed being back in Saltwater, in the sort of way a penitent enjoys self-flagellating. Reminders of Grace were everywhere I went and it seemed that each day a fresh wound opened up. I tried to focus on my wife's needs, but Grace Jeffrey kept seeping into the fabric of the thought, like blood through a bandage. She was always there, always the centre of attention. *Look at me. Look at me.*

Surprisingly, the most painful moment came not as I stood on top of the bluff again or revisited the bus shelter, but when I saw Grace's face scratched out in that childhood photo. At the time, I thought Pamela must have done it in a moment of sheer anguish, when the sight of her daughter's smiling face was more than she could bear. As I stared at the faceless little girl, it really hit me – the start of that black cloud descending, the weight of memories that are too dangerous to be faced pressing down on me.

I kept waiting for the Jeffreys to mention their daughter, but they never did; Michael even told Grace they didn't have any children. But then, on the last day of our stay, I ran into Pamela in the high street. She was coming out of the churchyard where, she revealed without any prompting whatsoever, she had been laying flowers at her daughter's grave. *Accidentally drowned*, she said, her face sagging with the weight of the words.

I told her I remembered Grace and feigned surprise at the news of her death, all the while feeling like a complete and utter bastard. As we walked back to The Anchorage together, Pamela talked almost non-stop about her daughter – about what a wonderful, loving person she'd been and how much she missed her. I kept quiet and just let her talk; if I'd tried to speak, I think I would have fallen apart.

Back at the guest house, Pamela invited me into the annexe for a cup of tea. She said she wanted to show me the plans for their building project, but I think it was just an excuse. Once inside, all she wanted to do was talk about Grace, like it was some sort of therapy. She even got out some old photos to show me, as well as a newspaper cutting of the funeral (Pamela was very proud of the fact that more than two hundred people attended). Meanwhile, Michael sat there, wordlessly, a look of torment collected on his face, like something dense and murky at the bottom of a drain.

It did occur to me that the Jeffreys might have lured me into their home under false pretences. That somehow they had cottoned on to the fact that I was the last person to see their daughter alive – and now, not unreasonably, they wanted answers. As we chatted about Grace, I felt like a fisherman, reeling in a huge fish on a delicate line, my muscles tense with the effort of trying not to jerk or show the strain. But, if they did have any suspicions about the part I had played in Grace's death, they weren't letting on.

I managed to hold it together while I was in the annexe, but as soon as I got outside, I broke down. I realised then that for the sake of my own mental health, I had to leave The Anchorage and all the painful memories behind. There was no doubt in my mind that if I stayed in Saltwater another day, all the festering cankers I'd kept so well hidden inside me would erupt. And then everyone would see the person I really was.

It took ten minutes of pacing up and down the street until I had composed myself sufficiently to return to my wife. Back at the guest house, as I faced her cross-examination, the lies oozed out of me like toxins.

I was forced to lie again, the other day, when Grace told me about the podcast. The truth is I already knew about the fire at The Anchorage; details of Kirsten's court case appeared on one of the newsfeeds I subscribe to. I was worried Grace would react badly if I told her, so I kept it to myself. She's come a long way since her accident and I thought that learning of the Jeffreys' deaths and our own narrow escape would set her back. She hides it well, but I know her insecurities are still there, like an underground ants' nest, waiting for something to disturb them.

In the event, she took the news surprisingly calmly; she must be tougher than I thought.

Then she asked about Grace Jeffrey. I said I didn't remember her because it's better that my wife never knows the truth. Better for her, and certainly better for me. I know she finds it odd that I don't talk much about my teenage years, but I don't need her to love the boy I was then – and I certainly wouldn't ask her to forgive him. *I* never have. Why should she? I only need her to love me now.

I have never believed in an afterlife. I've always thought that once you died, that was it: game over. But I have recently been forced to accept that some things cannot be rationalised.

I now know, beyond a shadow of a doubt, that part of Grace Jeffrey remains at The Anchorage. Hearing her voice again, after all these years, rocked me to my core. But the biggest shock of all was that she spoke to me with such tenderness. It offers me a crumb of hope that, if she has been able to forgive me, I will one day be able to forgive myself.

42

GRACE

I can't stop thinking about Grace Jeffrey. Perhaps it's just because we share a name – but it feels as if it's more than that.

Whenever I've got a few minutes, I often find myself scouring the internet, hunting for clues about her life – and death.

There isn't a huge amount. A school friend's touching tribute on a memorial website. A Facebook page that's frozen in time. It shows a girl with a thoughtful expression and dark-blonde hair, who loved bodyboarding and her pet cat.

Even more intriguing are the local newspaper reports from the time of her death. They reveal that Grace left her home on a blustery morning at the end of August without telling anyone where she was going. Her parents had only just reported her missing when the crew of a fishing vessel spotted her fully clothed body in the sea, about half a mile off the coast of Saltwater.

Despite being a strong swimmer, she had drowned – probably within minutes of entering the water. There were no injuries on her body, nor were there any signs of a struggle. The coroner recorded a verdict of death by misadventure. Case closed.

But just now, my googling yielded something new: a lengthy interview with Pamela's niece, a woman called Bethany Hall. It was published soon after the trial, in one of those women's weeklies that merge celebrity gossip with 'shocking' real-life stories.

The article reveals that shortly before her death, Pamela told her niece that she still felt Grace's presence at The Anchorage. This, Bethany claimed, was the main reason the Jeffreys were reluctant to sell the guest house, even though the business was foundering. Pamela also confided that she regularly talked to Grace – and that sometimes her daughter responded.

At the time, Bethany assumed that Pamela, in the depths of her grief, had simply imagined hearing her daughter's voice. However, the article revealed a small but intriguing detail, not disclosed in the podcast. During their search of Kirsten Masters' home, the police recovered a DVD, containing home video footage of Grace. Like Pamela's diary, it had been stolen from the annexe. Although Kirsten never admitted it, Bethany's strong belief is that she used audio from the footage to taunt her aunt, determined to drive the knife in as deep as she could. Pamela *had* heard Grace's voice – but sadly, it was nothing more than a recording, a memory, lost in the past.

Suddenly, my throat closes up and I find that I can't see properly; the tears in my eyes are making the room shimmer. I realise then that I can't keep doing this. I feel like a voyeur, feeding on the misery of others. Charles is right: I need to stop obsessing over the Jeffreys and focus on my own life.

I close the lid of my laptop and push it away. But something is niggling me, casting a shadow over the far corners of my mind. For a second, I can't think what it is. Then I remember. In the article, Bethany said that Grace always spent the summer holidays helping her mother in the guest house. And yet Charles insisted he'd never met her.

Something rises darkly inside me, a violent reverberation of unease. I push it back down, clenching my fists with the effort.

43

GRACE

A house as old as this must have seen so many amazing things over the years: epic parties, fairy-tale Christmases, declarations of undying love. It's been standing tall and proud up here on the bluff for so long now that I really thought it would be around forever. It breaks my heart to see the bulldozers moving in.

I must admit the house scared me shitless the first time I saw it. It was so creepy that the second I walked through the front door, I wanted to turn around and run straight back out again. But, as anyone who has ever lived here will tell you, this place has a sneaky habit of attaching itself to your soul. I have learned to adore its creaking floorboards and find beauty in its shadowy corners. It's hard to imagine living anywhere else, even after everything that's happened. Unfortunately, I don't have a choice: by this time tomorrow, The Anchorage will cease to exist.

It was horrible watching my parents die; a thousand times worse than the worst thing I could possibly imagine. I wish I could have done more to save them, but in my current state I have limited means at my disposal. As Mum knelt on the floor, trying to wake Dad up, I screamed at her to run. I know she heard me because she answered back.

'I'm not leaving him,' she said, as she grabbed him under the arms and started dragging him towards the stairs. Sadly, she didn't get very far.

I thought that once Mum and Dad had passed over, we'd have a great big family reunion, the sort of reunion I've been dreaming about for years. But apparently it doesn't work like that; we have to find each other first. Annoyingly, I haven't made much progress so far, but I'm throwing everything at it.

I miss talking to Mum. The first time I broke through it shocked us both. I suppose it was five or six years after I drowned, but I can't be sure. Time's a pretty meaningless concept when you're dead.

Mum was upstairs, hoovering the bedrooms. I was following her from room to room, enjoying the feeling of being close to her. I used to help out a lot in the house when I was growing up, especially during the summer holidays. My favourite thing was laying the tables for breakfast. I loved setting out the mini-jams and the tiny, foil-wrapped butters and folding the napkins just so. It meant a lot to me that Mum trusted me with such important tasks and she never got cross when I did things wrong – even when I accidentally dropped a whole jug of milk in a guest's lap.

My favourite place in the whole house has always been the smallest bedroom. It's on the top floor and it's got a sloping ceiling and a great view of the sea. I've spent a lot of time up there since I died, staring out of the window, remembering all the good times.

When Mum was working alone, she usually carried out her duties in complete silence, her mouth bunched up in concentration. But for some reason, as she cleaned the smallest bedroom on that particular day, she started talking aloud to herself. And the things she was saying were the exact same things she used to say to me.

'Don't forget the corners, love; that's where the spiders like to hide,' she said in a loud, clear voice, as she hoovered the strip of carpet between the wall and the chest of drawers.

Listening to her, I got that prickling sensation you have behind your eyeballs when you're about to cry, even though crying is a physical impossibility for me these days.

The hoovering completed to her satisfaction, Mum turned her attention to the bed. 'Give it a good shake,' she said, as she grasped the bottom edge of the duvet with both hands. 'Those feathers need a nice plumping.'

Afterwards, she went over to the portrait on the wall. 'Nice and gentle with Mrs Murrish, please,' she instructed.

I watched as she wrapped a microfibre cloth around her index finger, just as she'd taught me when I was eight years old, and began running it gently around the frame's inner edge. When I saw that, a tug of pain jarred loose the very deepest part of my heart – a place so secret I never went there myself.

'Always remember, love,' Mum added, in a softer voice. 'This painting is one of the most precious things in the entire house. So precious that it has to stay here forever.'

As a single tear rolled down her cheek, I reacted without thinking and reached out to brush it away, except of course I couldn't.

'I'm here, Mum,' I said, my words light as the tiny feathers from the duvet that were still floating in the air.

I knew in an instant I'd got through. Mum looked up and slightly to the right, which was exactly where I was. Then she cried – a great howl coming up from the bottom of her stomach. She cried so long and so hard that the walls shook with it.

After that, I talked to her quite often, especially when I could see that she was a bit down. It only worked sometimes, and I found I could never get more than three or four words out. But each time she heard me, her creased face would light up and her eyes would sparkle with tears.

I tried to talk to Dad too, but it was obvious he couldn't hear me. I reckon it's because his grief was too pent up, he was too afraid to let his emotions spill over. He put on a brave face, but I knew that inside his chest, his heart lay heavy, like a stone.

Mum and Dad never got over my death and missed me every second of every hour of every day. Despite this, they threw themselves into salvaging what was left of the business after the haters had done their worst. Bookings never really recovered, but after a few years and a lot of hard work, they were at least making a profit. Then that evil bitch got her teeth into them again.

At first, I found her antics funny. She was such an amateur; I couldn't believe anyone was falling for her crass dressing-up acts. The guests clearly didn't know that ghosts can't be seen by the living, although those with heightened senses will often be aware of them. It might be a heaviness in the atmosphere, a chill on the back of the neck, or an unexplained breeze in a room where all the windows are shut. And as for those recordings of sobbing kids and sea shanties she downloaded off the internet ... what a joke.

But then, when I saw the effect she was having on the guest house, I realised it wasn't funny at all. I was absolutely furious with her – and desperately worried for my parents as the bookings began to dry up. Unfortunately, there wasn't a fucking thing I could do about it. By their last summer, Mum and Dad were barely earning enough to cover the electricity bill. That's why they were so pleased when you rocked up. Me ... less so.

Unbelievably, your wife has the same name as me. Right from the start, you were all over her, always stroking her face and grabbing her hand; it made me want to puke. I liked her, though. I could feel her energy like it was a wind she'd set loose in the room, blowing back my hair. The Masters bitch suckered her in, which was a bit disappointing, but I brushed shoulders with my namesake a couple of times in the smallest bedroom and I know she felt it.

I still don't get how you had the nerve to come back here, after all this time. What did you want? To see how much Mum and Dad had suffered in the years since my death? To rub salt in their wounds, by showing off your pretty young wife? After all, *their* daughter was never going to get married or have children or a wonderful career and a deeply satisfying social life, was she?

My poor parents, not knowing any better, welcomed you with open arms and treated you almost as if you were a member of the family. You reminded them of happier times, before the village destroyed everything about The Anchorage that was good.

I wasn't surprised you had them bending over backwards for you; even as a teenager, you could charm the birds out of the trees. Inside, you were nervous, though. I could smell your anxiety coming off your skin. I tried my best to tell Mum about you, but every time I tried to say your name, the word lodged itself in my throat, hard and square, like a piece of apple, stopping me from saying any more.

I don't know what you've told your wife about me – if you've told her anything at all. Certainly not the truth, because if she knew what a monster you were, she wouldn't come within a hundred metres of you.

I know I was only a kid, but I was so in love with you, Charlie. I wanted to shout it from the cliff tops, but you insisted it had to be our secret. You said your parents had told you to stop chasing girls and focus on your GCSE coursework. You told me a lot of things over the course of those two weeks. You told me you loved me and that once you were back home, you would find a way to make it work. I believed every word you said. Why else would I have let you be my first?

It was only on our last day together, when I raised the possibility of coming to visit you in Salisbury in the half-term holidays, that the truth finally emerged: you had a girlfriend back home and I was just a bit of fun, a holiday fling. When I broke down in tears, too shocked even to speak, you told me to get a grip and accused me of being a hysterical little cow. I shoved you hard in the chest and ran from the bus shelter. I didn't think you'd come after me, but then I realised you'd be worried about the repercussions if I told my parents – and yours – that we'd slept together. More than once.

When I heard the abuse you were shouting at me, and the vile threats, I knew I had to get away. The tide was in, so I climbed onto the sea wall. My plan was to go to the lifeboat station where I knew some of the volunteers.

I was pleased when I glanced up at the bluff and saw you standing there, not making any attempt to follow me. But my relief was short lived because moments later, a huge wave came crashing down on the sea wall, sucking me into the water as it retreated.

I'm a pretty strong swimmer and very familiar with the currents round here, but the water was freezing and the waves were so powerful, I could barely keep my head above water.

As I struggled to stay afloat, I knew my life depended on one person: you. Because when I looked up, you were still on top of the bluff, looking right at me. I thought you would go for help, or call the coastguard, but instead you did nothing as I struggled and gasped and waved. And then, when I had no more strength left and my head disappeared under the water for the last time, you turned your back on me and walked away.

However you've managed to rewrite the story in your head, I know you haven't forgotten what you did. I know you felt my presence in the guest house too; you're clearly more sensitive than I gave you credit for. I saw how you flinched when I touched you that night – and when I said your name, you *knew*.

Then, like the coward you are, you turned and ran, before I had a chance to expose you.

Or was there another reason you were in such a hurry to leave? Everyone's convinced Kirsten killed my parents, but I'm not so sure.

I didn't see who started the fire; I was too busy watching over Dad and praying he wasn't badly hurt. But let's face it, Charlie, you certainly had the opportunity. As for the motive … I think you might have been scared that my parents were on to you.

I was there, you know. In the annexe when Mum invited you in to look at the plans for the new holiday cottage. I hated seeing you there, polluting my parents' home with your phony words and your fake sympathy, but what could I do?

Then Mum got out the newspaper article, the one she's kept all these years and hardly ever looks at because it makes her too sad. I watched you closely as you studied the photo of my friends gathered outside the church as my coffin was carried in, my girlfriends crying and clinging to each other for comfort. What were you thinking in that moment, I wonder … how lucky you were to get away with it?

Sitting on the sofa next to Mum, you said all the right things – how sorry you were for her loss, and how special I must have been to have such a big turnout at my funeral. You thought you were being so clever, so careful.

But not careful enough.

As you admired the beautiful wreath decorating my coffin, you made a fatal error. 'What beautiful flowers,' you said, as you leaned in for a closer look. 'Pink roses were her favourite.'

It was Dad who reacted first. 'What did you just say?' he asked, his eyes practically popping out of his head.

'*Pink roses were her favourite,*' Mum repeated, her voice rising at the end, as if she was in pain.

'You told us you barely knew Grace,' Dad said accusingly. 'How would you have a clue what her favourite flowers were?'

'I d-don't,' you stammered. 'I got my words muddled up. What I meant to say was, "Were pink roses her favourite?".'

You quickly changed the subject then and my parents didn't pursue it, but they knew you were hiding something; I could see it in the look they gave each other.

I think you saw it too.

I guess the million dollar question is, were you worried enough to take the drastic step of shutting my parents up? *Permanently*. It's a stomach-churning thought and I hope to God I'm wrong – but I alone know what you're capable of and I'm terrified that you'll hurt someone else.

You always underestimated me, Charlie. You have no idea what I am capable of. I bet you think I'm stuck here in Saltwater and that you're safely out of reach all those miles away, in your cosy little love nest. But the truth is, I can go anywhere I want. It's so easy, I just think of where I want to be, and *poof!* . . . there I am.

I was right there in the sitting room, when you two were discussing what happened in Turkey. As the details unfolded, alarm bells started ringing in my head. I'm sure you can see where I'm going with this, so I won't bother spelling it out. But believe me, Charlie McKenna, when I say that I am watching you. And if you ever harm one hair on that girl's head, I promise that I will find new and varied ways to make you suffer every day of whatever remains of your pathetic little life.

Looking out of the sitting-room window, I see that the bulldozers are here. It will be too depressing to stay until there's nothing left, so I'm getting ready to check out.

I can already see spots in my vision, like little twinkling stars, bright lights that crowd and fight for space in front of my eyes.

The infinitely precious, infinitely fragile reality I have inhabited for all these years has, in the space of a few seconds, begun to shrivel and collapse all around me.

And just like that, I am gone.

ACKNOWLEDGEMENTS

I owe an enormous debt of gratitude to my editor Sara Adams. It is no exaggeration to say I couldn't have done it without her. Thanks also to the wider team at Vintage, who have championed *The Guest Book* with such passion and energy. A special mention goes to Jade Chandler, Dan Mogford, Jane Kirby, Sarah Davison-Aitkins, David Heath, Dredheza Maloku, Sophie Painter and Bethan Jones.

penguin.co.uk/vintage